Praise for Alison Gervais and

The Silence Between Us

"A spectacular follow-up to *In 27 Days,* Gervais has written a beautiful contemporary YA novel featuring a strong female lead who isn't willing to change herself to fit in. A heartwarming own voices story about moving to a new school, making friends, and falling in love."

—KELLY ANNE BLOUNT, USA TODAY Bestselling
Author, Watty Award Winner

"Alison Gervais' *The Silence Between Us,* not only captures the anxiety most young people feel when they've been uprooted from their community of friends, but in Maya's case, it's exacerbated by the fact she is deaf and newly planted in a hearing school. As nervous as Maya is, her wonderful sense of humor enlivens the story for the reader. Gervais has a perfect grasp of the challenges facing Maya and fleshes them out empathetically. Her portrayal of Maya and the pitfalls she faces, in my opinion, are spot on. More subtle is Maya's natural defensiveness even against those students who attempt to befriend her, throwing up barriers when she suspects pity as their motivation."

—GINNY RORBY, author of *Hurt Go Happy*

"A spirited story about a girl trying to find herself and her place in the world. Gervais' writing is sure to inspire readers to always stand up for who they are."

—CHRISTINA JUNE, author of *It Started with Goodbye,*
Everywhere You Want to Be, and *No Place Like Here*

The Silence Between Us

Also by Alison Gervais

In 27 Days

The Silence Between Us

ALISON GERVAIS

MG+
6.5
11/95

BLINK

BLINK

The Silence Between Us
Copyright © 2019 by Alison Gervais

Requests for information should be addressed to:
BLINK, *3900 Sparks Dr. SE, Grand Rapids, Michigan 49546*

Library of Congress Cataloging-in-Publication Data
Hardcover ISBN 978-0-310-76616-2
Ebook ISBN 978-0-310-76630-8
Audiobook ISBN 978-0-310-76869-2

Interior design: Denise Froehlich

Printed in the United States of America

19 20 21 22 23 / LSC / 10 9 8 7 6 5 4 3 2 1

DEDICATION

For my parents, who didn't give up, and for Tyler, who thinks my hearing aid is cool.

CHAPTER *1*

hadn't set foot inside a hearing school in almost five years, and yet here Mom and I were, sitting in our minivan in the parking lot at Engelmann High School—a *hearing* school. We'd been waiting about fifteen minutes, and not once had my heart stopped pounding out a painful rhythm in my chest.

Mom reached over and tapped my knee, and I looked up from my lap where I'd been picking at a loose thread on my tie-dye T-shirt. She signed, READY?

I felt myself exhaling heavily. I was most certainly not ready, but it wasn't like I had much of a choice. Hearing school was definitely *not* my idea, but with the closest school for the Deaf being over an hour away from our new home near Parker, Colorado, we weren't left with many options.

READY, I signed. WAIT NOT HELP ME.

Yet again I found myself glad that American Sign Language was my preferred method of communication—it was short, sweet, to the point, and nowhere near as formal as English. I doubted I would have been able to string together any one sentence that would make an ounce of sense in English right then.

Mom gave an overly bright smile as she unfastened her seatbelt and opened the car door. DON'T WORRY, I saw her sign as I unbuckled my own seatbelt.

It was kind of hard not to worry when I knew I was about to become the weird new girl with the interpreter following her around all day. Talk about making an impression. I'd never had to worry about an interpreter before, because at the Pratt School for the Deaf—the school I'd gone to back in Jersey—90 percent of the staff were Deaf or Hard of Hearing, and those that weren't knew ASL and could communicate effectively.

At Engelmann High, I was going to be the one and only Deaf student—an honor I wasn't so sure I was ready to accept.

I grabbed my backpack and hoisted it up on my shoulder as Mom locked the car, and we began the slow walk toward my certain doom.

Okay, so maybe that was a bit dramatic, but the last time I'd gone to a hearing school, I'd actually been, you know, *hearing*. I'd gone to Pratt for so long and gotten used to being around Deaf or HOH people—people who spoke my language—and now I was going to have to resort to lipreading and struggling to follow basic conversation.

And then there was the matter of using my voice, which had me all but paralyzed with fear. I was oral because I'd lost my hearing long after I acquired basic language skills, but the issue was that I couldn't hear my own voice anymore.

Using my voice was sometimes a knee-jerk reaction when I was around people who didn't sign, like the home health care nurses that used to come over a few times a week back in New Jersey to help take care of Connor while Mom was busy working as an associate for a company that specializes in harnessing wind energy.

Even though there was nothing wrong with my voice—I hoped—using it was just downright *weird*. I couldn't hear myself speak, but I could feel the sound reverberating in my skull whenever I spoke. It was a sensation I wasn't all that fond of.

Last Friday, Mom and I met with my new teachers, the principal, and the interpreter the school district arranged to accompany me to all of my classes this year. And today, my interpreter would be the one introducing me to people, communicating with and voicing for me with teachers and which was a surefire way to end up a social outcast by the final bell.

The interpreter's name was Kathleen. She seemed nice enough, and she obviously enjoyed interpreting given how much feeling she put into it—a big part of signing to begin with. No matter how nice she was though, she was still a stranger.

Mom put her hand on my shoulder as we approached the main entrance of the school and signed, BREATHE. YOU FINE HERE.

I shrugged, biting my lower lip. There was no point in correcting her. Plus, my palms were starting to sweat because I was so nervous, and signing with sweaty palms was never fun.

K-A-T-H-L-E-E-N NICE, RIGHT? Mom signed before she held open the door for me. I KNOW YOU WILL LIKE HER.

FINE, I signed back, not wanting to press the issue.

I hated finger spelling long names, and I made a mental note to ask Kathleen what her sign name was. Sign names were typically representative of the individual, so I bet Kathleen's sign name had something to do with her fly-away red hair.

My sign name was technically the sign for *sweet* because apparently the Deaf teacher who taught my first ASL class thought I was sweet when she gave it to me. I didn't think that applied so much anymore. My given name—Maya—was a much better fit.

BUT? Mom pressed.

BUT HEARING SCHOOL, I signed, making a sweeping gesture around the school's lobby we were now standing in.

Rows of faded red lockers lined the hallway on either side of the entrance. Straight ahead was the main office, a huge clock bolted to the wall above the door displaying the time at 7:15, almost a half hour before school started.

NOT ALL HEARING SCHOOLS BAD, Mom signed, giving me an earnest look. I THINK YOU WILL LIKE SCHOOL HERE.

My new interpreter Kathleen came walking out of the main office to greet us, her mess of red curls pulled up into a bun. She signed, GOOD MORNING, with a perky smile.

I wasn't going to bother with a response, but I saw Mom's stern scowl out of the corner of my eye, so I forced myself to sign back, GOOD MORNING.

EXCITED? Kathleen asked me. FIRST DAY NEW SCHOOL.

I shrugged, signing, SURE.

DOCTOR R-I-V-E-R-A WAIT FOR US, Kathleen signed,

finger spelling the principal's name, and she gestured behind her to the main office. YOUR SCHEDULE READY.

WONDERFUL, I signed, though I wasn't sure if the expression on my face was as sarcastic as I wanted.

KATHLEEN NOT D-O SOMETHING WRONG, Mom signed as we followed after Kathleen. NICE, she added in a nonverbal threat, pointing a finger at me.

ALWAYS NICE, I signed to Mom, resting my hand on my chest and batting my eyelashes.

Mom rolled her eyes, and I knew she was giving one of her world-weary sighs by the way her shoulders slumped. I officially lost my hearing when I was thirteen, four years ago, but I still remembered what *some* things sounded like, and Mom's dramatic sighs were firmly ingrained in my memory.

The school secretary was seated behind a massive desk just inside the office, and she nodded to Kathleen when we walked in. I watched her say, "Good morning," as Kathleen pulled open a door that led into the inner part of the main office where the principal, Dr. Rivera, other school administrators, and the nurse worked.

Dr. Rivera's office was small and dimly lit with the blinds pulled down, which had made lipreading difficult when we met with him last Friday. I had an interpreter with me, sure, but at the same time I wanted to at least appear like I could understand what was being said. I wasn't incompetent.

Dr. Rivera was standing behind his desk when the three of us entered his office. This time the bright overhead lights were on, the small accent lamp on his desk turned off. Standing beside the one window in the room, arms crossed and looking just about as uncomfortable as I felt, was a girl with a high ponytail wearing a dressy skirt and blouse.

I froze in the doorway. Had Engelmann assigned me a second interpreter? Or was this girl fresh out of 'terp school, here to shadow Kathleen and add to my already awkward entourage?

TWO INTERPRETER? I signed frantically to Mom. DON'T NEED TWO INTERPRETER.

Before my mom could reply, Kathleen jumped into the conversation, signing NOT INTERPRETER, pointing to the girl by the window.

The girl was wearing stylish square-rimmed glasses, but I could see her dark eyes flicking over to the door like she wanted to make a break for it but was forcing herself to stay put.

You and me both, girlfriend, I thought.

HER NAME N-I-N-A T-O-R-R-E-S, Kathleen finger spelled, still pointing to the girl.

Nina clearly didn't know a lick of sign language, but she sure knew we were talking about her with all the pointing we were doing.

DON'T UNDERSTAND, I signed to Mom and Kathleen. WHO SHE? WHY SHE HERE?

Dr. Rivera was talking quickly now, picking up on the tense atmosphere, but I couldn't even think of lipreading at the moment. I wanted to know what this girl Nina was doing here.

Kathleen brushed her fingers up along her forearm, the sign for *slow*, and Dr. Rivera paused, pink in the face. He'd probably never dealt with a Deaf kid—like everyone else in this school, I was willing to bet—and I could tell he wasn't quite sure what to do.

N-I-N-A WONDERFUL STUDENT, Kathleen was signing as Dr. Rivera gestured to Nina, who still looked beyond embarrassed with her cheeks a blazing red. WE ASK HER B-E YOUR PEER MENTOR FOR YOUR FIRST TWO WEEKS HERE.

DON'T UNDERSTAND, I signed in confusion, shaking my head.

Dr. Rivera waved his hands around like he was giving some dramatic Shakespearian monologue as he explained what a "peer mentor" was. I only caught a few words of what he was saying, like "great student" and "grades" and something about student council. He hadn't really seemed to pick up on the whole *you need to slow down so the Deaf kid can understand you* thing.

N-I-N-A SHOW YOU YOUR CLASSES, Kathleen explained to me. WALK YOU AROUND SCHOOL. MAKE SURE YOU HAVE GOOD TIME.

I should have seen this coming.

SHE MY BABYSITTER? I signed, jabbing a finger at Nina. WALK ME AROUND, HAVE HEARING KIDS MAKE FRIEND WITH NEW DEAF GIRL?

Mom was pursing her lips, looking uncomfortable while Kathleen relayed what I said to Dr. Rivera and Nina. I watched Nina's face fall as she listened to Kathleen, and I felt a momentary twinge of guilt.

I wanted to get used to the idea of being in a hearing school again at my own pace. Not just be thrown to the wolves and expected to make friends with the first hearing kid to cross my path.

NOT LIKE THAT, Kathleen interpreted as Nina started to speak. WANT YOU ENJOY E-N-G-E-L-M-A-N-N.

IMPOSSIBLE, I signed back immediately.

I saw Mom give another one of those sighs and scrunch her eyes closed. She took a moment to collect herself and signed to me, WORK WITH HER. I KNOW YOU NOT HAPPY, BUT TRY. PLEASE.

It was the expression on her face that ultimately made me back down. She looked so tired and worn down, and I knew it was partially because of me. I hadn't made things easy on her since she announced we were moving. I knew she was doing everything she could to make a good life for us out here, and she had enough to worry about with my little brother, Connor. When you have a son with cystic fibrosis, somehow your Deaf teenager ends up being the less difficult one—maybe not so much attitude-wise though.

OK, I signed, reaching over to squeeze her forearm. SORRY.

OK, Mom signed, a wobbly smile on her lips.

We sat in the two chairs in front of Dr. Rivera's desk as he sat down again, looking relieved the storm had passed. Kathleen beckoned Nina closer before moving behind Dr. Rivera's desk, standing directly in my line of sight to interpret.

This was pretty much the last thing in the world I wanted to be doing, but probably the sooner I accepted this whole hearing school thing as my new "normal" the better off I might be.

Despite what Kathleen promised, having Nina around was still a bit like having a babysitter.

Nina took her position as peer mentor very seriously and was quite thorough as she led Kathleen and me on a tour around Engelmann. Every classroom, hallway, and office were described in painstaking detail, even though Engelmann wasn't all that different from Pratt—just bigger. And every time I looked up, either Nina or Kathleen was watching me like they were escorting a toddler instead of a seventeen-year-old.

To be fair, I'd had a split second of panic saying goodbye to Mom before Nina took us off on the tour. I was thrown into a flashback of my first day of kindergarten, terrified to see Mom go and leave me behind in a foreign place with total strangers. I'd wanted to hug her, take in the comforting scent of her amber perfume, beg her not to make me do this. Instead I squeezed her hand three times and signed, SEE YOU LATER.

It was difficult to stay focused on Kathleen while she was interpreting what Nina was saying when students started trickling inside the closer we came to the first bell.

People gravitated to their lockers that lined the hallways, chatting with one another or shuffling around still half asleep. At first, none of them noticed me. But Kathleen was very into her signing, and she threw her whole self into it with the facial expressions to match. I appreciated her enthusiasm, but it attracted attention more than I would've liked. It didn't take very long before heads were turning as we passed through the halls.

Kathleen waved a hand to get my attention for what was probably the sixth time, redirecting me toward Nina. We'd just reached the back door beside the cafeteria and Nina was talking animatedly, using her hands almost as much as she would have if she were signing.

SHE TALK A LOT, I signed to Kathleen, and her lips twitched like she was fighting back a smile.

The last stop on our tour of Engelmann was my locker before we were required to be in the gym for a first-day-of-school assembly to bolster our excitement for the new school year. I was probably the only person excited about the assembly, because it meant I could sit quietly and anonymously for a few minutes of this wacky day.

It took some jiggling to get my locker door to unstick, and as soon as it popped open I understood why. Whoever had the locker before me hadn't been the tidiest; a bunch of old assignments lay crumpled at the bottom, a variety of gum and food wrappers sprinkled on top. Gross. Gingerly, I hung my backpack on the hook inside, wondering if the universe was actually conspiring against me. It probably was.

ASSEMBLY NOW, Kathleen signed for Nina as I swung

my locker shut. SOMETIMES BORING, BUT STUDENT COUNCIL LIKE CANDY.

Oh, well, as long as there's candy involved, I thought.

By the time we reached the gym almost all the bleachers were full, and my desire to end up in the very back row was thwarted. Nina raced across the floor toward an empty portion of the first row of bleachers, motioning for Kathleen and me to follow. She waved at a bunch of people by a table set up underneath one of the basketball hoops as we ran by, then threw herself down on the bleachers as Dr. Rivera stepped into the middle of the gym, microphone in hand.

I quickly sat down in the empty space next to Nina, and Kathleen stood a few feet off to the side, ready to interpret when the assembly started. Dr. Rivera was too far away for me to try to lipread, but he looked like he was trying to get the students to quiet down with how he was making a shushing gesture with his free hand.

I couldn't tell if people were following his instructions because the conversation, the constant movement, and the dull tremble of microphone noise reverberated in the bleachers where I sat. Kathleen only got a few signs into Dr. Rivera's speech when I turned my hearing aids off.

I didn't actually hear much of anything with my hearing aids like some people seemed to think. At best I could hear *some* ambient noise, like a quiet *thud* if someone slammed a door. My hearing aids really only served to help me be somewhat more aware of my surroundings and weren't a cure-all—just a temporary solution to a permanent problem.

If I just closed my eyes, hearing aids off, I was entirely alone in the world, and sometimes I preferred it that way instead of being sucked into all the hubbub around me. It was one thing I enjoyed about being deaf—the ability to disconnect from everything.

After only a few minutes, I could tell from Kathleen's signs that Dr. Rivera's speech was similar to every "it's the first day of school so let's do our best" speech I'd gotten at Pratt. I tuned most of it out, though I did pay attention when Kathleen mentioned something about lunchtime, because . . . food. I also perked up when a couple of guys threw candy into the bleachers and a Snickers landed in my lap. It was by far the best part of my strange and stressful morning.

As soon as Dr. Rivera finished his speech, Nina placed a hand on my shoulder, pointing to the person walking toward us. It was one of the guys who'd been throwing candy a minute ago, but he had a black T-shirt in hand now. I could see the outline of a green Spartan soldier on the shirt, the words ENGELMANN HIGH printed above it. This guy was tall and a little gangly—awkward even. His dark hair was a mess, like he'd just rolled out of bed, and yet it seemed stylish in an I-don't-care kind of way.

Smiling, the guy said something to Nina first and then he turned to me, a rush of color flooding into his cheeks as he said *hello*. Whatever he said next was totally lost on me given how quickly his lips were moving, so I settled for doing the universal sign for *I can't hear you*—pointing to my ear and shaking my head, making sure to frown in confusion.

MY FRIEND, Kathleen signed for Nina, jumping into the introductions when she realized I wasn't absorbing anything the guy was saying. NAME B-E-A-U W-A-T-S-O-N. STUDENT BODY PRESIDENT.

NICE TO MEET YOU, I signed, keeping it simple.

I wasn't sure what kind of name *Beau* was but it seemed fancy, a name you might expect the student body president to have.

As he spoke, Beau's cheeks went from pink to crimson while I lip-read what he was saying. The focus it took to lipread sometimes tended to make people uncomfortable, which I secretly found hilarious.

"It's nice . . . you. Great to . . . here. I thought you . . . T-shirt? You know . . . thing and . . . that."

I looked to Kathleen, unable to decipher all that he was saying to me.

HE BRING SCHOOL T-SHIRT FOR YOU, Kathleen signed. WELCOME GIFT.

Somehow, I wasn't surprised to see the look that came over Beau's face as he watched Kathleen sign to me. It was a mixture of confusion and surprise, but mostly confusion. Usually what followed what I called *the look* was the shouting, as if they spoke loudly enough I might actually be able to hear them. Either that or pity once the realization that I couldn't hear sunk in.

But I had enough T-shirts stuffed in boxes filling up my new room at the moment so my response was to sign, NO, THANK YOU, with a shake of my head.

Beau bit his lip as Kathleen told him the message. He looked to Nina like he didn't know what to do next.

Nina introduced Kathleen instead, and I caught a few words of what she was saying, like "interpreter" and "classes."

"Oh," Beau said. "That's . . . cool."

Watching him get all uneasy as his eyes darted back and forth from me to Kathleen was strange. It was clear he didn't know who he should be talking to—me or her. This wasn't the first time someone spoke to an interpreter instead of to me, like I wasn't literally right in front of them and perfectly capable of being included in the conversation. But I had hoped I'd make it further into the day—preferably after first period—until it happened here.

HEY, I signed to Kathleen. ASSEMBLY ALL DONE? CLASS START NOW, RIGHT?

There were thundering footsteps shaking the bleachers as students scrambled their way out of the gym. First period had to be just minutes away from starting.

I was on my feet the second Kathleen signed, ALL DONE.

I made a sweeping gesture to let Nina know she was free to lead the way to first period. Nina waved to Beau as she grabbed her bag and Beau gave a halfhearted wave in return before we quickly exited the gym, using our elbows to get around a few people. Kathleen somehow fell behind us, and when she caught up out in the hallway she had that shirt Beau tried to give me a minute ago.

I raised an eyebrow in a silent question. What did she expect me to do with it?

NICE GIFT, Kathleen signed with one hand, holding out the T-shirt to me. HE LOOK LIKE NICE BOY.

Actually, Beau looked like a scared—albeit very

tall—rabbit. I'd only signed *nice to meet you* and *no, thank you* to the guy, and he'd looked at me like I was speaking Klingon. Not a very nice feeling.

I took the T-shirt from Kathleen and made a mental note to stuff it in my backpack once I retrieved it from my locker. If Mom started up another box of donations to be taken to a thrift store while we were unpacking, I was going to toss the shirt into it.

Nina directed us to my first period class—AP Statistics—in the math wing. She hovered outside the doorway, looking apologetic.

I HAVE DIFFERENT CLASS NOW, Kathleen signed for Nina. I COME BACK WHEN CLASS ALL DONE, WALK WITH YOU NEXT CLASS.

OK, I signed, and because I didn't want to come across as totally ungrateful I added, THANK YOU FOR YOUR HELP.

"No problem," Nina said, to *me* instead of to Kathleen.

I was so surprised, I actually smiled at her. This girl really must be smart if she'd figured out the art of interpretation. It was . . . something. But still not enough to convince me this whole hearing school thing wouldn't turn out to be a complete and total disaster.

CHAPTER 3

READY? Kathleen signed, nodding toward the open door.

I was so *not* ready, but I signed, SURE, anyway and gave a shrug.

My first class at a hearing school was about to begin, and more than anything I wanted to turn tail and run as fast as my legs would carry me.

Kathleen just gave me a smile and squeezed my shoulder. I couldn't decide if her perkiness was encouraging or annoying but at least it was reliable. Consistency had to count for something when your whole life had been turned upside down.

The bell must have just rung with the way people straightened up in their desks, looking toward the front of the classroom. The teacher, Mrs. Richardson—whom I'd already met last week—was sitting at her desk up front, shuffling stacks of papers around. She looked up with a smile as Kathleen led me over.

I watched her say, "There . . . are, Maya."

EXCITED FOR CLASS? Kathleen added when Mrs.

Richardson spoke too quickly for me to understand what she was saying.

YES, I signed. I wished people would stop asking me that.

SEAT FOR YOU HERE, Kathleen interpreted as Mrs. Richardson got to her feet, pointing to the other side of the classroom up in the front.

The desk Mrs. Richardson was referring to was currently occupied by a girl who had somehow mastered the art of the flawless makeup, messy bun, jeans, and T-shirt look I'd seen on Pinterest lately. I could see her texting on the iPhone not-so-tactfully hidden in her lap and she didn't look up until Mrs. Richardson tapped a finger on her desk to get her attention.

Mrs. Richardson had her back to me, so I couldn't lipread to try and figure out what was being said. Whatever it was made the girl scowl.

"I like here . . . spot . . . the best . . ." the girl said, though the gum she was chewing on made it difficult to lipread.

I gave Kathleen a look, giving a pointed glance toward the girl.

Kathleen took a moment to listen in, then began to sign, TEACHER SAY GIRL NEED MOVE, WHY? YOU NEED SEAT NEAR TEACHER. GIRL NOT MOVE, WHY? SHE HERE FIRST.

Wow. Class hadn't even started yet, and already we were running into issues. That had to be some kind of record.

Normally I wouldn't have bothered picking a fight over a stupid seat, and I would've happily sat in the back of the room, but I actually *did* need to be up front. It was easier to see the teacher and be more aware of what was going on in class, especially since this teacher didn't sign.

The girl stopped arguing with Mrs. Richardson when the guy sitting behind her leaned forward. I zeroed in on his lips as he spoke and saw him say, "Just move . . . not . . . deal . . ." and the girl finally gave up and grabbed her things to move to an open desk a few rows over.

Mrs. Richardson went to grab an extra chair so Kathleen could sit a few feet in front of my desk to interpret. I took my seat at the now-vacant desk, dropped my backpack beside me, and turned around to thank the guy behind me for intervening.

It was Beau, the T-shirt guy. Of course.

THANK YOU, I signed to him, a little reluctantly.

Beau understood that much and nodded as he said, "No problem." He smiled, dimples flashing. That smile transformed him from an awkward rabbit into a surprisingly cute guy, and for a second I forgot how much he'd annoyed me earlier.

Then I felt a hand on my forearm, and when I turned around, Kathleen was signing, CLASS START NOW.

AP Statistics wasn't actually so bad with Kathleen interpreting, much to my surprise. I understood the material, and Kathleen's peppy signing helped me get a feel for how Mrs. Richardson spoke. Mrs. Richardson must've remembered some of the tips Mom handed out at our meeting

Friday about interacting with the Deaf, like making sure to face me when speaking and not to cover her mouth when she spoke. When the five minutes we were given to complete a practice problem were up, Mrs. Richardson even flashed the lights to get my attention.

But as nice as Mrs. Richardson was, I was massively uncomfortable. I could feel everyone's piercing gaze fixed on us as Kathleen signed and I watched intently. But if anybody was making fun of us, it wasn't like I could hear them anyway. Still, I couldn't help but think they were talking about me, whispering behind my back or making comments about how my neon blue hearing aids clashed with the color of my hair or something.

Thankfully, class was over in fifty-five minutes, and once Mrs. Richardson jotted down our homework on the whiteboard and passed out textbooks, we were given the okay to leave. There was a rush to get out the door, but I lingered, taking my time as I packed up my things. I didn't want any more run-ins with Beau or my other classmates.

Kathleen waved to get my attention and pointed behind me as I shoved my textbook into my backpack. Beau was standing there behind me when I glanced over my shoulder, and Kathleen came forward to interpret as he started to speak.

Great, I thought, trying not to let my irritation show. This guy just couldn't take a hint.

YOU ENJOY CLASS? Kathleen signed.

I shrugged. EASY, I signed, then pointed to myself. MATH GENIUS.

With the way the corners of his eyes crinkled and his

cheeks lifted, Beau must've laughed when Kathleen told him what I signed. I was able to make out most of what he said next, something like, "Good . . . Mrs. Richardson . . . tough."

Maybe it was a little bit of an exaggeration, but I *was* good at math. I'd been in accelerated classes since freshman year. Good thing too, seeing as my math and science grades needed to be above and beyond average if I wanted to make it as a respiratory therapist, my dream job. It would be hard enough getting into the medical field being Deaf, so I had to make sure I had the smarts to prove that not being able to hear wouldn't stop me from helping save lives.

I'd spent more than my fair share around respiratory therapists—they were a huge part of Connor's treatment team for cystic fibrosis. Everything about the disease sucked, from the constant pain to the medications to the special vest Connor had to use that made him hack up fluid and mucus in his lungs. But the therapists helped make Connor's hospital stays as easy and comfortable as possible. I wanted to do the same thing for other kids with CF.

I felt a smattering of guilt when I realized Kathleen was still interpreting the conversation with Beau and I'd been too wrapped up in my thoughts of Connor and respiratory therapy to pay much attention.

NEXT CLASS? Kathleen signed as Beau continued speaking to her.

He still didn't seem to catch on that he should be looking at me, not Kathleen. He was three feet from me, and I was almost positive I saw him say, "Tell her . . ." I had to make a conscious effort not to start grinding my teeth out of annoyance.

I pulled my crumpled class schedule out of my back pocket to check what class was next. A-P U-S HISTORY, I signed.

Beau was flashing those dimples as he smiled again when Kathleen voiced what I'd signed, then said, "Me too."

COOL, I signed back. I wasn't sure if I meant it.

OK IF I WALK WITH YOU BOTH? Kathleen signed for Beau as he jabbed a thumb toward the door.

N-I-N-A TELL ME SHE WALK ME T-O NEXT CLASS, I signed in response.

Beau nodded as Kathleen relayed what I signed to him and said, "Nina is . . . girl. She's . . . friend."

Kathleen raised her eyebrows at me as Beau fell into step behind us on our way to class. She didn't need to sign anything for me to get what she was hinting at.

CUTE, I KNOW, BUT NOT FOR ME, I signed to Kathleen, making sure not to look Beau's way. DON'T SAY ANYTHING.

This was one of those times when I appreciated that nobody else around us knew sign language.

WHO, ME? Kathleen signed, but she left it at that.

Nina was waiting for us just outside the classroom, leaning up against the row of lockers with her cell phone in hand. She gave us a smile when she asked how class had gone, and I gave her the same answer I'd given Beau—math genius here.

On the way to AP US History, I got stuck behind Nina and Beau, and I could tell they were talking about me. Not because I could hear them or because I could read their lips, but because neither of them included me in the conversation.

Every so often Beau would glance back and say something to Kathleen—*still* not to me—but that was it.

CONFUSED, I signed to Kathleen, frowning at her.

TALK ABOUT CLASS, Kathleen signed, pointing up at Nina and Beau.

ME? I signed next.

Kathleen paused for a moment, listening, and nodded.

I grimaced.

This is what always happened whenever I was with hearing people. They were always so talkative and impatient, so busy bouncing around from one place to the next that they never think to slow down and take the extra step needed to communicate with a Deaf person.

Kathleen put a hand against my arm for my attention and signed, THEY DON'T KNOW HOW COMMUNICATE WITH DEAF PEOPLE. NOT YOUR FAULT.

Kathleen was right, but it was still difficult to wipe the grumpy expression off my face.

Mr. Wells, the AP US History teacher, came rushing forward the second I walked into his class. When he grabbed my hand to give it a vigorous shake, I was so startled I took an immediate step back.

"Wonderful . . . excited to . . . always wanted . . . sign language . . ."

He was talking far too quickly for me to understand everything he was saying, so once again Kathleen stepped in and signed, SLOW, like she had in Dr. Rivera's office.

Rather than trip up in embarrassment like a lot of people, Mr. Wells just kept on talking, and I could tell by the overly exaggerated way he moved his lips and leaned forward that he was shouting when he said, "I'm . . . sorry!"

His voice must have been *really* loud, because Nina and Beau stopped on their way to two open seats and looked back at us, and every other person in the classroom directed their gaze toward us too.

I was mortified.

Kathleen looked disgruntled when she waved at Mr. Wells and signed, YOU NOT NEED SHOUT. TALK NORMAL. I INTERPRET FOR HER.

DON'T MATTER IF YOU SHOUT, I CAN'T HEAR YOU, I signed to him, maybe a little more forcefully than I should have. I wanted to make the point here, and how I was not going to take this shouting thing lying down. STUPID T-O SHOUT A-T DEAF PEOPLE.

For as much as Mr. Wells seemed completely oblivious, he understood from the agitated way I was signing I was most certainly annoyed.

CAN I HAVE SEAT NOW? I signed, pointing to the open desk beside Nina.

Mr. Wells bobbed his head as Kathleen spoke for me and quickly stepped aside so I could go sit down. I snatched a notebook and pencil out of my backpack while Kathleen went to grab an extra chair to sit in front of me again.

When I sat upright, I saw Nina sliding her own notebook across her desk toward me, and I noticed she'd scribbled something down on the front page.

Mr. Wells is a doofus. Don't worry about him.

I fought back a tiny smile as I took my own pencil and

THE SILENCE BETWEEN US

scribbled down a response to Nina before passing her note-book back.

He's not the first person to shout at me, and he won't be the last. But thanks.

Nina grinned when she read my note and said, "You've got this."

It was a simple statement, one I'd been told a lot in the past few weeks. But it meant just a little bit more coming from a person who wasn't my mother or an interpreter.

A t Pratt, lunch had been my favorite part of the day. At Engelmann, I was pretty sure it was going to be my absolute *least* favorite part.

OK IF I SPLIT FOR LUNCH? Kathleen asked as I followed Nina into the cafeteria.

FINE, I signed. PROMISE. MEET AGAIN AFTER LUNCH.

SURE? Kathleen repeated.

YES, I signed again.

It was not as if I publicly announced I was Deaf—my interpreter and the signing and my hearing aids kind of made that obvious—but I wanted to have a normal lunch without having everyone stare at me or whisper about me. Having Kathleen sitting at the same table, interpreting lunchtime conversations, would kind of make that impossible.

Kathleen and I parted ways outside the cafeteria, and Nina led the way to the food line. The place was already crowded with old friends sitting together catching up on their summers. Everyone had their place and seemed glad to return to the same groups with the same friends.

Suddenly, I felt very homesick.

Nina found us a spot in line behind a rather short guy with smooth brown hair and a lean physique that suggested he was into sports. He and Nina exchanged pleasantries—maybe they were friends?—and then the guy turned toward me. A smile that was probably meant to be charming, but looked a little too practiced, crept over the guy's face as he eyed me.

"Well, hello there. Who . . . have here?"

I inwardly cringed as I shook his hand, already predicting how this encounter would play out.

"Jackson, this . . . Maya," Nina said, introducing us. Something about the expression on her face made it seem like she was trying to tell him off. "She just . . . New Jersey."

"Wonderful!" the guy called Jackson said, and he winked at me.

The only person who ever winked at me was my Grandpa Sully back before he died, and usually it was when he was sneaking me candy behind Mom's back. Having a guy my age wink at me was weird—and creepy.

Nina shifted slightly so I didn't have a good look at her face, but I could tell she was trying to fill Jackson in on my situation. Whatever she was saying didn't seem to bother Jackson as he said, "Now that's just . . . Nina. I . . . little . . . sign language."

His eyes moved to me again and he started to finger spell his name, although he wound up with the letter *m* instead of *n* when he got toward the end. "Jackson," he said, leaning toward me, a telltale sign he was raising his voice.

I smiled politely at Jackson and decided to respond to his overly dramatic introduction in the same fashion. I took my time signing, I DON'T LIKE HEARING BOYS, but it was all I could do to keep from busting out laughing when Jackson nodded and gave a thumbs-up, the cheeky smile still in place as he moved forward with the line.

"Sorry . . . that," Nina said when she turned back to face me. "Jackson's . . . lady's man."

I shrugged. Wasn't like I hadn't met one of those before. I tapped the backs of my index and middle fingers to my forehead, the sign for *stupid*, and pointed at Jackson. When Nina kept staring at me in confusion, I very clearly mouthed the word without using my voice, and then she looked like she was holding in a laugh once she understood.

I bought a sad-looking roast beef sandwich and a bottle of lemonade when we reached the food and somewhat anxiously trailed after Nina. She was my only lifeline in this school so far, and I wasn't bold enough to break off on my own and sit at a table alone. When I saw the table we were heading toward, I almost wished I had. Beau was sitting there with Jackson close by, along with a whole bunch of people I didn't recognize.

I took a seat at the table beside Nina, across from Beau and thankfully away from Jackson. I unwrapped my sandwich and took a bite, doing all I could to ignore the eyes fixed on me. Nina mentioned she and Beau were on the student council, so it wasn't a stretch to figure out the rest of the people at this table fell into the same category.

Nina placed a hand on my shoulder for my attention, and I watched her introduce me to everyone saying, "This . . . Maya. She just moved . . . New Jersey."

I gave a small wave as some people presumably said

hello and quickly returned to my sandwich. I had this bad habit of eating super-fast when I was nervous, and at my current pace I was going to finish my sandwich in under a minute, tops.

I gave a start when Nina nudged me with her elbow, and when I looked over at her she nodded toward Jackson. He was leaning toward me across the table, two seats down from Beau, and he was talking to me, fast and with no breath in between.

It could've been because I was already exhausted from lipreading, trying to remain alert, and overly paranoid that people were talking about me behind my back that I spoke, because it was the quickest way of getting my point across.

"I'm assuming Nina told you I'm Deaf, right?"

I saw Beau's eyes widen, and I could tell the next words out of his mouth were, "You can talk?"

And in that split second after Beau said those words, my mood went from uneasy and unsure to *pissed off.*

"Of course I can talk! A lot of Deaf are oral, but it's our choice whether we want to use our voices," I told Beau, my glare fierce. "Just because I *choose* not to talk doesn't mean I can't do it. I'm not stupid or anything, you know. I'm just as capable as you are."

I was angry at that unbelievably thoughtless comment, but lurking on the periphery was the fear that my voice sounded so bad and was somehow so surprising it caught Beau off guard.

Beau started to say what I was sure was going to be some lame excuse, but Jackson started tapping on the table in front of me, wanting my attention again. When I turned my glare on him, he seemed oblivious to my anger, saying, "If you . . . talk, why do . . . sign language?"

"Why don't *you* use sign language?" I snapped at him.

I snatched my backpack off the back of my chair, grabbed my sandwich and lemonade bottle, and was off like a rocket. The hallway outside the cafeteria was blissfully empty, so I just took off, not caring if my shoes were slapping extra loud on the tiled floor. I wanted to put as much distance between me and that lunch table as possible. It was a shame walking all the way back to New Jersey was out of the question.

I'd never gotten, "You can talk?" before. As if my being able to talk was somehow supposed to be impossible because I was Deaf? What did *that* have to do with anything?

I felt myself growing more and more irritated with myself because I was actually *embarrassed* about having spoken in front of Nina and Beau and those other total strangers at that lunch table.

Don't think about it, don't think about it, I chanted to myself as I kept on down the hallway. These people didn't mean anything to me. I didn't care what they thought or said. At least, I didn't want to.

Taking up a post at my locker, I picked at the rest of my sandwich and took a few sips of lemonade, though my appetite had all but disappeared after that little display in the cafeteria. As I ate, I debated the merits of going out and getting a job to buy a car so I could drive myself to that school for the Deaf. It wouldn't be the same as Pratt, but at least there I could be around other people who "spoke" my language. It was a nice thought that kept me going through next period's art class, though I knew it wasn't exactly realistic. Even if I found a job in the next few weeks, I doubted I could save up enough to get a car before I graduated.

Mom's attempts at reassuring me everything was going to be great at this hearing school already hit a brick wall on the first day. How could she have ever thought this would turn out okay?

CHAPTER 5

YOU OK? Kathleen signed to me on our way out of chemistry class, the last class of the day. SAD, she added, pointing to me with raised eyebrows.

FINE, I signed back. TIRED.

Not a total lie—I was exhausted. I'd forgotten how tiring it could be to lip-read so much, trying to make sense of what people were saying around me. I had to put forth way more effort into communicating than the hearing people at this school. It was depressing to think I was going to have to do it for almost eight hours a day, five days a week, for the next several months.

TOMORROW NEW DAY, Kathleen signed to me, smiling encouragingly.

I KNOW, I answered. BUT I FORGET HEARING PEOPLE WEIRD WITH DEAF.

Kathleen signed, I KNOW. She didn't offer any other words of encouragement, just gave my shoulder one of those squeezes, and I was grateful she was leaving it alone.

We parted ways, promising to meet in front of the school tomorrow morning, and I made the trek all the way back to my locker on the other side of the building.

I kept my head down and quickly gathered up all the textbooks and homework I received throughout the day. I'd already been assigned a few hours' worth of homework, and I was weirdly grateful. The work would be a temporary distraction so I wouldn't have to think about how awful coming back to this stupid school was going to be.

Mom was waiting outside in the pickup loop, and I wrenched open the passenger side door and leapt in, throwing my backpack down between my feet with a little too much force.

I leaned back in my seat to wave hello to Connor sprawled out in the back with several bags of groceries Mom must have picked up, looking a little tired after his first day of school but otherwise just fine. He signed, HELLO, followed by a smile where he stuck his tongue through the gap where his two front teeth used to be—one of his favorite things to do since he lost them a couple weeks ago.

Then Mom had her hand on my shoulder, and I twisted back around to look at her. By the expectant look on her face, I could tell she was silently asking, *so how was it?*

AWFUL, I signed to her. I started listing off everything that went wrong as she put the car in gear and maneuvered out of the parking lot. GIRL ANGRY WITH ME FIRST CLASS, WHY? TEACHER HAVE HER MOVE FOR ME. DIFFERENT TEACHER YELL AT ME. LUNCH SOME HEARING BOY TRY F-L-I-R-T WITH ME, AND DIFFERENT BOY NAME B-E-A-U SURPRISE I TALK. HE REALLY SAY, 'YOU CAN TALK?'

If Mom were not familiar with the way I signed she

probably wouldn't have a single clue about what I was telling her given how frantically I was signing, but she got it. She had this disappointed look on her face as she drove, turning to look at me so she could reply when we reached a stoplight.

REMEMBER, YOUR FIRST DAY, she signed. THINGS STRANGE FIRST DAY. HEARING SCHOOL NEW FOR YOU AGAIN. BUT SORRY THAT HAPPENED.

SAME, I signed, sinking my teeth into my lip. I felt frustrated, angry tears pricking my eyes, but I refused to let those jerks get to me by making me cry.

NOT MEAN KIDS, Mom continued. THEY DON'T KNOW ABOUT DEAF.

SHOULD KNOW, I told her.

Mom pursed her lips in thought, and it wasn't until we reached another stop sign that she signed, TEACH THEM.

Connor's small hand squeezed my shoulder tight before I could respond, and immediately I felt my anger begin to disappear.

Despite how thin and pale Connor always seemed to be, he was probably the happiest little kid I knew. He had this mess of brown hair that stuck up everywhere despite how much Mom tried to tame it, a bunch of freckles, and he was always smiling.

Connor didn't know much sign, but he gave it his all whenever we were around each other. A lot of the time he would write notes to me, so we had a special spiralbound notebook covered in Marvel comic book stickers for that exact purpose.

HELLO, Connor signed to me again. MISS YOU TODAY.

THE SILENCE BETWEEN US

SAME, I signed with a grin, then said aloud, "How was your first day of school, squirt?"

Connor was one of the few people I didn't mind using my voice in front of. He was too young to remember what it was like when I was still hearing, so to him I'd always been his Deaf big sister.

"Awesome!" I watched Connor say excitedly. He gave another big thumbs-up with his toothy smile. "I have . . . new friend . . . teacher put us . . . name . . . Trevor. Likes . . . Spider-Man!"

"That's great!" I said, thinking that at least Connor enjoyed his new school even if I hated mine.

A handful of minutes later we were pulling up into the driveway of our new home.

This house was smaller than our home in New Jersey, but it was still cute—painted green with a nicely kept front lawn and a big sweetgum tree out front. It was maybe the one thing I liked about moving so far.

Inside was still a total mess, with us navigating around the stacks of moving boxes everywhere. We'd gotten the couches arranged in the living room and the entertainment stand set up with the TV, but everything else was still chaos.

I started in on my homework once all the groceries were put away, setting up camp in the living room with Connor. He didn't have any homework and was perfectly content turning on some cartoons and plopping down on the couch, making sure to turn on closed captioning for me. I was caught up outlining the chapter in my AP US History textbook about corporations in early twentieth century

America when Mom popped her head into the living room to tell us dinner was ready.

DINNER, Connor signed at me when I didn't immediately get up, making the letter "D" with his fingers and tapping the side of his jaw.

Mom already had the table set in the dining room just off the kitchen when Connor and I joined her. A shrimp pasta with a side salad was a welcome change from all the take-out we'd been having since we moved.

I sat across from Mom for any necessary interpreting and dug into my plate of food.

As we ate, every so often I would look up and see Connor in conversation with Mom, and then I would feel that little twinge of sadness I always did when my family was speaking around me and I didn't have any idea what they were saying.

I didn't blame Connor or Mom for not always signing when they spoke because that wasn't an easy thing to do when your first language was English. I never felt sorry for myself because of it, but sometimes it was impossible to put a cork in it. I didn't hate being Deaf—it was part of who I was—but sometimes my lack of hearing made me feel painfully alone.

Once dinner and cleanup were finished, I grabbed my things from the living room and went upstairs to my new bedroom, which was all the way at the end of the hallway beside the bathroom I shared with Connor.

Rather than dive back into my homework, I hung up a few posters, mostly reprints of Van Gogh and Picasso masterpieces that always made me marvel. I got sheets properly fitted on my bed, put more clothes away in the dresser beside the window, and then decided to give up and FaceTime my best friend Melissa.

Melissa picked up after a few rings, waving her hands excitedly as she came into view on my iPad. Melissa and I met at Pratt shortly after I transferred there, and we'd been close friends ever since. Unlike me, Melissa was born deaf, which meant ASL was her first language. It had taken a while for me to stop thinking so much in English since it was my first language—and sometimes I still thought I wasn't fluent in ASL—but this had never been a problem for Melissa.

Melissa was spunky and bubbly and never failed to see the positive side of the equation—something I could definitely use at the moment. And after this mess of a first day at Engelmann, I was hoping Melissa's self-confidence in her identity as a Deaf person might rub off on me.

MISS YOU, was the first thing Melissa signed to me. COLORADO, YOU LIKE?

FINE, I signed back. BEAUTIFUL MOUNTAINS.

HEARING SCHOOL? Melissa signed next, raising her eyebrows in question.

AWFUL, I told her honestly.

I wasted no time giving Melissa a play-by-play account of everything that happened my first day of hearing school. She watched me intently as I signed, twirling a strand of her dyed black hair around her finger. When I got to the part about lunch, the creepy hearing guy, and Beau, the expression on Melissa's face went from interested to annoyed.

HEARING PEOPLE, she signed, and gave a disgusted shake of her head as if that said it all.

I KNOW, I signed in agreement. AND I STUCK HERE NOW. EIGHT MONTHS BEFORE GRADUATE.

STRONG, Melissa signed, pointing at me. BELIEVE IN YOU.

THANK YOU. I attempted a smile even though I felt like bursting into angry, frustrated tears all over again. MISS YOU SAME.

Melissa and I spent the next half hour catching up. As we were signing, it was almost like I hadn't moved and was back in my old bedroom in New Jersey, procrastinating doing my homework with Melissa. She promised me we would FaceTime again after her first day back at Pratt, which wasn't until next week, and fill me in on everything I missed.

It was eleven o'clock east coast time by the time Melissa and I signed off. I hated saying good-bye, but I still had homework to finish. And even though getting to see her face made me feel better, it somehow made me feel worse too. Our call reminded me that I had left so much behind in New Jersey—a life that had been happy and comfortable and full of people who understood me. If my first day at Engelmann had proven anything, it was that I was completely, utterly different from everyone else.

And there was no chance that was going to change.

CHAPTER 6

When I lost my hearing, Mom got her hands on an assistive technology catalogue and bought me a new alarm clock called a Sonic Bomb. It was geared toward those with hearing loss and came with a vibrating disc you slipped under the mattress that would shake the bed when the alarm went off. The thing even had a red flashing light.

It was a nifty piece of technology, but it had a tendency to yank me out of sleep every morning and send my heart kicking into overdrive. It was the same way I woke up every morning in New Jersey, and now in Colorado, except instead of heading off to Pratt, I was going to be on my way to another dreadful day at Engelmann. That thought alone kept my heartrate from slowing back down to normal.

I rested my head against the car window on the way to school, focusing more on the way the bumps of the car were rattling my skull than what I was about to face on my second day of school.

HEY, Mom signed when she parked the van at the curb outside Engelmann. YOU WILL HAVE GOOD DAY. PROMISE.

I was very doubtful of this, but it was nice of Mom to say so anyway. I signed, SEE YOU LATER, as I unbuckled myself, blew a kiss at Connor in the backseat, and dragged myself out of the car toward school.

Kathleen was waiting for me by the main entrance and signed, HELLO, a coffee cup in her free hand. I was one of the first to arrive in AP Statistics, happy to take my seat at the same desk as yesterday without any hassle this time. As I waited for class to start, I did a quick scan of last night's homework, wanting to make sure I'd completed each problem correctly.

I was checking the second to last problem when someone tapped my shoulder. I twisted around in my seat and made a face when I saw it was Beau sitting behind me again.

"What do you want?" I said aloud.

I had this strange desire to keep using my voice around this guy, if only to prove I was perfectly capable of talking.

My eyes widened when Beau very carefully made the sign for *sorry*—a closed fist moving in a circular motion against the chest.

There had to be some kind of ASL website open on Beau's laptop, because in the next minute he went through a handful of signs, clearly struggling to remember the ones he wanted. I was both in awe and baffled as to why Beau would be attempting to use sign language with me. And when he accidentally used the wrong sign, I couldn't help but bust up laughing.

"What did . . . wrong?" Beau demanded, looking nervous.

I made the letter "W" and tapped the three fingers to my lips. "This means water," I said, then put my pinky up

47

and tapped four fingers against my lips. "This means talk. You said I don't need to water around you."

Beau clapped a hand over his eyes, sinking down a few inches in his chair. His embarrassment was oddly adorable. "Okay . . . credit for trying . . ."

Maybe a little credit was due. Compared to the random strangers who liked to stop me and finger spell the whole alphabet just to show me they could, Beau had done a fairly decent job conveying his message to me.

"If you're trying to say you're sorry for yesterday, I get it," I said, hoping my voice was somewhat quiet. I could never be sure of how loud I was being. "But just . . . maybe when you're practicing ASL online again, you can google things you're not supposed to say to a Deaf person."

Beau's cheeks had gone all kinds of pink, but he nodded, saying, "Right. Maybe I . . . look that . . . too."

I think I might have smiled at him before I turned back around in my seat.

⌒〜

Like yesterday morning, Nina was waiting for me outside once the bell rang.

"How are . . . this morning?" she said, all smiles.

It was beyond me how cheery she was so early in the morning, but then again, I'd only finished half my cup of coffee at breakfast and it was hard for me to be cheery without copious amounts of caffeine.

FINE, I signed, Kathleen standing nearby to interpret. ENOUGH HOMEWORK YESTERDAY. TIRED.

SAME, Kathleen interpreted while Nina spoke. AND THAT BECOME WORSE FROM HERE.

Thankfully, when we arrived in history, Mr. Wells didn't single me out again the second I walked into his classroom. In fact, he wasted no time jumping into today's lesson, a continuation of yesterday's discussion over the establishment of big businesses in the US at the turn of the century. I was only halfheartedly taking notes, since I'd covered most of the material back at Pratt. I ended up getting halfway through a doodle of a miniature Hogwarts, complete with boats full of first-years on the lake, when Kathleen leaned over and started tapping on my desk.

GROUP TIME, she signed when I looked up at her.

I stared at her in confusion, unsure of what she meant, and she signed, TEACHER WANT YOU ALL TALK ABOUT EARLY U-S BUSINESS. HOW BUSINESS CHANGE WITH NEW TECHNOLOGY.

This was quite possibly a Deaf person's nightmare—"Group time." There was no way Kathleen or I would be able to keep up with the rapid flow of conversation from multiple people, and only rarely did some people not seem to be annoyed by the small delay interpreting could cause. This was going to be like putting a hearing person in between two Deaf people arguing in sign language and expecting them to understand what was going on.

I was hoping I'd be in the same group as Nina, but I wound up with two girls who looked like they'd rather be anywhere else and a half-asleep guy leaning back so far in his desk I was sure he was going to fall over.

Kathleen dragged her chair over to our circle of desks by the whiteboard at the front of the class.

TOILET, she signed to me, telling me she was going to use the restroom.

Great timing, I thought.

I nodded, trying to squash the feeling of unease stirring in the pit of my stomach.

When Mr. Wells came over to dole out instructions, Kathleen still hadn't returned. It didn't matter that Mr. Wells was facing me, he was still talking too quickly and animatedly for me to understand a word of what he was saying. He gave me a thumbs-up when he finished, looking expectant with wide eyes, so I just mustered up a smile and did a thumbs-up of my own.

The lone guy in the group slid lower in his seat and put his hands behind his head when Mr. Wells wandered off, like he was getting ready to take a nap. The two girls started laughing, and I figured the boy must have cracked a joke or made some sarcastic comment. I couldn't be sure because I couldn't really see his face.

What was I supposed to do now? The group discussion was starting without me, and where was Kathleen? This was only the second day of school and I was determined not to let myself start falling behind already, even if this was just some silly group discussion. For all I knew, they could be having the most intelligent, thought-provoking group discussion of the last decade.

But how was I supposed to offer input if I couldn't even figure out what they were saying? What if I mispronounced the name of some business magnate or company or talked too loudly? That would get me even more weird, *interested* stares from that guy Jackson; he was sitting all the way across the classroom and I could still feel his eyes on me.

I looked up from my tightly clasped hands when I saw a figure tip back in their seat to stick their head into our group. It was Beau, and he was speaking to the girls. I only caught a few words of it. Something like, "You . . . she's deaf, right? You should . . ."

"Hey!"

Beau and the two girls looked surprised when they turned my way.

"You don't need to speak for me. Stop sticking your nose in my business."

I might have spoken a little too harshly—wasn't like I could tell—because Beau looked like he'd been struck across the face. He started fumbling around for words, saying something like, "I wanted . . . help. I was just trying . . ."

"I don't want your help," I snapped, and I meant every word of it. "I don't need your help. And I am perfectly capable of contributing to the conversation. Like, I don't think John D. Rockefeller was a very good person even if he was an amazing business man. See?"

This was the exact moment Kathleen arrived, seeming alarmed at the tense atmosphere she just walked into.

WHAT HAPPENED? she signed to me.

NOTHING, I signed back. WAIT FOR YOU BEFORE WE START TALK.

Kathleen did not look convinced, but she nodded, taking her seat, ready to interpret. Beau took this as his cue to return to his own group now, his eyes avoiding mine.

Who said I needed him to be stepping in for me like that? It was obvious to the rest of the class I was Deaf, so where was the point in reminding my group of that?

I decided his apology in sign language didn't matter. Beau didn't know anything about my world, and I sincerely doubted he ever would.

CHAPTER 7

Two weeks into the semester I was finally able to meet with my new guidance counselor, Mrs. Stephens. When Mom first announced we were moving to Colorado, I began extensive research on nearby colleges, searching for the best respiratory therapy programs to apply to. The result of my search was Cartwright College, a small school with an average class size of 25, about a twenty-minute drive away. This would allow me to live at home and still help Mom take care of Connor.

It was crucial I saw Mrs. Stephens as soon as possible. The more time I had to make sure she understood every aspect of my plans for college and just how important this was to me, the better. I intended to apply to Cartwright early decision, so I would hopefully know by the end of the semester if I'd been accepted.

After chemistry, Kathleen followed me down the hallway to the main office at the front of the school.

MEETING ABOUT COLLEGE? she signed to me as we walked.

I nodded, giving her a quick rundown of the plan I had

mapped out for the four years ahead of me. Kathleen was beaming when I finished.

SMART, she signed, pointing to me. YOU NOT NEED WORRY. BELIEVE THEY ACCEPT YOU.

I gave a wobbly smile, signing, THANK YOU.

Despite all my worrying in the beginning, Kathleen was steadily moving into the category of acquaintance rather than stranger. I was thinking more and more that my classes might not be all that bad if I had her to interpret for me. My classmates were the bigger problem, and I noticed Kathleen had a habit of giving a steely eyed glare to anyone that so much as had a weird look watching us sign. Not really what an interpreter was supposed to be doing, but it was nice she was looking out for me.

When we reached Mrs. Stephens' office, Kathleen knocked on the door before I could. There must've been some response from inside because Kathleen opened the door a beat later and ushered me inside.

Mrs. Stephens was seated behind her desk and got up to greet us as we walked in. She was stern looking with thick-framed glasses and black hair cut short in a bob, but she smiled when she shook our hands.

She said something like, "Nice to . . . you, Maya."

SAME, I signed, taking a seat in one of the chairs by her desk.

Kathleen began to interpret as Mrs. Stephens started talking, clicking around on the computer on her desk.

I SEE YOUR WORK FROM OLD SCHOOL. WONDERFUL GRADES, Kathleen signed to me for Mrs. Stephens. HOPE YOU LIKE NEW SCHOOL.

I gave a one-shouldered shrug and signed, DIFFERENT, BUT OK.

TELL ME YOUR HOPE FOR COLLEGE, Kathleen signed next for Mrs. Stephens.

APPLY EARLY FOR R-T PROGRAM WITH C-A-R-T-W-R-I-G-H-T, I signed.

Mrs. Stephens appeared startled at my response.

WHY R-T PROGRAM? Kathleen signed Mrs. Stephens' question.

I hesitated, not sure if I wanted to share anything about Connor, but I decided being honest would be best. If she knew how important this was to me, maybe she would be an ally.

I told her about Connor's diagnosis and how difficult dealing with his illness could be, not only for him, but for the rest of the family too.

I WANT TO HELP ALL KIDS WITH C-F, I finished, signing with feeling.

Mrs. Stephens was nodding along as Kathleen interpreted and said, ". . . think what you want . . . wonderful. Promise . . . help you . . ."

I watched Kathleen interpret the rest of what Mrs. Stephens was saying. It was almost surreal that Mrs. Stephens was saying that with my grades and above average SAT scores, she believed I had a very real shot at getting into Cartwright, where it was not uncommon for students to be put on a waiting list for more than a semester or two.

It was hard not to flop back in my chair with a heavy sigh of relief. I think I signed THANK YOU about nine times. Planning for college had been one of my major worries about coming to a hearing school. My guidance counselor at Pratt was Deaf too, so he understood the obstacles lined up for me when graduation rolled around. Mrs. Stephens did not—at least not from firsthand experience—but she seemed more than willing to try working with me.

I had a genuine smile on my face as the meeting wrapped up, and it was almost a struggle to keep from bouncing off the walls. This was going *much* better than I thought it would. The type of person who didn't bat an eyelash or bring up barriers when a person with a "disability" shared their dreams was definitely someone you wanted on your side.

We made an appointment to get together again in two weeks' time to start working on my application for Cartwright, and Mrs. Stephens promised she would do some investigating into the college's accommodation policies.

GOOD MEETING, Kathleen signed when we walked out the door.

WONDERFUL MEETING, I signed in agreement. HAPPY FOR HER SUPPORT.

Things had gone well, but that didn't mean I was out of the woods. I had enough trouble keeping up with the goings-on in my classes here, even with Kathleen interpreting. Lip-reading was not a perfect science. In those few moments when Kathleen stepped out to use the restroom, I could never be sure what I was missing. There was always some type of conversation going on around me that I knew was happening but couldn't hear. And once I got to college I would be expected to keep pace with everyone else while someone interpreted the professor's lecture for me. If I had a hard time keeping up in a regular chemistry class, what was going to happen when I hit college?

Kathleen gave my shoulders a squeeze and signed, WHY SHE NOT SUPPORT YOU? WE ALL BELIEVE I-N YOU.

I mustered up another smile but quickly averted my eyes. It was good that we were getting a head start on this, but this was far from over.

Mom texted me during lunch to tell me Connor had an appointment at Children's Hospital in Aurora with his new doctor and that she might be late picking me up from school. To kill time, I dragged myself to the library after saying good-bye to Kathleen. My attempt at getting some homework done was proving to be an unsuccessful endeavor, since my mind was still on college and my future. It was hard to focus on chemistry when my head was spinning. I jumped a little when I felt a gentle hand on my shoulder and looked around to see Nina standing beside me.

"Hi," she said with a smile. "You okay?"

I nodded, signing, GOOD.

I could definitely see myself becoming friends with Nina, really the first person I'd met at Engelmann who had potential. Nina knew I was *here*, and most surprising of all, I didn't mind so much using my voice in front of her. She hadn't seemed fazed one bit when I used my voice in front of her for the first time, unlike Beau, who apparently thought my being able to speak was a miracle of epic proportions. Nina's casual attitude toward my voice made all the difference for me, and I was a little tempted to ask her what my voice sounded like.

"Cool," Nina said. "We're about to . . . council meeting. Love it if . . . stay."

Nina gestured to the people now coming over to the table, notebooks and backpacks in hand, chattering away with one another. And then there was Beau, who always seemed to be somewhere in the background with those green eyes and dimples of his.

Beau had not tried to sign to me again since that incident in Mr. Wells' class, and I was happy about that. I think he got the picture when I snapped at him to keep his nose out of my business. I did *not* need him to stick up for me or tell people they needed to be nice to me because I was Deaf. Being coddled because I couldn't hear was the last thing I needed in my life.

Beau stopped when he saw me sitting at the table, then pulled out a chair across from me and sat down, dropping his giant notebook down on the table.

I was not expecting him to sign, HELLO to me, followed by, HOW ARE YOU?

Apparently, my temporary reprieve from Beau's signing was up.

FINE, I automatically signed back.

He seemed very unsure of himself, but he kept going, signing the words, NICE DAY? next with his eyebrows raised in question.

What was he doing? A sad attempt at an apology in sign language was one thing, but now this? No way was

Beau actually learning ASL to hold a conversation with me. ASL wasn't a particularly easy language to learn as it was, even with a teacher to guide you. Some website and YouTube tutorials weren't always the best way to learn a language like ASL.

"What are you doing?" I said, not caring there were a whole bunch of other people sitting at the table now.

I expected Beau to turn the color of a tomato any time I spoke or signed to him, and he did not disappoint this time. But there was a determined set to his mouth as he tried to sign what I think was supposed to be, I WANT TO LEARN SIGN LANGUAGE, but came out more like, ME SIGN LANGUAGE.

"Did you mean to say, 'I want to learn sign language?'" I asked, incredulous.

When Beau nodded and signed, YES, I demonstrated the correct way to sign that sentence, going through the motions slowly to make sure he understood me. I was about 50 percent sure this was some kind of elaborate prank, but I might as well make sure he was signing things the right way.

THANK YOU, Beau signed when I was done.

Someone started tapping their hand repeatedly on the table by us, and when I turned to look around there was some guy with carefully gelled hair and a blue polo shirt leaning toward me. He was facing me directly, so it wasn't difficult to figure out he was telling me, "This . . . members only."

This was perfectly fine by me, and I wasted no time gathering up my things, sweeping them into my backpack. It wasn't like I wanted to sit through some student council meeting where I'd be the recipient of all these *looks* because I signed or even if I used my voice. I could just as easily go wait outside for Mom.

Beau caught my arm as I was zipping up my backpack and very clearly said, "Stay," and added a PLEASE in sign.

NO, THANK YOU, I signed, lying when I added, MY MOTHER HERE.

I waved good-bye to Nina and got five steps toward the library exit before there was another hand at my shoulder. I turned around and came face-to-face with Beau.

"There's . . ." Beau started to say, but then slowly finger spelled the words S-T-U-D-E-N-T C-L-U-B F-A-I-R. ". . . Friday. Will you come?"

My immediate response was to say *no*. Homework combined with the mountain of unpacking we still had to do made for little wiggle room in my schedule, but I started thinking of the playdate Connor had with one of his new classmates this past weekend.

My eight-year-old little brother was making an effort to meet new people and involve himself at school, CF or not, and the most I'd done was spend some extra time chatting with Nina. As his older sister, didn't I have a responsibility to set a good example for Connor? Show him I was making the most of our move to Colorado too?

So instead I settled for saying, "Maybe."

Maybe if I could hang out with someone like Nina during this student fair thing it might not be so bad, though I certainly saw enough of Engelmann during the almost eight hours five days a week I was required to be here.

There was this glimmer of hope in Beau's expression,

those dimples slowly appearing as he smiled and said, "Okay. Cool . . . see you . . ."

As I left the library, I couldn't decide what I was supposed to think about Beau trying to learn sign language to "talk" to me. His signing was basic, but there was no doubt he'd been practicing with how fluid his movements were becoming. I had to appreciate the effort, but what was he expecting? That he could just learn a few signs online and suddenly we'd be best friends? It was one thing to learn and use ASL, and something totally different to understand the people and culture ASL belong to.

I pulled my phone out of my pocket before sitting on the curb outside the main doors to wait for Mom. I sent a text message to Melissa to get her advice.

Hearing boy is trying to learn sign to talk to me . . . what am I supposed to think of this??

Melissa's reply was almost instantaneous, in choppy English like a lot of Deaf people use when their first language is ASL.

Hearing boy cute??

I huffed out a sigh as I waffled over my reply. Of course, that would be Melissa's first question.

Very tall, very green eyes, . . . and dimples, I finally replied.

So, he cute then, Melissa texted back.

Yes, but he is a HEARING boy!

So? If he learn sign what it matter?

I was saved from texting anything else when Mom pulled up to the curb. Instead of getting into the front seat like I normally would, I opened the door to the back, already knowing what I would find.

Connor was stretched out across the backseat, dozing with his head pillowed on his arm, looking a little paler than usual. I felt my insides twist when I looked at the portable oxygen tank on the floor at his feet and the cannula inserted in his nose to make sure he was getting enough air.

BAD APPOINTMENT? I signed to Mom when she leaned around in her seat to face me.

She gave a grim smile and a small shake of her head. OK, she signed. MOVE HERE HARD FOR HIM. DOCTOR SAY NEED TIME FOR HIM FEEL BETTER.

I carefully set my backpack on the floor next to the oxygen tank and climbed in beside Connor. He jerked awake as I buckled myself in and looked around sleepily.

"Hi, buddy," I said with a smile. "Sorry to wake you up."

He didn't respond. He put his head on my lap instead and was out again in a matter of seconds.

When we got to the house, I had to gently coax Connor from the car while he struggled to keep his eyes open, unsteady on his feet. Mom carried the oxygen tank and my backpack, one step behind us as Connor leaned heavily against me while I led him into the house.

Melissa had texted me about Beau again, but I didn't reply. There was only one hearing boy in my life I cared about, and it wasn't the one with dimples and green eyes.

On Friday, Mom took a half day at work and came home early, leaving the car up for grabs. I figured it might just have been the universe's way of telling me I needed to go to the student club fair after school.

I'd told Beau that *maybe* I would come. Well, *maybe* this was the motivation I'd been waiting for.

Mom straightened up where she sat at the kitchen table pouring over some work documents when I signed, HEY, at her, followed by, BORROW CAR?

She looked equal parts suspicious and excited when she signed, WHY?

I had to fight to keep back the frustrated sigh threatening to break loose while I signed, STUDENT EVENT . . . THING. FOR SCHOOL.

Mom spent about thirty seconds signing, YAY! with such a happy smile on her face it was a wee bit difficult not to start feeling better about my decision to go to this thing at Engelmann in the first place.

WITH FRIEND? she signed in question, leaning forward with interest.

I had to take a second to think about that. I decided

that ultimately, yes, I could call Nina a *friend*. She'd done so much to make me feel welcome at Engelmann—even if she didn't know half the signs Beau seemed to have picked up in two weeks—and she hadn't even batted an eyelash when she heard me use my voice for the first time, which was a major thing for me.

So I signed, YES, to Mom, but quickly added, I THINK.

This time she signed, YAY! for about a minute straight.

I was smiling and groaning in exasperation. If nothing else, at least my mother was thrilled I was being somewhat social now since the move.

NOT STAY LATE, I signed to Mom as I grabbed the car keys from her purse on the chair next to her.

MAYBE YOU GO WITH BROTHER? Mom signed, jabbing a thumb toward the living room where Connor lay sprawled out on the couch.

It looked like he'd melted down into the cushions he'd been there so long, clutching the remote in one hand. I could see that glassy look in his eyes that came from binge watching TV.

This was going to be a student fair type thing with a bunch of high schoolers, but it might do Connor some good to get out of the house and away from Nickelodeon for a little while.

SURE, I signed to Mom, tucking the car keys in the back pocket of my jeans. BRING HOME PIZZA FOR DINNER?

There was never a bad time for pizza, and this way Mom wouldn't have to tear herself away from work to make dinner.

Mom nodded in agreement and dug around in her purse

for a few crumpled bills which she passed over to me. I tucked those away in my back pocket too.

"Hey, squirt," I said to Connor, sitting down on the couch next to him. "What do you say to going to a student fair with me at my school?"

Connor propped himself up on an elbow, his eyes narrowing at me in suspicion. "What's . . . student fair?"

Good question.

"Um. It's a super fun event they do for school clubs. Lots of music and candy and stuff."

This was a bogus lie, so hopefully they *did* have candy there. If Beau was in charge of the event, probably he'd be there throwing more Snickers at people.

The word *candy* seemed to do the trick, and Connor perked right up.

"Okay!" I watched him say excitedly, carefully getting to his feet. He pointed to the corner of the living room where we kept a giant box of spare oxygen tanks for him and signed, HELP ME?

Connor went to fetch the backpack he used for his smaller, portable oxygen tanks when he didn't want to wheel one around, and we got him situated with a tank and a new cannula before we said our good-byes to Mom and left the house.

I kept an eye on Connor in the rearview mirror on our way to Engelmann. I felt a growing sense of relief to see some color coming back into his cheeks.

Most student events at Pratt were typically held in the gym due to its massive size, so it was a bit of a surprise to see Engelmann's student fair taking place smack dab in the middle of the parking lot.

As I drove down the street looking for a parking spot I could see the marching band in their vibrant green uniforms with their glistening instruments, a balloon arch or two, and a bunch of tables set up to advertise school clubs or sports teams.

I spent a few nerve-wracking minutes trying to parallel park the van down the street and gave myself a mental pep talk as I helped Connor get his backpack and oxygen tank situated.

This won't be so bad, I told myself. *Nobody's going to notice you anyway. There's too many people here.*

Connor and I easily mixed into the crowd of people in the parking lot once we reached it. I noticed some of the student body seemed to share the same idea of bringing their siblings to this student fair thing, because Connor wasn't the only one under fourteen here.

I kept an arm around Connor's shoulders as we strolled through the row of tables checking out all the materials and photos student clubs put out in the hopes of getting people to join their organizations. I was definitely right about the candy bit, and I had to cut Connor off when he swiped a huge pile of peanut butter cups and Milky Ways off the Key Club table and dumped them in his backpack.

This was kind of awkward, wandering up and down the rows of activity tables and not seeing any familiar faces, but it wasn't *uncomfortable* like I'd been expecting.

"Can . . . do soccer when . . . high school?" Connor asked me when I looked down at him, pointing to a nearby table where two guys in uniforms where kicking a soccer ball back and forth.

I hesitated answering his question. The honest answer was *probably not*. Connor's lungs had to work so much harder than the average person's, and physical exertion like playing soccer would put even more of a strain on him.

I settled on saying, "Sure, squirt. You can try to do anything you want."

This was the motto I tried to live by at least.

I came to a sudden halt when I saw Nina a couple tables away, talking with some girls that had to be freshmen. I waved without thinking, and it only took a second for Nina to catch sight of me. Her waving was far more enthusiastic than mine had been.

Connor glanced up at me and signed, WHO? and pointed to Nina.

N-I-N-A, I finger spelled for him before leading him over to the student council table.

"You came!" Nina said when we reached her, giving a thousand-watt smile.

"Well, we didn't really have anything else to do this afternoon," I said, which was a half-truth.

Most of the time you could find something worth watching on TV.

I was waiting for that familiar spasm of panic to zip through me watching Nina say hello to Connor, ready to pull him behind me and shield him from inquisitive eyes or nosy questions like always. But that moment strangely did not come. She didn't even seem to notice Connor was on oxygen.

And then Beau was suddenly there too, his smile as genuine as ever as he introduced himself to Connor. Beau wasn't sneaky as he took in Connor's oxygen tank, and my heart skipped a beat in anticipation of the inevitable barrage of questions about to be thrown at me, but that didn't come either.

Beau turned to me and said, "Didn't think . . . come."

"We went out to get pizza," I said quickly. "Thought we'd stop by."

Wasn't like I was going to tell Beau I'd come all the way out here with the express intent of running into him or Nina.

Connor whipped around at this, looking beyond thrilled. "We're . . . pizza⸮!"

It looked like Beau and Nina both laughed at Connor's enthusiasm.

LATER, I signed at Connor, and I watched him give a huff and then dive into the candy bowl on the table.

"So . . ." I did a quick glance over all the brochures and announcements their table had put out, ones with lots of colors and stock photo teens with overly enthusiastic smiles. "What is it that you do exactly⸮"

"Everything," Nina answered, and she laughed again.

Beau waved at me for my attention and started to say, "Student council, DECA, sometimes speech . . . debate."

I was a bit stunned.

Beau was an honors student in advanced placement classes, not to mention the student body president, and he voluntarily took on all these extra clubs⸮ That sounded horrific to me.

WHY? I signed back, my eyes going wide.

I LIKE STAY BUSY, Beau signed with a shrug.

I mean, so did I, but *geez.*

"Don't forget . . . !" Nina added, grabbing a clipboard and passing it over to me.

It was a pink piece of paper decorated with a bunch of balloons, the words *Join the Homecoming Committee* written across the top in bold letters. I felt myself start to grimace, not surprised to see Beau's name toward the top of the paper.

What didn't this guy do? I wanted to be annoyed by it, but I was a little impressed too.

I immediately thrust the clipboard back at Nina. "Dances aren't really my thing."

"No?" Nina said, frowning, and then a look of understanding zipped across her face. "Sorry . . . forget music . . ."

I tried not to sigh here, biting down on my lip. I understood where Nina was coming from, but it wasn't as if music was something off limits to Deaf people. A lot of Deaf people enjoyed music, myself included.

"I like music," I said to Nina. "I can't hear it, but I can still feel it if the beat is strong enough. I'm just not good at dancing."

SAME, Beau signed, and I smothered a laugh.

Beau seemed a little too uncoordinated with his uneven walk to be much of a good dancer.

". . . still . . . fun night," Nina said, returning the clipboard to the table.

"Sure," I agreed halfheartedly.

There wasn't an opportunity to sign or say anything else with the arrival of some preppy looking girl with straight brown hair and a glittering smile, decked out in all sorts of Engelmann High spirit wear. She was pretty—a bit over the top if you asked me, but who was I to judge when this girl looked like she was having a good time?

"Hi! . . . Erica," the girl said when she laid eyes on me.

I mumbled out my name as I shook Erica's hand, and she launched into what I was pretty sure was a detailed description of all the clubs they were advertising. I didn't even bother trying to lip-read what she was saying. I was more interested in the way she kept glancing up at Beau after every few words, almost like she was trying to make sure he was watching her.

If it weren't for the green and black paint—the school colors—decorating her face, I would've thought Erica was blushing.

Connor started tugging on my hand for my attention as I began to wonder just how many clubs and activities Erica did with Beau. She seemed like the type of peppy over-achiever who would be after Beau based on their shared interests.

Except Beau wasn't watching Erica talk. I felt his eyes fixed on me while Connor started signing up at me, a Milky Way stuffed in his mouth.

Connor looked ready to ditch the student activities fair, signing, PIZZA? with a bored expression.

SURE, I signed back. PIZZA NOW.

Any excuse to make a break for it. It looked like Erica had just figured out I hadn't heard a word of what she just said and seemed mildly embarrassed.

"Sorry, but we have to go pick up dinner," I announced suddenly.

OK, Nina signed and gave a thumbs-up, saying something about seeing me in class on Monday.

"Nice to meet you," I said to Erica before turning to Beau and signing, SEE YOU LATER.

Beau nodded with a small smile. "Glad . . . came."

"Sure."

"High school . . . weird, huh?" Connor said to me on our walk back to the van.

"Yeah," I agreed without a second thought. "High school is *so* weird."

High school was plain strange whether you went to a hearing or a Deaf one.

And wasting time wondering about Erica's relationship with Beau certainly wasn't going to help the situation.

CHAPTER 9

The first month of school faded into the second, and autumn gripped the city in its chilly clutches. The days passed, and I grew more accustomed to life at a hearing school, but I still never felt quite like I truly belonged at Engelmann.

Nobody, apart from Nina, seemed interested in getting to know me. I repeatedly told myself this was a good thing—Nina was great, so what did it matter? But it stung more than I wanted to acknowledge. I didn't know if the communication barrier made people uncomfortable around me or if I had the words GO AWAY stamped across my forehead in flashing neon lights, but the rest of my classmates kept their distance.

Nina started picking up signs the more time we spent together at lunch or during downtime in class. She wasn't fluent by any means, but we could hold mini conversations. Nina was without a doubt my first hearing friend in years, something I previously thought impossible. Not to mention it was easier than I thought telling her about Connor and his CF when she'd politely asked why he was on oxygen.

She'd just squeezed my arm and told me how great it was I looked after him, no sign of pity anywhere.

And then there was Beau.

That day during the first week of school when he started signing to me had just been the beginning. Every other day or so he would have a few new signs for me, asking things like YOUR HOMEWORK HARD? or SLEEP GOOD?

I would correct him if he signed something wrong—he usually did—and never gave more than a one- or two-word response. I'm sure my facial expressions were never that enthusiastic when I was signing back, but that never seemed to deter him.

I saw enough of Beau on a daily basis that I had formed a pretty good picture of his life. Beau was Engelmann's golden boy with all his student council work and academic achievements, and he definitely knew it. He even had this "cool guy" way of sitting in class with his right leg stretched out in front of him, leaning back in his chair.

His world and my own belonged in two different solar systems. That's why I couldn't help but feel I was some sort of charity case—a good line for his resume or some essay for college applications. *Look how awesome I am helping a Deaf classmate!*

One day toward the end of September, I returned from the bathroom after Historical Literature, a class I shared with Beau, and found him talking with Kathleen. They were just a few feet away, and because Kathleen had her back to me I couldn't see her response to Beau's question of, "Then why . . . Maya like to . . . back?"

73

I went marching over to them, peeved Beau wanted to talk about me when I wasn't present.

WHAT'S UP? I signed to Kathleen, raising my eyebrows.

Beau offered a HELLO in sign, but I ignored him, waiting on Kathleen.

HE ASK WHY YOU NOT SIGN WITH HIM, she finally signed to me, looking away from Beau.

I rolled my eyes so hard they almost disappeared into the back of my head.

WHY HE CARE? I signed. I knew with his limited knowledge of ASL Beau wouldn't be able to understand what I was signing, but I made it a point to sign quickly just in case. HE NOT BUSY WITH HIS FRIENDS RIGHT NOW? SCHOOL?

For one second Kathleen looked like she was about to smile, but her face remained impassive as she replied, SIGNING NOT THAT BAD, nodding toward Beau.

DOESN'T MATTER, I signed back. I NEVER ASK HIM LEARN SIGN LANGUAGE. WE GO CLASS NOW.

OK, Kathleen signed, and turned to Beau to say, "See you later," signing as she spoke.

I shot off down the hallway without waiting for Kathleen, but she was at my side again once I rounded the corner. We were seated for the final class of the day, chemistry with Mr. Burke, when Kathleen decided to sign, B-E-A-U NICE BOY, RIGHT?

I dug my pencil into my paper, deepening the lines of the doodle I was making in the margins. My answer was an indifferent shrug.

Kathleen tread carefully as she signed next, WHY NOT SIGN WITH HIM MORE? HE LOOK EXCITED.

DON'T CARE, I signed back. I SIGN WITH N-I-N-A, THAT ENOUGH.

TRUE, Kathleen signed with a nod. BUT MAKE NEW FRIEND NOT HURT.

DON'T WANT NEW FRIEND, I told her firmly. HERE FOR SCHOOL, NOT BOY.

Kathleen looked like she wanted to keep this conversation going, but she went palms up in defeat when Mr. Burke flashed the lights, his new way of calling class to attention. I was happy to put this topic to rest, and I was hoping it was one we would not ever resume.

⌀

The day after my run-in with Beau, Nina and I were carrying on one of our half lip-reading, half signing conversations during lunch.

"Do you want . . . over this . . . ?" she asked me as she popped the top off the salad she bought for lunch and dug in.

"What?" I said aloud, confused. I couldn't fill in the blanks I'd missed.

Beau leaned over, waving his hand to sign HEY to get my attention. He started to sign what Nina said slowly, struggling a little to come up with the right words.

SHE ASK IF YOU . . . Beau frowned, biting his lip as he concentrated. I noticed there was that same determined look in his green eyes whenever he was trying to sign. WANT MEET . . . ?

"You want to hang out this weekend?" I guessed, and Beau signed, RIGHT.

"For . . . Mr . . . midterm," Nina said.

I seemed to be off my lip-reading game, so I turned to Beau and signed, HOMEWORK?

He nodded, adding, FOR W-E-L-L-S. M-I-D-T-E-R-M.

The midterm for AP US History was to be a presentation on the historical importance of one major event that took place during twentieth century America. I wasn't sure how my half of the presentation was going to go in sign language, since I was definitely *not* going to use my voice for this. It was nerve-wracking enough giving a presentation if your hearing worked perfectly.

"Sure," I said to Nina. "We could do that."

"Great!" Nina said, smiling all big. "Want to . . . my place?"

Going to Nina's house was the better alternative than her coming over to mine. Most of the unpacking was done, but Connor was still struggling to adjust. Moving to a higher elevation made it harder for him to get enough oxygen, which meant he now had to be on oxygen 24/7, and he did not like that one bit. He was grumpy most of the time now since being put on oxygen, kicking up a minor fuss whenever we had to change his oxygen tanks or get him a new cannula.

When we were at home, he attached himself to my hip and wanted to watch cartoons. This made it a little difficult to get homework or chores done, but I would do anything to make sure Connor got some peaceful rest. If that meant staying up late to finish my homework, I had no problem making more than one pot of coffee in the morning.

Not that I thought any of this would bother Nina, but still, not a great work environment for midterms.

SURE, I signed to Nina.

"I'll . . . my address," Nina said, tapping her phone, and I nodded.

Nina and I texted a lot, mostly about homework and class assignments, but we did find enjoyment going off on tangents over how ridiculous our classmates could be or college plans after graduation. She'd been nothing but supportive when I told her I was determined to get into the best respiratory therapy program possible.

It took me far longer than I would've liked to write my letter of intent to include in my application to Cartwright, but Mrs. Stephens was pleased with the result. We'd submitted the finished application this past week, and I was thinking I wouldn't get a good night's rest until I received a response from the admissions office. It was probably a good thing I had midterms to obsess over.

My gaze fell on Beau as I picked at the peanut butter and jelly sandwich I brought from home. Jackson was sitting next to Beau like always, chatting about whatever it was the school's baseball star and his friend did, but Beau didn't seem to be paying attention to him at all. He was fiddling with his sandwich wrapper, and by the way his lips were only moving once in a while, he was giving Jackson one-word responses.

Beau looked up as Jackson gave him a friendly jab to the side, wanting him to participate in the conversation. He raised his eyebrows when he noticed I was watching him, and I couldn't look away fast enough before he signed, WHAT'S WRONG?

NOTHING, I signed back. I kept it as basic as possible when I signed, J-A-C-K-S-O-N TALK A LOT.

Beau frowned, shaking his head as he signed, DON'T UNDERSTAND.

I pointed to Jackson and moved my hand up by my mouth to mime someone blabbing their head off, and that time Beau understood. It looked like he was trying not to start laughing with the way he pressed his lips together tight, the corners of his eyes crinkling.

YEAH, Beau signed, nodding his head toward Jackson. THAT HIS FAVORITE THING.

Jackson hadn't missed all the pointing we were doing and looked uncomfortable as his eyes moved back and forth between me and Beau. When he leaned toward Beau, I caught a bit of what he was saying, which was something like, "Can you not . . . me . . . right here."

Whatever Jackson was saying, he was clearly a bit annoyed.

"Don't worry . . . we just . . ." Beau said, but the apology was ruined by the smirk on his face.

I went palms up, doing my best not to smile too. This was the amusing bit about two people knowing a language—or at least some of a language—and using it around other people who had no idea what was being said.

Nina put a hand to my shoulder then, and I looked up as she pointed to the ceiling. The bell must've rung since everyone around us was getting up from the table, collecting their trash and backpacks. I realized Beau and I had just been sitting there, smiling at each other, and I didn't know why.

I quickly averted my gaze and gathered up my things, ready to make my escape. My next period was art, a class

I thankfully did not share with Beau. I wasn't an artist by any stretch of the imagination, but it was the only time during the school day I was able to fully relax.

I waved good-bye to Nina and went off to class with Kathleen, who'd been waiting by my locker for me. Class was held in an art studio somewhat like a warehouse, with concrete floors and high ceilings, years of students' artwork covering every inch of the walls.

Kathleen began to interpret as the teacher, Ms. Phillips, got to her feet, walking around her desk to come to the front of the studio.

TODAY WE DO SELF PORTRAIT, Kathleen signed as Ms. Phillips spoke. DRAW WHO YOU THINK YOU ARE.

Who am I? That was not a question I could answer very easily anymore. I had ambitions for my future, but who am I right now? A Deaf girl suddenly dropped into the middle of a hearing world I was positive I didn't belong in anymore.

I kept running the question over and over again in my mind as I collected a bunch of charcoal pencils from the supply shelf and pulled out my sketchbook. Kathleen explained that Ms. Phillips was letting us use whatever was in the art studio to complete the self-portrait. My more ambitious classmates were pulling out lumps of clay or paintbrushes and blank canvases.

I flipped open my sketchbook to a clean page, still at a loss of how I was going to do this. Ms. Phillips wanted a self-portrait. Did that mean a representation of who I saw when I looked in a mirror or something that showed who I felt like I was on the inside?

Ms. Phillips made a stop at my table as I was drawing

thick, loopy lines with a charcoal pencil, getting absolutely nowhere.

She waved Kathleen over to interpret and Kathleen signed, WHAT'S WRONG?

CONFUSED? Kathleen added, pointing to me.

YES, I signed quickly. VERY CONFUSED.

Ms. Phillips' frown deepened when Kathleen told her this, and she said, "How can . . . help?"

I thought about how to respond to this question for one long beat, and signed, I FEEL I DON'T KNOW MYSELF.

Ms. Phillips looked thoughtful as she pulled out the stool across the worktable from me and sat down. Kathleen hovered nearby.

"That's . . . normal. A part of . . . life," Ms. Phillips said, resting her chin in her hands. "It's okay . . . take your time."

Ms. Phillips leaned across the table to pick up the charcoal pencils next to my sketchbook, staring down at them, lost in thought again.

YOU SEE YOURSELF I-N BLACK AND WHITE? Kathleen signed when Ms. Phillips finally spoke.

NO, I signed in answer. DON'T KNOW.

I mean, I liked color. I *loved* color. That's why I had so many reprints of Van Gogh and Picasso paintings on my bedroom walls. You don't have to hear colors. When I looked at their artwork, I wasn't missing anything.

Ms. Phillips got up and crossed the studio to the massive industrial shelves where she kept every kind of art supply known to man. She rummaged around for a bit before she came back with two trays of bold-colored paints.

"Try . . . these," she said, tapping the trays.

OK, I replied hesitantly.

I was decent enough at sketching, but I'd never attempted painting before. This was just supposed to be a basic art class, so I hoped Ms. Phillips wasn't expecting the next "The Starry Night" out of me for this.

Ms. Phillips gave me a reassuring smile and drifted off to the next worktable to see how things were going.

I sat there staring at the tray of paints in front of me, full of bright reds, greens, and blues, and finally I got up and went to grab the last easel resting in the corner of the studio beside a pile of canvases. The least I could do was try.

CHAPTER 10

There was a breakfast of chocolate chip pancakes on the table when I trudged downstairs Saturday morning still half asleep. Connor was chowing down on his pancakes and gave a happy wave when I plopped into the chair beside him.

Mom gave a dramatic start when she saw me, a hand at her heart, and signed, YOU AWAKE BEFORE NOON. WOW.

FUNNY, I signed with an eye roll. COFFEE?

KITCHEN, Mom signed back.

She'd put a stack of pancakes and syrup at my spot on the table when I came back from the kitchen with a steaming mug of coffee and my favorite hazelnut creamer.

BUSY DAY TODAY? I asked Mom.

She shook her head, cutting into her own stack of pancakes. CONNOR WANT MOVIE DAY, she signed, nodding toward my little brother, who was still stuffing his face. I TRY WORK FROM HOME. YOU BUSY?

I was nervous to tell her about Nina's invitation to work on our midterm project for Mr. Wells' class at her house. Mom and I hadn't really talked much about me making hearing friends, and I didn't know if she'd be excited or nervous for me.

BORROW CAR? I signed to Mom in a rush.

Mom looked taken aback by my question and signed, WHY?

FRIEND ASK IF I WORK WITH HER TODAY FOR M-I-D-T-E-R-M, I explained. WE PARTNERS.

A wide smile broke out across Mom's face as she signed, FRIEND? SAME FRIEND FROM BEFORE?

YES, I signed with a huff. WE HAVE CLASS TOGETHER.

Mom was firing off rapid questions now, like WHO SHE? and NAME? and WHAT SHE LIKE?

N-I-N-A, I told her. YOU MET HER. SHE MY STUDENT MENTOR WHEN I START SCHOOL.

I SEE, Mom signed with the same enthusiastic smile. WONDERFUL. YOU GIVE HER SIGN NAME? Mom asked curiously.

I shook my head, signing, NO. I hadn't planned on getting close enough to anyone to give them a sign name, but Nina had proved to be a pretty stand-up friend. She could probably do with one.

YOU SHOULD, Mom signed.

I shrugged. MAYBE.

HAPPY YOU MAKE FRIEND, Mom signed, and now a rather interesting expression was taking over her face as she smiled. WHAT ABOUT BOY?

The bite of pancake I'd just taken stuck in my throat, and I nearly choked. I stole Connor's milk and took a big gulp to wash it down.

DON'T UNDERSTAND, I signed once I could breathe properly again. NO BOY.

Mom's smile was slowly morphing into a smirk. BOY SIGNED SEE YOU LATER THAT DAY YOU WAIT OUTSIDE FOR ME AFTER SCHOOL ALL DONE.

I did *not* want to mention Beau's name to her because I would never see the end of it. Mom never directly came out and said she was worried I was going to be eighteen at the end of next January and I'd never been on a date, but I had a strong suspicion that thought floated around her brain every so often. This was a conversation I wanted to avoid at all costs.

TALL BOY, Mom signed to me while I started shoving bite after bite of pancake in my mouth. CUTE.

DON'T KNOW, I signed again.

Mom slumped back in her chair, and I knew she was giving a huff of exasperation. NOT HURT YOU IF YOU TRY MEET BOY, she signed, her expression moving from curious to serious.

FINE WITHOUT BOY, I told her honestly.

Mom threw up her hands and signed, FINE. BUT ONE DATE NOT HURT YOU.

I returned my attention to my pancakes, ready to be done with this whole thing. Besides, Mom knew as well as I did I would prefer to date a Deaf boy—hearing, or lack of hearing, was a huge thing to have in common with someone—and as far as I knew, there weren't any of those at Engelmann.

Mom tapped the table in front of my plate again, and when I looked up she signed, IF YOU DATE HEARING BOY, THAT NOT BAD.

I shook my head, now viciously stabbing at my pancakes with my fork. MY FOCUS SCHOOL, I signed after I stuffed a huge bite of pancake in my mouth. HOMEWORK, COLLEGE. NO TIME FOR BOY.

She finally let it go, signing, FINE IF YOU BORROW CAR.

THANK YOU, I signed, relieved to have tabled the subject.

Knowing my mother, she would bring it back around eventually, especially if she ever saw Beau when she picked me up from school again. But for now I was going to refuse to think about it.

I helped Mom clean up the breakfast dishes and went upstairs to shower and dress while I finished the rest of my coffee. Nina had told me it was fine to come over whenever, but the sooner we got to work on this midterm, the better. Mr. Wells was a bit of an airhead, but there were rumors about him being a harsh grader, and a low grade on a midterm was the last thing I needed mucking up my transcript.

COME HOME AFTERNOON, I signed to Mom as I swiped the keys from her purse on the kitchen counter.

Mom was on the couch watching a movie with Connor, who already looked like he was falling asleep. Looking at him I felt a pang of sadness zip through me. He was having a really tough go of it. I'm sure the thought had already occurred to Mom, but maybe it was time to reach out for some help and get another home health care provider for Connor worked into our schedule.

WE GO T-O PARK LATER, Mom signed to me as I put on my jacket.

FUN, I signed, forcing a smile. It was supposed to be

another crisp autumn day, but it would be good for Connor to get out of the house for some fresh air.

SEE YOU LATER, I signed, and bent down to plant a kiss on Connor's forehead. He waved halfheartedly, torn between his movie and rest.

It was a ten-minute drive to Nina's. The majority of houses in her neighborhood seemed upscale, the lawns well-kept and cars in the driveways that cost more than a year's college tuition. Nina's house was at the end of a cul-de-sac, a brown, two-story home with a porch swing and a row of potted plants leading up to the front door.

The door swung open while I was on my way up the walkway to the porch and Nina stepped outside, dressed as nicely as she always was at school.

She ushered me inside as she signed, HELLO.

NICE HOME, I signed, inspecting my surroundings.

The décor was made up of soft cream colors, with leather furniture in the living room and an impressive flat screen TV mounted on the wall above their fireplace. Nina had never mentioned what her parents' jobs were, but I was willing to bet those jobs paid *very* well.

"Go ahead . . . shoes," Nina said, gesturing to the neat shoe rack beside the front door.

I was embarrassed about my mismatched cartoon socks when I took my shoes off, but Nina didn't seem to notice. I followed after her as she rounded the corner, away from the living room.

I assumed we were going to set up camp at the massive bar in the kitchen where Nina's history textbook and notebook were, so I set my backpack down on one of the barstools.

Nina got us some water bottles from the fridge, and I saw her say, "Hey," when she swung the fridge door shut.

I looked over my shoulder and saw a woman who was obviously Nina's mother, dressed in brightly-colored exercise clothes, walk into the kitchen. Her hair was the same color as Nina's, pulled back into a high ponytail, and she had similar square-framed glasses.

"Mom, this . . ." Nina was saying, gesturing to me. "She's . . ."

I was caught off guard when Nina's mom turned my way and signed, HELLO. NICE T-O MEET YOU, with a pleasant smile.

SAME, I signed, still taken aback. YOU SIGN?

A LITTLE, Nina's mom signed back. COLLEGE CLASS.

I was a little overly excited when I signed, COOL!

MY NAME J-A-C-K-I-E, Nina's mom signed, introducing herself. "And that's . . . finished," she said with a laugh.

I busied myself with pulling out my school things while Nina conversed with her mom. She joined me at the bar after Jackie left the kitchen.

"Ready?" Nina asked me, reaching for a highlighter. "Mom went for . . . jog, and my dad's . . . work."

"It's just us?" I guessed as I sat on the barstool beside her.

Nina nodded. "Thankfully," she said. "My brother's away . . . Stonybrook . . . in New York."

COOL, I signed, flipping open my textbook.

". . . brother . . . kind . . . genius," Nina said, pulling her own textbook toward her. "Less pressure . . . me."

"Do you want to go to New York too?" I said, interested to learn a little more about Nina.

THE SILENCE BETWEEN US

She gave this dramatic shudder and shook her head. "No . . . prefer Colorado. Close . . . home."

I couldn't say I preferred Colorado when I'd been here less than two months, but I could relate to wanting to stick close to home. Mom and Connor—they were my home.

SAME, I signed with a tiny smile. "So where do you want to go to college?" I asked aloud next.

Nina held up one finger, signaling me to wait, and then very carefully began to finger spell, C-U B-O-U-L-D-E-R.

The effort she put into finger spelling made my smile widen, so I signed, FOR? back at her.

"History," she said aloud. ". . . want . . . work . . . museums."

She ended her sentence with a word I couldn't quite make out, so I imagined she'd said something about wanting to be a curator or director or something.

WONDERFUL, I signed to her.

"Well, let's get . . . work," Nina said with a happy smile, tapping a finger on the textbook. "Promise . . . have snacks . . ."

The next hour or so passed quickly, but we made little progress. Nina and I were wearing identical frowns as we poured over our books. We'd narrowed down the list and had talked about how we would do a presentation, but we weren't any closer to picking a final topic.

"What . . . we . . . do? The . . . century . . . huge," Nina said while she scribbled out half a page of notes about famous events scattered throughout the twentieth century.

Nina grabbed the piece of scratch paper we'd been using to jot notes to each other when speaking or signing wasn't cutting it and wrote: *How did presentations at your old school go?*

I shrugged, unsure of how to answer. "Normal, I guess?"

Apart from being done in sign language.

Nina made a sour face and shoved her textbook away, hopping down from her stool. FOOD, she signed, heading over to the refrigerator.

I checked the time on my phone and noted it was nearly noon. Hard to believe we hadn't picked a topic for our presentation after two hours.

"We have time to work on this," I said to Nina, following after her. "We'll figure it out."

With my stocking feet on the kitchen floor, I felt the reverberation when Nina slammed the refrigerator door shut after pulling out a cup of yogurt. She ripped the foil lid off, grabbed a spoon from a drawer nearby, and dug in.

I didn't understand why she signed, SORRY, once she finished the yogurt, which she did in about a minute. That sour look was still on her face while she chucked the empty yogurt cup in the trash.

"Is everything okay?" I asked hesitantly.

Nina flopped over onto the kitchen counter, holding her face in her hands. "I always . . . worked up about school. I feel like . . . perfect grades. And . . . love history . . . but still . . . all classes . . . important. Need . . . ace this."

I was getting the impression that this conversation was about to move into more personal territory, and yet I still felt weirdly comfortable speaking with Nina being so open about herself. That didn't always have to be a bad thing.

"I feel that way too," I said. "Literally all the time."

Sometimes it seemed like I drove myself to the edge trying to ace every homework assignment and test thrown my way. Somewhere along the way I'd convinced myself having perfect grades was the only way I'd get into a reputable RT program and actually get to do what I'd dreamed of for years. It didn't help that I was never fully awake until at least fourth period, when two of my AP classes were done and over with. Staying up late each night to muddle through a mountain of homework made me groggy all morning, even with multiple cups of coffee.

"My mom is . . . and my dad . . . doctor," Nina was telling me. "Big shoes . . . I need to . . . good school. Boulder . . . not . . . easy school . . ."

"Nina, I think you'll have no problem getting into Boulder," I told her, hoping my voice sounded firm and confident. "You're beyond smart. You'll be fine."

"Thanks, but I think . . . will get into . . . before me," Nina replied.

When I just stared at her in confusion, not understanding who she was talking about, she finger spelled, B-E-A-U.

"What about him?" I said, trying to keep from frowning like I did every time somebody mentioned Beau.

"He wants . . . Yale," Nina said. "It's like, all his dad . . . for him." Her eyes crinkled up at the corners when she laughed and said, "I think that's . . . we get along . . . well. We're both . . . over-achievers."

I figured Beau was smart, but Ivy League? I couldn't help but be a little impressed.

"But at least my . . . aren't on me . . . like Beau's dad . . ."

Nina said with a small shake of her head. "All he does is try to . . ."

"Try to what?" I said, suddenly anxious to know what she had said about Beau.

Nina held up a finger, signaling for me to wait, and went to grab the scratch paper off the bar. She took her time writing something down before passing the paper over to me.

Beau's dad is pretty intense when it comes to college. Half of Beau's family went to Yale, so that's what his dad wants for him too. I think it makes him sick sometimes, thinking about what will happen if he doesn't get in. I don't think he'd even be on the student council if his dad hadn't told him it would look good on college applications.

I didn't know how to respond to Nina's note.

I could at least understand the pressure Beau must feel about getting into the college of his choice, even if in my case, *I* was the one laying on the pressure. But this information didn't quite match up to what I knew of Beau. He always seemed so self-assured, confident even, when he was signing and clearly struggling with finding the right word. But if someone else was dictating his life, maybe he didn't have it all together like I thought.

WHAT'S WRONG? Nina signed when I finally tore my gaze from her note.

NOTHING, I signed immediately.

She stared at me a few more moments, her lips pursed like she was trying to refrain from speaking.

"What?" I asked, feeling uncomfortable.

"Nothing," she finally said and gave me such a bright

smile I thought I was going to get whiplash from her sudden change in mood. "So, are you . . . homecoming next . . . ¿"

I didn't need to be hearing to know what she was asking. I shouted, "No!" before she'd even finished speaking. "I told you at that student fair thing I don't like dances, remember¿"

Nina threw back her head and laughed. I failed to see what was so funny.

"Well, homecoming will be . . . than homework," she said, nodding to the mess of textbooks and notes on the counter.

"Homecoming is better than Mr. Wells' midterm¿ Impossible!" I said firmly.

I think that made Nina laugh even harder.

"Come on, girl, let's . . . finished," she said. "But first . . . need more snacks."

"Yeah," I agreed. "Food first. Always. But I think I have an idea on what to do for our presentation."

I was pretty sure no high schooler would choose working on midterms over chitchat about homecoming, but getting good grades was higher up on my list of priorities than some dance.

And besides, I was pretty sure I had an idea in mind that might get my classmates to get a little more comfortable with sign language.

CHAPTER *11*

Even if I managed to steer Nina away from talk of homecoming that one time, it didn't count for much at school the following Monday. Suddenly *everything* at Engelmann seemed to be about homecoming. I was a bit stunned I hadn't noticed it sooner. There were brightly colored, glittery banners and fliers plastered throughout the hallways, and somebody had even started up a countdown in the cafeteria.

All this excitement for homecoming just served to remind me of the one disastrous dance I went to at Pratt my sophomore year. The guy I'd been crushing on at the time, Jake Perkins, asked me to go with him in the middle of math class, only to ditch me halfway through the dance for some other girl. I spent the rest of the dance as a wallflower, feeling sorry for myself. I was not eager to repeat the experience, and besides—how different could homecoming at a hearing school really be?

I should've been preoccupied with upcoming midterms, and in a way I definitely was, but it was hard to shake off thoughts of homecoming with so many reminders everywhere. Even Beau—who claimed he wasn't good at dancing—was in on the homecoming babble and seemed genuinely excited.

I was sitting across the table from him at lunch, probably paying more attention to him than I should have, as he spoke with Jackson. Beau talked with his hands a lot even when he wasn't keeping up with his signs, and sometimes watching him was more interesting than anything else going on at Engelmann.

Beau wasn't facing me head-on, so I couldn't be positive, but I was pretty sure I saw his lips form the word *homecoming* a time or two.

Jackson was easier to get a read on, and maybe it was rude of me to think, but the guy had a big mouth. Lipreading whatever he said didn't take much effort. My interest was definitely piqued when I saw Jackson say, ". . . should ask Erica . . . homecoming."

I figured Jackson must've been talking about the Erica I'd met at the student fair event a while back. I'd seen her a couple of times in the hallways and she'd wave hello to be polite, but that was about it for our interaction since I didn't have any classes with her.

Beau just rolled his eyes at Jackson, saying something like, ". . . don't like . . . like that."

So Beau didn't like Erica? That was . . . interesting. She kind of seemed like the type of girl Beau would date, being the student body president and all.

When Beau glanced my way a second later, I quickly averted my gaze and tried to engage Nina in a conversation in sign. Somehow it was significantly more embarrassing getting caught lipreading when it was Beau's mouth that I was watching.

When lunch was over, and Kathleen and I were on our way to art class with Ms. Philips, my mind was stuck on Erica and why Jackson thought Beau should ask her to homecoming, so I wasn't absorbing much of what Kathleen was signing at me. Something about homecoming too, I think. I couldn't fault Kathleen for being so nice and peppy, because sometimes seeing a friendly face was a relief, but did my interpreter really have to show so much interest in a school dance?

This was turning into one of those days when I was eager to jump into working on my self-portrait rather than focusing on everything else going on around me. So far, I'd come up with a decent outline of *someone* on my canvas, but I was struggling with how to make that someone *me*.

When we walked into the classroom I went straight for the supply shelves and got out the trays of bright paints Ms. Phillips suggested I use the other week. I'd been afraid to touch the colors for fear of messing up somehow, but this assignment's due date was quickly approaching.

I got myself a variety of paintbrushes and a cup of water for cleaning them, then set up my canvas on an easel toward the back of the classroom. I didn't want anybody to see me while I worked, but I could feel Kathleen's presence behind me, peering over my shoulder as I inspected the trays of colors resting on the easel in front of me.

Kathleen signed, COLOR TODAY? when I looked up at her.

I shrugged.

MAYBE, I signed back. DON'T KNOW.

Kathleen tapped a finger to her lips in thought while her eyes swept over my canvas.

I felt myself frown when she signed, BLUE, after a moment and pointed to the corresponding color on the tray.

WHY? I signed in confusion.

Kathleen curved her index finger and tapped the top of her ear twice, the sign for *hearing aid*. YOU, RIGHT? she added in sign with raised eyebrows.

She has a point, I thought.

My hearing aids *were* a rather big part of myself, and in my opinion neon blue was a pretty awesome color. It didn't seem like it would be too difficult to incorporate that color into my self-portrait.

OK, I signed to Kathleen after a moment. I TRY THAT.

Kathleen gave one of her big smiles and a thumbs-up, and then the moment was ruined when she signed TRY DANCE? next.

The expression on Kathleen's face was so earnest I couldn't find it in myself to outright sign, NO. So I settled for signing, MAYBE, again.

Homecoming probably wouldn't be so bad if Nina and Beau were there. They did know some sign language. And at least I knew homecoming dances were never like what you saw on TV—no one breaking out into choreographed dances or songs, no embarrassing confessions of love from the homecoming king.

At the very least I knew I'd make an okay wallflower.

Nina ended up wearing down the last of my resistance about going to homecoming. She was nothing if not persistent, and she assured me homecoming at Engelmann was always a good time and the homecoming committee—which she was a proud member of—put on a good show. That was all fine and dandy, but I still had serious doubts I would end up enjoying myself.

But I went along with it anyway because it *was* nice hanging out with a friend when homework or school assignments were not involved. Nina had done so much to make me feel welcome at Engelmann, and if she wanted me to go to homecoming with her as her "friend date," how could I say no?

Mom had a smile about a mile wide stuck on her face as she drove me to Nina's house early on Saturday evening, a few hours before homecoming. Connor was in the backseat, engrossed in a video game. He still had plenty of time before he had to brave the perils of high school dances.

At a stoplight around the corner from Nina's place, Mom turned to me and signed, YOU KNOW I BUY YOU NEW DRESS IF YOU WANT.

I HATE GO T-O M-A-L-L, I reminded her. Clothes shopping was the worst and had never been a favorite pastime of mine. I FINE BORROW DRESS FROM N-I-N-A.

SHOP FUN, Mom disagreed.

SOMETIMES, I signed back.

Mom pulled up into the driveway of the Torres' house, and the front door whipped open a second later. Nina came bounding over to greet us, a peppy bounce in her step.

Mom rolled down the window to greet Nina, and she

THE SILENCE BETWEEN US

leaned into the car, waving happily. I tried to smile back, but I was still feeling a little iffy about this whole homecoming thing now that it was finally upon us.

"Promise . . . have good time," Nina was saying to Mom, and Mom was laughing, nodding along as she spoke. "Homecoming always . . . fun."

Nina peeked into the backseat next and waved to Connor, who somehow managed to return the wave without looking up from his Nintendo 3DS.

I grabbed my bag off the floor by my feet and gave Mom a fleeting hug before getting out of the car, promising to keep her updated throughout the night. She gave one massive yawn as she signed, SEE YOU LATER, and I stood there on the driveway for a beat, looking at her more closely. It wasn't something I did often, but that yawn caught my attention.

Mom had dark circles under her eyes, and her hair looked greasy pulled back into a messy bun. The lines around her eyes and mouth, from laughing and smiling, seemed more pronounced, like she'd been aging faster than normal.

I felt both guilty and sad seeing how rundown Mom was. She wasn't taking care of herself, and I knew it was because she devoted all her time and energy to Connor, making sure he was healthy and as comfortable as possible, on top of being our family's sole financial provider. And there I was, her daughter who certainly hadn't made life any easier, kicking up a fuss about moving to Colorado and going to a hearing school.

I had to make it up to her somehow.

HEY, Nina signed to me when we were in the entryway of the house and I'd kicked off my shoes. YOU OK?

"I'm fine," I said aloud, holding my bag tightly to my chest. "Just distracted."

"Don't worry," Nina said, leading me toward the stairs. "Homecoming will be . . . you'll love . . . promise."

"Sure," I said. "It'll be great."

Nina dragged me up to her bedroom on the second floor, and I could tell from the second I walked in that she'd been taking her time preparing for homecoming. She had all sorts of makeup carefully lined up across her dresser, a curling iron plugged in, a bunch of hair products out, and a handful of dresses laying in a neat row across her bed.

"I think we're . . . same size," Nina said as I set my bag on the floor. "I pulled out . . . dresses I think . . . might like."

I went over to the bed to inspect the dresses. She'd set out four for me to look over, and they were all far more stylish than anything I'd ever worn. One was purple with a lot of lace and a little too low cut for my liking, two were black and simple but would probably fall a few too many inches above my knees since I was taller than Nina, and the last was yellow, more like a sundress than something you would wear to a school dance. It seemed like the perfect fit for me.

"This one," I said, trailing my fingers along the fabric. "I like it."

"I . . . you might," Nina said with a sly grin. "Try it . . . !"

I took the dress, and Nina showed me to the bathroom down the hallway where I could change. I was careful to fold my jeans and T-shirt and set them on the counter as I tried on the dress. The bathroom was full of extravagant towels, soaps, and potpourri, and I didn't want to mess anything up.

Nina was right about us being the same size. The dress fit perfectly, cinched at the waist and falling a few inches past my knees. I looked at my reflection in the bathroom mirror before going to show Nina. I still recognized myself, so that was a good thing. I didn't think my neon blue hearing aids were a good fit with the yellow color of the dress though, but there was nothing to be done about that.

"I knew it!" Nina clapped her hands and did a little dance when I came back to her room, my clothes tucked up under my arm. "You look . . . pretty!"

"Thanks," I said awkwardly.

"Come on . . . down," Nina said, ushering me over to the chair she put in front of the mirror propped up on her desk. "I'm going to . . . your hair first."

I pulled out my hearing aids and set them carefully on the desk, then gave Nina the go-ahead to pull my hair out of its twist. I used the mirror in front of us to lip-read when she started to speak.

"I didn't know . . . hair was . . . long!" she said, eyes wide as she started working out some knots with a comb.

"I like to keep it up," I said. "My hair gets tangled around my hearing aids a lot."

I gave Nina full permission to do whatever she wanted with my hair and makeup and let her work her magic. I never bothered doing anything with my hair in the morning besides throwing it up in a ponytail, and after the one time Melissa gave me a disastrous makeover sophomore year, I didn't see the point in makeup either.

I purposely did not look in the mirror while Nina worked, instead focusing on eating the pizza her mom bought us for dinner. Nina must have had more patience than I gave her credit for because she wound up doing a fabulous job curling my hair, something Melissa had declared impossible.

Nina went light with the makeup and used lip gloss to make my lips shinier than usual.

"I know you're . . . nervous," Nina said to me as I spent longer than I should have inspecting my reflection in the mirror. "But I promise . . . will have . . . great time."

I wasn't used to seeing myself with eyeshadow or mascara, but it made my eyes look brighter, my lips a shiny pink from the lip gloss. I looked . . . *different*, but still somehow like myself. Not hideous or anything like that, but maybe a little misshapen—like my self-portrait.

"Right," I said, not meeting her gaze as I put my hearing aids in. "A great time."

CHAPTER 12

The parking lot at Engelmann was packed when we arrived. Nina spent a few minutes cruising through row after row looking for a spot, singing along to whatever song was blasting from the radio. She turned the volume up loud enough to where I could feel the entire seat vibrating underneath me, which was not helping to calm me down.

We finally found a spot way in the back. I let Nina lead the march into school, feeling a bit like her awkward shadow. She looked like a knockout in the red sheath dress she wore with dangly gold earrings and her hair pulled back into a ponytail. It was a simple and elegant look, and she carried herself with a confidence I tried to mimic as we walked through the parking lot. Just because I was a nervous wreck didn't mean everyone else needed to know it too.

Once we got inside, Nina gave our tickets to the front office receptionist who had the bad luck of chaperoning, then wiggled her way into the gym, itching to start dancing. There were strands of twinkle lights cascading down from the gym ceiling and a lot of dark blue and black balloons everywhere. Pretty much everyone was already dancing or stuffing their faces with snacks from the refreshment tables in the back of the gym.

Nina was shouting something to me, but I couldn't make out what she was saying because the lighting was too dim to lipread. She caught my wrist and led me across the dance floor to the refreshment tables, and I quickly figured out why. Beau was there.

I felt awkward and uncomfortable wearing a dress as nice as this one, but it looked like Beau felt the same way in the dress pants and red button-down shirt he was wearing. His face was all screwed up in a frown as he ate a cookie, giving a side-eyed glare to the nearby couple dancing a little too enthusiastically.

He dropped the second cookie that was in his hand when he saw Nina and me approaching and swallowed down the rest of the cookie in his mouth. It was too dark to tell, but I was sure he was blushing.

Nina greeted him with a friendly punch to the shoulder and must have commented on his appearance by the way he started fidgeting with the collar of his shirt. His eyes moved to me as he gave Nina a response, and whatever he was saying fell short.

I almost started squirming under his gaze. Why was he looking at me like that? I stared back defiantly, signing, WHAT'S UP?

Beau didn't seem to think twice about signing the word for *beautiful*, a circular motion with the fingers around the face, and then pointed to me.

I didn't know how else to respond but to sign, GOOFY, and point right back at him.

THE SILENCE BETWEEN US

Beau cracked a smile at this and signed, THANK YOU.

YOU'RE WELCOME, I signed back.

I didn't know what to do with the fact Beau thought I looked beautiful. He wasn't paying much attention to what Nina was saying to him, his eyes still on me, and I was torn between feeling flattered and wanting to tell him to knock it off. I never got much notice from boys, Deaf or hearing. This was weird. Even weirder was this weightless sensation taking me over, making me curl my toes from the way Beau was looking at me.

HAPPY YOU HERE, Beau signed next.

From the genuinely pleased look on his face, I had to think he meant that.

Now I wasn't sure if I wanted to giggle or hide my face in embarrassment. I knew my cheeks were hot already, but at least the lighting was poor and he couldn't tell.

Rather than sign something I knew Beau wouldn't understand, I said, "I'm not doing anything else tonight."

SAME, he replied in sign. He tried signing something else, and it took me a moment to figure out he was trying to ask me if I liked dancing, but he floundered on the last word, his lips pursed again.

I was trying not to grin as I showed him how to properly sign the word for dance—the tips of the middle and index fingers moving back and forth across the palm a few times.

NO, I then signed in answer to his question, adding, I HATE DANCE.

SAME, Beau signed again with the same grin as before.

Nina had her hands on both our forearms, snagging our attention, and said, "Do . . . guys want . . . dance?"

Beau and I both started laughing.

Nina was determined to hit the dance floor, and that was my cue to excuse myself to go to the restroom. I hid in the bathroom playing Fruit Ninja on my cell phone. Not really what you were supposed to be doing at homecoming, but the more time I could kill, the less time I'd have for dancing.

I figured my time was up after fifteen minutes. I wouldn't put it past Nina to come hunt me down and drag me back out there. And seeing as she was my ride, it wasn't like I could make an early escape.

Eventually I began making my way back toward the dance, but I took my sweet time doing it. I was still some distance from the gym, but I could feel the bass vibrating the tiled floor—not enough to pick up any distinct rhythm, but it was enough to tell it was some upbeat, fast-paced song. I thought about finding a new hiding spot, but I stopped when I caught sight of Beau.

He had apparently snuck off too and was partially hidden behind the mountain of jackets and shoes on the folding tables where the receptionist had sat taking tickets. I could see him in the corner, his mess of hair and his shoes with his long legs stretched out in front of him a dead giveaway.

There was a book open in his lap, and he seemed lost in the pages as he absentmindedly munched on the cookie in his hand. I stood there watching him long enough for it to get creepy, but it was weirdly fascinating to see him outside his natural habitat. He just kept turning page after page, pulling a cookie from the stack he had on a napkin next to him. He seemed oblivious to all the noise around him while he was reading, like he'd checked out from everything—the same thing I liked to do.

I took a few steps closer, but he still didn't look up from his book. Between his fingers I could see the title: *Canterbury Tales.* This guy was doing the reading for our Historical Literature class at homecoming.

"Are you really reading Chaucer at a school dance right now?" I asked him in disbelief.

Beau looked up in surprise and nodded, signing, YES.

"Why?" Beau probably had a lot of friends wondering where he was, and more than a few girls wanting to dance with him. Probably Erica that Jackson had mentioned the other day for one. "Don't you want to go hang out with your friends? Or have some student council thing to take care of?"

FORGET, Beau signed, giving his book a little shake. NEED FOR HOMEWORK.

"So?" I said. "There's always time for homework tomorrow."

He gave a slight smile and signed, TRUE. BUT NOW WORK FOR ME.

I settled myself on the floor beside him without really thinking about it, snagging a cookie from the pile on the napkin and taking a bite out of it.

"Nina says you worry about school a lot," I said around a mouthful of cookie.

The conversation I had with Nina during our sloppy

attempt at putting together a presentation for our history midterm last weekend had been illuminating to say the least.

Beau's lips pressed together tightly as he snapped *Canterbury Tales* shut, signing, TRUE, again.

I was frowning as I finished off the last of my cookie and reached for another one. Why was Beau not using his voice? I appreciated the signing, but I got the feeling Beau felt the same way about signing that I felt about using my voice. It was awkward and maybe uncomfortable, but we both kept doing it anyway.

I decided to go along with it in the moment. Besides, if we both didn't use our voices, that meant we could keep eating cookies.

WHY YOU WORRY ABOUT SCHOOL? I signed to Beau.

I had to repeat myself twice before he understood what I was asking. It took him a minute or two to come up with an answer. I could practically see the cogs whirring in his brain while he tried to come up with the signs he wanted to use.

NEED GO TO GOOD C-O-L-L-E-G-E, he finally signed, reaching for another cookie.

I KNOW, I signed. Y-A-L-E.

YES. HOW YOU KNOW? Beau signed, his brows pulled together in confusion.

N-I-N-A TELL ME, I answered. TELL ME YOU REALLY SMART.

I had to finger spell the word *smart* for him, and he went pink in the face once he got it. His response was, MAYBE.

NO LIE, I signed, trying to hide a smile. YOU KNOW YOU SMART.

Beau shrugged, wiping a bit of frosting from the cookie off his pant leg.

I leaned over and nudged him gently with my elbow, wanting his attention. WHAT'S WRONG? I signed when he finally looked at me.

He immediately started to finger spell the word *nothing*, and I stopped him before he got too into it, showing him the proper sign. *Nothing* was kind of a weird sign; making the letter *o* with your fingers and shaking your hand back and forth.

Beau just signed it again, NOTHING.

LIE, I signed right back at him.

Why couldn't he just tell me what was eating at him?

FINE, Beau signed quickly. NOT LIE. TRUE.

I pulled a quizzical face, channeling Sherlock Holmes as I narrowed my eyes and put my chin in my hand.

This made Beau laugh, and for one split second I wanted to know what that laughter sounded like. His dimples appeared, and I felt my stomach give a huge flip before the moment was over.

HATE SCHOOL, Beau signed once he was done laughing. DON'T LIKE.

SAME, I agreed. BUT LAW SAY WE NEED SCHOOL.

I KNOW, Beau signed. BUT I . . .

He paused, gnawing on his lip as he struggled to convey what he wanted to tell me.

"But what?" I said aloud because it seemed easier that way.

Maybe Beau's signing wasn't exceptional, but he was trying to communicate with me nevertheless. He knew more sign than Nina did. I could at least meet him halfway, right?

"I don't know . . . I want . . . my life," he said, looking agitated as he reached for another cookie. Our supply was quickly dwindling.

"You don't know what you want to do with your life?" I repeated, hoping I got it right.

Beau signed, YES.

It was an unusual thought—at least for me—not knowing what you wanted to do with your life. I had it in my mind I wanted to become a respiratory therapist even before I became Deaf. It was just something that had always been there, that ambition, and it was strange to think of what it would be like if I hadn't had that epiphany that day I spent at the hospital with Connor when he was barely four years old.

"I think that's okay," I said to Beau after a moment of thought. "I mean, you're what, seventeen, eighteen? It's not like you have to have everything mapped out right now."

I could tell Beau was laughing again, but it wasn't a happy laugh like before.

MY FATHER THINK THAT, he signed, his frown deepening. HE WANT ME . . .

Nina mentioned Beau's dad was more intense about the whole college thing than most parents, but it seemed like whatever it was his dad wanted really aggravated him. Sometimes peoples' facial expressions said it all.

"Well, you're the one that'll be taking out all those

massive student loans, right? Might as well go off to college to do what you want," I told Beau.

"Maybe," Beau said. "I just . . . to . . . Yale. My dad will . . . if I don't."

I'd always had the unfailing support of my mom, which made it a challenge for me to put myself in Beau's shoes for this.

"So?" I finally said. "It's not like it's his life to live."

Beau's eyes widened, his lips parting as if he were about to speak. But whatever he was going to say fell short when I gave a yelp of surprise at the hands that suddenly came down on my shoulders.

I tried to break free and whip around to see who was behind me, but I wound up painfully smacking my head on the row of lockers next to me.

Jackson was standing there, and quickly inched back a step at the dirty look I sent his way. My heart was pounding hard, my breathing uneven. I could not stand it when people snuck up behind me like that.

Anytime it happened, it was like one of my biggest fears was being realized. I'd get flashes of this dark scenario—of someone creeping up behind me late at night as I'm walking to my car in some empty parking lot, and I'd never know. I'd never know because I'm never entirely aware of my surroundings without being able to hear.

"Sorry," Jackson said with wide eyes.

"Don't do that," I snapped, using the lockers as support to pull myself up to my feet. "Don't sneak up on me like that."

"Sorry," Jackson repeated, and maybe he looked like he

meant it, but that didn't change the fact he'd just scared the living daylights out of me. "I just . . . see what . . . up to. Maybe want . . . dance?"

Seriously?

Beau got to his feet too, and rather than looking frustrated or sad like moments before, he looked angry. "Dude. Why would you . . ."

Jackson went palms up like he was surrendering. "My bad. I didn't . . ."

HEY, I signed to Beau to get his attention when he very much looked like he was about to go off on some rant, telling Jackson off. STOP.

Jackson stopped mid-sentence, and a curious expression took over his face as he watched me sign to Beau. I did not care for his staring. Not only because it made me uncomfortable—as if I didn't get enough staring at this stupid school—but also because I had a strong suspicion Jackson was maybe a bit more than just a *ladies' man*, like Nina mentioned.

I'd seen one girl in AP US History flat-out turn him down, but that hadn't stopped him. Either he was exceptionally dense, or he was the type of guy who didn't take no for an answer. And a guy who didn't take no for an answer wasn't really someone I wanted to be around.

WHY YOU FRIEND WITH HIM? I signed to Beau. NOT REALLY NICE.

He looked conflicted as he finally connected the dots, making sense of what I signed. NOT BAD PERSON, he signed, carefully choosing his signs. HE . . .

WHAT? I demanded. I was a little angrier than I

thought. My hands were trembling. HE COOL FRIEND YOU THINK YOU NEED?

NOT TRUE, he signed back after I had to repeat myself. I NEED . . .

I didn't care to stick around long enough to find out what Beau needed. I was tired of being subjected to Jackson's *interested* gaze. I would take dancing over standing between these two.

SEE YOU LATER, I signed to Beau, and just because I could, I grabbed the last of his cookies before I marched off.

I flopped down onto the bleachers in the gym and ate the last cookie, thankful the noise from the dance in full swing was lost on me. I felt all the vibrations from the music sinking into the bleachers, but that was easy enough to ignore.

Here I had thought I was just having a genuine conversation with Beau, both in sign and using our voices, and now I was starting to wonder if I'd been wrong. And I didn't *want* to be wrong.

Beau was the only hearing boy at this school who'd taken the initiative to even learn a few signs to try to talk to me. He wasn't fluent in ASL by any means, but I'd felt more of a connection with him out there in the hallway, signing and eating cookies, than with any of the Deaf boys I'd met back at Pratt.

And after that talk we just had, I did not think I could ignore that fact any longer. The hearing boy with all his books, the one destined for Yale, seemed just as vulnerable and scared as I felt most of the time at this school.

I sat upright when I saw a pair of bare feet heading my way and was relieved to see it was Nina walking up.

OK? she signed, looking concerned.

FINE, I replied.

"Where's Beau?" she said, looking around.

DON'T KNOW, I signed with a shrug.

Nina gave up with a shrug too and said, "You want . . . dance?"

"Sure," I said, suddenly feeling like I had nothing to lose. "Let's dance."

I let Nina pull me out onto the dance floor. Despite my earlier hesitation, it only took a few moments before I got lost in the beat I couldn't hear and let go.

CHAPTER 13

B eau must've said something to Jackson after our little run-in out in the hallway Saturday night. That Monday after homecoming I didn't feel Jackson's noticeable stare during AP US History, and he didn't once glance my way during lunch. It came as a relief, but I was also stupidly curious, wondering if Beau had played up the *leave the poor Deaf girl alone* angle.

I'd immediately pegged that thought as *dumb* the second it flitted across my mind. Even if I still had a laundry list of questions about him, there was no getting around the fact that Beau was just a genuinely *nice* guy.

I could have spent a lot more time contemplating the mysteries still surrounding Beau, but with midterms the following week and that homecoming incident, my conversation with Beau had to be forcibly shoved to the back of my mind.

With our presentation just on the horizon, Nina and I spent every spare moment in the library doing research and practicing our speech. We'd decided to present on a major event from the twentieth century . . . but not one that was in the history book. Deaf President Now—or DPN—was a huge turning point for the Deaf community back in the 1980s. DPN was a student-lead protest at Gallaudet University (the first all-inclusive university in the United States for the Deaf and Hard of Hearing) where they'd protested the appointment of yet another hearing president who didn't even know sign language.

At that point in time, not once in Gallaudet's 124-year history had there ever been a Deaf president. Over a hundred years, and there'd never been a person in charge who could understand the students in a way no hearing person ever could. It took days of protests and thousands of people marching on Capitol Hill to make the Deaf students' demands heard.

I had this idea that by making our presentation about DPN we would get my classmates to understand that just because a person was Deaf it did not mean they were incapable of living a successful, meaningful life. I hoped this presentation would inspire people to treat me like a normal person, like I had felt at Pratt.

So, I had reason enough to be nervous about the presentation for Mr. Wells' class, but then there was the midterm for Mr. Burke's chemistry class to throw on top of that. Chemistry was a pretty essential subject in the medical field, and I was on the border of an A-/B+ in the class. A good exam would push me to an A, but a bad one could tank my grade.

NERVOUS? Kathleen signed as we walked into the chemistry classroom.

A LITTLE, I answered.

If the midterm was going to be a multiple-choice test or

something, I would've been okay, but Mr. Burke announced last week that our midterm was going to be a lab. Labs got me nervous. There were far too many ways to get off track. My lab partner, Eli Collins, never seemed keen to do labs with me either, so it was anybody's guess how this was going to go.

I took my seat at the lab table beside Eli, who was repeatedly tapping his pencil on the tabletop. He looked more nervous than I felt, barely giving me an acknowledging nod.

Once Mr. Burke was ready, we put our lab aprons and protective glasses on and were given the go-ahead to start.

HAVE 5-0 MINUTES, Kathleen signed with one hand, skimming over our instruction sheet.

". . . beakers," Eli said, nodding toward the lab table where our supplies sat. "You . . . math."

"Deal," I said, settling myself on the stool.

It was more difficult than I thought to split my attention between the lab and Eli, looking back and forth between him and the equations I was attempting to work on about every thirty seconds, watching him to make sure I wouldn't miss anything he might be saying to me.

Kathleen was there to interpret for me, but she was a few feet away on the sidelines to give us space to complete the lab rather than hover.

You can handle not having Kathleen here to interpret everything. *So far so good*, I kept telling myself, tapping out a beat on the tabletop with my pencil as I worked through my equations. *Math genius here.*

Eli's attention had been solely fixed on the test tubes

since the start of the lab, measuring out a baking soda and vinegar mixture, handling the pressure sensor. So far so good.

I kept a tight grip on my pencil as I pounded out each equation, making sure to press down on the paper hard so every number and letter was perfectly legible.

I had no way of knowing how much time had passed when Kathleen's hand suddenly came down on my shoulder, and then Eli had me around the arm, yanking me to my feet, pointing to the beaker full of the sodium bicarbonate solution now overflowing onto the table, spilling over the side and onto the floor.

Kathleen was signing, OK, FINE, NOT HURT, but Eli wasn't having any of it.

"I told you . . . watch . . . pressure sensor!" He had to be shrieking at me, all scarlet in the face. "What the . . . wrong with you?!"

"I'm sorry . . ." My voice felt funny coming up my throat and out of my mouth.

Everyone was fixated on us, their own labs forgotten as they watched Eli tear me apart.

"I want . . . new lab partner," he said to Mr. Burke, who was now working quickly to mop up the mess on the lab table.

I stood there in a daze, my feet glued to the floor. I didn't know what to do. Eli was freaking out, people were staring, and this was *my* fault. I ruined the lab and probably tanked the midterm too, and it was all because I couldn't hear Eli tell me to watch the stupid pressure sensor.

"Eli, calm down," Mr. Burke said, holding a sopping

mess of paper towels in both hands. "We'll . . . cleaned up. You . . . retake the midterm."

I'd almost forgotten Kathleen was there, a foot away from me, until she approached Eli. She didn't look all that thrilled.

WHY YOU NOT ASK ME INTERPRET? she signed, and it looked like she was raising her voice to match Eli's with the way her eyebrows shot up and her mouth opened wider. YOU KNOW M-A-Y-A DEAF, WHY YOU THINK SHE HEAR YOU NOW? WHY YOU NOT CATCH HER ATTENTION?

"Everything . . . okay," Mr. Burke said when he returned from tossing the paper towels. One of my classmates had taken the overflowing beaker to a nearby sink. "I'll let them retake . . . midterm."

". . . not the point!" Kathleen said, forgetting to sign.

Mr. Burke didn't respond, instead turning to me and reaching over to pat my hand. He didn't look angry.

"It's fine, Maya," Mr. Burke told me. "Don't worry."

I knew I was about to burst into frustrated tears, and I didn't want to break down in front of my classmates. I hurriedly signed, TOILET, to Kathleen, pulling off the lab apron and my glasses. I walked on unsteady legs to the bathroom down the hallway. Breathing made my chest hurt. My eyes hurt too with the effort it took to keep back the tears threatening to fall.

I had no idea where I was going or what I was supposed to be doing, but putting as much distance between myself and that classroom felt like the best idea I'd ever had. In less than two minutes I was out of the science hallway, halfway across the school, walking right into Ms. Phillips' classroom.

Maybe I unconsciously knew I'd find the classroom empty because this was Ms. Phillips' planning period. She was sitting at one of the worktables sketching and did not look up until I approached and tapped a finger on the tabletop.

"Can I paint?" I said when she looked up at me, pointing toward the corner of the room where our self-portraits were being kept.

For whatever reason, Ms. Phillips didn't seem surprised by my request. Rather than fire a bunch of questions at me, she must've gotten everything she needed to know from the look on my face, and she simply nodded, smiling. She gestured toward the pile of canvases as if to say *have at it*.

I turned my hearing aids off after I got settled with a water cup and fresh paints, wanting nothing more than to be left alone in my own world of silence right then. And now that I was sitting down in front of my half-completed self-portrait, I wasn't sure if I wanted to finish the thing or ruin it with a bunch of paint. It looked sloppy somehow, and all the colored paints I'd been trying to incorporate looked dull.

I could barely think straight as it was, so trying to pick what colors I wanted to use or what feature of the painting I wanted to focus on was pointless. The only thing I could hone in on was what if that chemistry midterm was just a preview of what would happen if I got hired on at a hospital as a respiratory therapist?

Sodium bicarbonate was just baking soda, so it wasn't the end of the world that there had been an accident during that lab. It could be cleaned up and forgotten. But what would happen if I were at work in a hospital and somebody

THE SILENCE BETWEEN US

went into respiratory failure and I didn't hear the alarms? That person could die, and it would be my fault.

To reach the point of even being able to get a job at a hospital would take *years* of busting my butt to prove myself, graduating from college and completing internships, and to have that suddenly snatched away in an instant because I couldn't hear a simple alarm? The thought was terrifying.

I gave a start of surprise at the sudden gentle touch to my shoulder and almost groaned when I looked over to see who was standing beside me now, staring at my self-portrait on the easel.

"What're you doing here?"

Beau kept staring at my self-portrait, and a lifetime seemed to pass me by before he finally looked at me.

YOURS? he signed, nodding toward my portrait.

YES, I signed, curling my fingers tightly around the paintbrush in my left hand.

I LIKE, Beau signed with his usual smile and the dimples, and then I started to feel like I was collapsing in on myself again.

Beau stayed put when I didn't say or sign anything to him, and he signed, WHAT'S WRONG?

NOTHING, I signed back, but I couldn't even get through the sign without my lips trembling.

Beau raised one eyebrow, clearly not accepting my response. The heavy rise and fall of his chest indicated he must have sighed when I didn't exactly respond. He went and grabbed a stool from the closest worktable, dragged it over, and sat down beside me.

WHAT'S WRONG? he signed again.

"What are you even doing here?" I asked, blowing off his question. "Shouldn't you be in class?"

"I'm . . . office . . . this period. Running . . . for Mrs. . . ." Beau said, and when I just stared at him in befuddlement, he finger spelled, E-R-R-A-N-D-S. I felt another sigh escape when he added, WHAT'S WRONG? again in sign.

"Ask me what's wrong one more time, I swear . . ."

Beau paused, and a grin broke out across his face as he signed, WHAT'S WRONG?

I couldn't help but throw my head back and laugh, then immediately regretted it when I almost lost my balance and fell off my stool.

Beau watched me with a small smile and waited until I was done grumbling to say, "Seriously. Can you . . . me what happened?"

I didn't mean to spill my story, but I didn't have the energy to squabble with him anymore.

"I just had my chemistry midterm," I began, and I could feel the hitch coming out in my voice.

Beau raised his eyebrows as if to say, *and?*

"It . . . it didn't go well. Actually, it was a freaking disaster if I'm being honest."

WHY? Beau signed immediately, leaning forward with interest.

"I think my lab partner, Eli Collins, forgot I'm Deaf," I told him. "He asked me to watch the pressure sensor we were using for this sodium bicarbonate solution, but, you know, obviously I *didn't hear him* ask me."

It took half a second for Beau to get where the rest of my sad little story was heading, and he started to frown, his lips tightening. I felt like I didn't need to finish explaining how messy everything got after that.

Rather than signing, Beau mimed something like an explosion going off, and by the way his cheeks puffed out I knew he'd added some type of sound effect there.

"Correct," I said, fighting back a little smile.

Beau gave his head a disgusted shake. "Eli is a . . ."

"A what?" I said, adding, AGAIN, in sign so he could repeat himself.

He gave a dismissive wave. "Never mind. Maya, that wasn't . . . fault."

I shrugged. "Maybe. Maybe not. But you can't deny it only happened because I can't hear."

It was enough to shake my confidence—something that hadn't been all that stellar to begin with.

"Seriously," Beau said. "Just ignore Eli."

"He wants a new lab partner now, so that shouldn't be a problem," I said with an eye roll.

GOOD, Beau signed, and said, "You're better . . . without . . ."

"Sure."

Beau tapped me on the knee, wanting me to look him in the face as he signed, YOU SMART. NO WORRY.

WORRY A LOT, I signed, pointing back at myself.

SAME, Beau agreed with a crooked smile. BECOME BETTER SOON.

Soon? I almost laughed. I didn't see myself feeling unworried anytime soon. Maybe not until the end of college at the earliest.

YOU SIGN BETTER, I told Beau after we sat there for a

few moments and I'd been swirling my paintbrush around in some green paint.

Beau seemed surprised at this as he signed, REALLY?

I nodded, suppressing the urge to smile. PRACTICE A LOT? I asked him.

I had to finger spell the word *practice* for him before he understood, and he gave a nonchalant shrug, signing, MAYBE.

I was hesitant to ask, but the question had been bugging me for ages.

WHY YOU LEARN SIGN? I signed to him slowly, not meeting his gaze.

Beau didn't answer for some time. He just sat there staring at me, head tilted to the side.

It felt anticlimactic when he just swiped two fingers against his nose—the sign for *fun*.

We were sitting there now, not signing or speaking, and it was both weird and . . . *calm*. Normal, almost. Like we were friends.

Beau looked up suddenly and then got to his feet, pointing a finger up at the ceiling. "Bell rang," he told me.

SEE YOU LATER, I signed to Beau. I STAY.

FOR? he signed, pointing to my self-portrait.

"I'm feeling . . . inspired," I answered.

HAVE FUN, Beau signed, giving a small wave. SEE YOU LATER.

I started smiling when I swiveled back around to face my self-portrait again.

This time as he walked away it sort of felt like I was looking forward to seeing Beau again.

CHAPTER 14

Wait. What do you mean, you have to leave?"

Nina rocked back on her heels with her hands clasped behind her back, a thoroughly apologetic look on her face. It took her longer than a minute to finger spell the words *academic decathlon* as I waited impatiently beside my locker.

"Our presentation for Wells is tomorrow," I pointed out.

Less than twenty-four hours before we were supposed to give a presentation to class for our AP US History midterm, and Nina was telling me she had to leave for some academic decathlon? Nina was always on top of her game when it came to schoolwork; why hadn't she mentioned this before? With the chemistry mess behind me, I couldn't survive another exam screw-up.

"Here's . . . thing," Nina said. "I talked . . . Mr. Wells . . . because Beau's partner . . . with me too, he . . ."

I turned to Kathleen, desperate for her to interpret.

Nina launched into some explanation, including her apparent remedy for our presentation for Mr. Wells tomorrow. I learned my partner was bailing on me to go to an academic decathlon in Greeley, over an hour away. Apparently so was

Beau's partner, Kyle Matthews. Mr. Wells agreed to let Nina and Kyle write an essay in place of presenting, and his wild solution was that Beau and I were now partners. Apparently, we were being given the choice to present on the topic Nina and I picked, or the one Beau and Kyle had chosen.

Nina kept signing, SORRY, and said, ". . . warned Mr. Wells . . . might happen, but . . . didn't think . . . get . . . finals for . . . last minute . . . another school dropped . . ."

I started to space out, blanking on the rest of Nina's explanation.

I could take comfort in the fact Beau took his grades *very* seriously and would want to give as professional and well-planned a presentation as possible, but this was *so* last minute. And what if Beau didn't care one iota about our presentation topic? That I would not stand for.

The universe was definitely conspiring against me.

I gave a start when Nina got hold of my forearm and squeezed gently.

". . . fine," she said. ". . . total faith . . ."

TRUE, Kathleen signed when I glanced her way. GIVE B-E-A-U CHANCE.

I bit down on my lip to keep from huffing out a disgusted sigh.

I supposed Beau did deserve a chance. I didn't completely understand his reasoning behind wanting to learn sign language, but he was getting pretty good at it. And it *was* fun talking with him, annoying Jackson during lunch with our overly dramatic signing and pointing toward him.

If he was that interested in sign language, maybe he'd catch on to DPN just as quickly.

"Fine," I said. "But you owe me."

"Deal," Nina said, shaking my hand.

"This is hardly necessary," I told Beau, standing beside his car in the student parking lot with my arms crossed.

Beau's car was the nicest one out here, and I was hesitant to get in for fear of somehow accidentally ruining the leather seats I could see through the tinted windows. Whatever Beau's dad did for a living obviously came with a hefty paycheck.

DON'T WORRY, Beau signed, looking my way over the roof of his car. DRIVE SAFE.

"That's not the problem," I said through pursed lips. "It's this stupid presentation."

Beau gave a nod of agreement, and I only caught a few words of what he was saying which was something like, ". . . we can . . . your idea . . ."

I didn't bother with a response and got into the passenger seat of the car, carefully buckling myself in. Rather than dump a pile of questions on me when I'd sent a text informing her of the change in plans, Mom seemed thrilled I was working together with another "friend" for my school project.

My plan was to force Beau to stay put in the driveway while I ran inside to grab my laptop which currently had the PowerPoint presentation on DPN saved to the desktop. Then we would head straight to the library.

At a stoplight a block from my house, I peeked into

the backseat to finish out my inspection of Beau's car. Somehow, I was not surprised to see the gigantic stack of books taking up most of the space. I could see library stickers on most of the books, some of which were in rather shabby condition. Before I turned back around to face forward, I caught a couple of titles like *The Old Man and the Sea* by Ernest Hemingway and *Brave New World* by Aldous Huxley.

"I like . . . read," Beau said when he saw me eyeing his collection of books.

"I've noticed," I said with a tiny smile.

We pulled into my driveway then, and Beau looked over at me after he parked the car.

MY MOTHER . . . Beau signed, glancing at his books in the rearview window. SHE ALWAYS READ.

LIKE? I signed curiously.

When he finger spelled the words *Harry Potter,* I signed, YAY! because who didn't love Harry Potter? I'd finally found something Beau and I could agree on wholeheartedly.

"We went . . . library . . ." Beau continued, using his voice. "She loved books."

"And you do too," I said, speculating.

YES, Beau signed with a nod.

"I bet that makes her happy."

". . . wouldn't know."

Beau slid the keys from the ignition, turning them over in his hand. I had to lean closer to lip-read the rest of what he wanted to say.

"She's been dead . . . long time."

I felt my heart give a painful lurch in my chest. I realized

127

Beau had spoken to me more than once about his dad, but never about his mom. It never occurred to me that it was because his mom had passed away. All the books and the reading made even more sense now. It was a way he could hold on to his mom. I'd done the same thing when my parents divorced when I was eight. I kept one of my dad's old checkered ties carefully folded in my dresser.

SORRY, I signed, and then I repeated the word aloud.

The word and the gesture felt inadequate, but I didn't know what else to do.

FINE, Beau signed, but I wasn't convinced by the smile he forced onto his face. PAST.

Beau suddenly gave a polite little wave, and I felt myself make a noise of surprise when I looked around and saw Mom standing there in the driveway, tapping the car window with a finger, a delirious smile on her face.

"Well, this is obviously my mother," I said unnecessarily. *My mother who is home surprisingly early,* I didn't add.

I held tight to my backpack as I stepped out of the car, trying to keep myself anchored. I could tell Mom was getting the wrong impression here and that a full-fledged parental interrogation was about to take place.

After stepping out of the car, Beau introduced himself, shaking Mom's hand, and my stomach started freefalling when Mom gave a come-follow-me gesture, pointing up at the house.

STOP, I quickly signed to her, hoping Beau wasn't paying attention. WE GO T-O LIBRARY, NOT STAY.

FINE, Mom signed breezily, and just like my first day of school at Engelmann, she added, BE NICE.

I marched on ahead, itching to grab my laptop and get out of there as quickly as possible. It probably was not the smartest idea to leave Mom behind with Beau, but small sacrifices were occasionally necessary. I waved to Connor who was on the couch watching cartoons, his homework spread out on the coffee table in front of him, and sprinted up the stairs to nab my laptop off my bed and wrap up the charger.

Beau was waiting by the front door, and I tripped off the last step, not because he'd been talking with Mom and Connor, but because he was standing in front of my self-portrait from Ms. Phillips' class that Mom insisted on hanging in the living room.

I guess I hadn't minded so much when Beau stumbled across me painting when my self-portrait wasn't complete, and I'd been messing around with a bunch of colors. But this was different. All in all, I didn't think the end result was that bad. I'd been pleasantly surprised, and I think Ms. Phillips had been too.

There was the same messy outline of a person in the middle done in black, and if it weren't for the person's out-stretched hand holding two neon blue hearing aids, you wouldn't have been able to tell the person was me. The other hand was covering the eyes, blocking out the explosion of bold colors covering the rest of the canvas and dripping down around the person like rivulets of water.

It seemed like the best way to describe one major thing in my life—how all I had to do was take out my hearing aids, close my eyes, and the world was mine. There were no limits to my imagination when it was just me and the

THE SILENCE BETWEEN US

universe. And I was only seventeen; in what world was I supposed to know who I truly was at this point in time? So the misshapen outline of myself made sense.

ALL DONE? Beau signed when I came over to him.

I signed, YES, in response.

Beau inspected my painting for another few moments, and I just stood there, gnawing on my lip, wanting him to look away already. I was beginning to feel too vulnerable like this, having Beau examine my self-portrait so closely. Here he was looking at a representation of what I'd truly come to think of myself, and I was just waiting for him to come up with some criticism of it.

All he ended up signing was, BEAUTIFUL.

THANK YOU, I signed back awkwardly.

Mom came over to see us off, still all smiles. When Beau had his back turned to open the front door, she signed, CAREFUL, like maybe she thought I needed to be on high alert because I was going to work on some school project with a boy.

PROMISE, I answered back.

I waved good-bye to Connor and sprinted out of the house after Beau, laptop tucked under my arm.

LIBRARY, RIGHT? I signed to Beau once I was buckled up in the front seat of his car again.

Beau had this funny little look on his face when he glanced at the clock on the dashboard and shook his head.

LIBRARY CLOSE NOW, he signed, nodding toward the clock. TIME 4.

You've got to be kidding *me*, I thought, looking at the clock too and seeing that it was currently 4:03.

"You're not actually suggesting we go back inside to do this project, are you?" I blurted. I was sure there was a note of panic in my voice even if I couldn't hear it. "I mean, my mom . . ."

Beau pressed his lips together tight then, and I realized a beat later it was because he was trying hard not to smile. This was so *not* funny. My mother wasn't a helicopter parent by any means, but she had perfected the art of hovering to the umpteenth degree.

When Beau signed, YOU OK WITH MY HOME? color came flooding into my cheeks once the notion that going to Beau's house to work on this project might very well mean it would just be the two of us. *Alone.*

"Um . . ."

"Don't worry," Beau said quickly, and his cheeks were just as red as I knew mine were. Not that he was thinking about us being alone together or anything . . . right?

". . . promise . . . not . . . and we have . . ."

I signed, DON'T UNDERSTAND, with a shake of my head, and Beau took a minute to think something through, whatever it was, before he signed, YOU T-R-U-S-T ME?

It wasn't what I thought he'd been about to say, but I signed, YES, without even stopping to consider the question.

I *did* trust Beau, even though I didn't know him half as well as I was starting to want to now. Weird.

Beau gave what I think was supposed to be an encouraging smile before he put the car into gear and backed out of the driveway.

The car ride was less than ten minutes, but I felt myself

growing apprehensive when Beau turned a corner and all the houses lining the streets started getting *a lot* bigger.

All the lawns were well-manicured despite it being knee-deep into autumn, the houses all two stories with fresh coats of paint, and beyond intimidating. Ultimately it wasn't too much of a surprise when Beau pulled up into the driveway of a house that could've graced the cover of some gaudy architectural magazine. The house before me was done in a stylishly dark stucco color, with the same immaculate lawn and what looked like a lighted path leading up to the front door.

I was holding tightly to my laptop when Beau parked his car and I felt him shut the engine off. He was watching me with a guarded look on his face, like he was just as nervous as I was to have me here at his home. As important as acing this midterm was, I couldn't shake thoughts of what Beau thought of this whole thing, maybe being alone with me, if he thought something was going to happen . . . or if I even wanted something to happen.

"What does your dad do for a living again?" I asked Beau, turning to face him.

P-E-D-I-A-T-R-I-C S-U-R-G-E-O-N, Beau finger spelled for me, taking his time, then said aloud, "He works . . . Children's Hospital."

I knew Children's Hospital very well. Connor had visited the one back in New Jersey regularly for treatment and was now going to the one nearby in Aurora.

"Wow," I said. "That's impressive."

There was that tight set to Beau's mouth again as he reached around to grab his backpack from the floor in the back, shoving his keys in his pocket. It was clear he was done talking about his dad.

I followed suit, grabbed my backpack and laptop, and went up the path to the front door alongside Beau, wondering what on Earth I was about to walk into.

CHAPTER

Once inside the house, standing there in the foyer, Beau motioned for me to slip off my shoes and hang up my jacket in the hall closet. I took my time inspecting the Watson household as Beau led me from the foyer. Some interior designer must've gone through this place trying to make it homey and inviting with warm colors and expensive furniture.

Except something was still missing here.

There were no pictures of any kind anywhere. The walls were completely blank, no photos of Beau and his parents or one of those awkward school photos from the third grade. There weren't even any of Beau's certificates or academic medals put on display, and I knew he had plenty.

This made me sad.

The second you walked through our front door, there was barely any empty space anywhere with all the family pictures, art projects, and rainbow ceramic pieces Mom insisted on putting up. Our house was *full*—or messy, if you wanted to get technical—and you could tell people lived there and had made the space their own.

Beau took me to a state-of-the-art kitchen just off the

side of a spacious living room that had a large marble fire-place, mood lighting, leather furniture, and the whole fake potted plants deal. There was someone already in the kitchen though, and it wasn't Beau's dad.

The woman currently at the kitchen sink, stacking cups and plates into the nearby dishwasher, was short and plump with gray curly hair, wearing an oversized purple T-shirt, jeans, and sneakers. She turned around as we entered and gave Beau a warm smile. I didn't catch whatever it was she was saying to him. She gave a little start when she saw me and grabbed at a dish towel to dry her hands, coming forward to greet me.

D-A-N-A, Beau signed to me, pointing at the woman as I shook her hand. SHE HELP COOK AND CLEAN SOMETIMES.

This woman Dana didn't even bat an eyelash at Beau's signing, just smiled at me as she very clearly said, "Nice . . . meet you!"

It made me wonder if Beau had ever spoken about me to her.

"You too," I said aloud.

"Want . . . snack?" Dana asked us both. "Don't mind . . ."

"Sure," Beau said. "Thanks."

I wasn't going to decline the offer—why would I ever pass up food?—so I thanked Dana and followed Beau into the living room to start setting up, ready to work on the project at hand.

FAMILY FRIEND? I signed to Beau after I booted up my laptop, gesturing toward Dana.

He nodded, a grin tugging at his lips, and he signed,

SHE HELP WHEN MY MOTHER DIE. MY FATHER ALWAYS BUSY.

I watched Dana bustling about the kitchen as she made us what looked like a tray of celery sticks with peanut butter and raisins, and I imagined that she was humming some sort of tune while she worked. Maybe some Disney song. Dana just looked like one of those people that was simply *happy*.

As much as I was starting to feel a twinge of disappointment that Beau and I weren't going to be working alone together, I was glad he had Dana.

We both thanked her when she brought the tray of celery sticks and peanut butter over along with glasses of water. She wished us luck on our project before heading back to finish up the dishes in the kitchen.

"Okay," I said to Beau once I got the PowerPoint pulled up on my laptop. "Here's what we have so far."

The presentation had about twelve slides so far and contained the bulk of information Nina and I pulled together about DPN, mostly from online sources. To the rest of the world, I doubted DPN was significant enough to make even a tiny blip in history, but there was so much more to it than that. It was a turning point in the Disability Rights movement and let the world see just how driven and capable Deaf people are. It set the precedent for how future presidents of Gallaudet would be chosen and let students *finally* have their say.

Beau took his time examining each slide as I went through them. By the fifth slide he was leaning forward in his seat, a fascinated glint in his eyes as he held his chin in his hand. When we hit the end of the slideshow, Beau sat back, slapping a hand on his thigh.

"What do you think?" I asked, hoping I didn't sound too anxious.

"Brilliant," Beau said, giving a thumbs-up.

YAY, I signed, not sure of what else to sign or say.

". . . there . . . news reports?" Beau asked, then signed, VIDEO, MAYBE?

DON'T KNOW, I signed back. Nina hadn't seemed too concerned with getting anything other than the hard facts surrounding DPN. TRY Y-O-U-T-U-B-E.

Beau shrugged, absentmindedly munching on a celery stick as he leaned over to pull up YouTube on my laptop. He was signing something with his free hand, but I couldn't even think to pay attention when I suddenly realized just how close he was sitting next to me.

Close enough that I could see he had a chicken pox scar by his left eye, that his hair was starting to curl just past his ears, and that he smelt strongly of some type of cinnamon spice. He was frowning in concentration as he clicked around on YouTube, but it wasn't such a bad look on him. Cute even.

You're so stupid, *Maya*, I thought the moment I realized I'd been unconsciously leaning toward Beau, trying to inhale more of his enticing scent.

We were a little over two months into the school year and only now was I willing to admit that my feelings for Beau were steadily moving past the "just friends" territory.

I felt some noise of surprise escape my throat when Beau touched my knee and it finally clicked in my brain that he'd been trying to get my attention for some time.

OK? Beau signed, this alarmed expression on his face. ". . . lost you."

"Toilet!" I blurted out, and immediately I wanted a sink-hole to appear in the floor and swallow me up. "I mean, can I use the bathroom?"

I was grateful Beau didn't laugh at my embarrassing outburst, just nodded and stood up, a little unsteady on his feet as he led me to the bathroom around the corner and down the hall.

I didn't really have to go to the bathroom—the bathroom here was just as nice if not nicer than Nina's with the fancy towels and decorative soaps—but I needed the few minutes to snap myself out of this weird stupor I was caught in.

"Get a *grip*," I muttered to myself after I splashed cold water on my face and used a fancy hand towel to dry off. "You're being ridiculous."

Sitting there on the couch next to Beau, so close I could feel every one of his smallest movements, I was far too aware of his presence.

I had never been so preoccupied by a boy before—hearing or Deaf—and so far it was proving to be a major distraction when I had this dumb midterm to worry about.

After a few minutes in the bathroom I returned to the living room, but came up short when I saw Beau sitting with his right leg stretched out in front of him, his pant leg pulled up to his knee. It was almost the same way he always sat during class, but this time he was pressing his fingers along his shin as if massaging the skin there. Even from where I stood I could see a scar that ran the length of the lower half of his leg. Given how pink and smooth the scar looked, it had to be years old, but by the way Beau was massaging it, I'd bet it still caused him pain.

It took effort to recall the task at hand, and I made sure to slap my feet against the hardwood floor as I walked into the living room, announcing my presence. This didn't seem like something Beau wanted me to see, and I wanted to give him the chance to straighten himself up in peace.

The scar was covered, his pant leg back down when I took my seat next to him on the couch again. He'd forced a smile on his face when he looked my way, no dimples in sight.

"Find anything?" I asked, nodding toward my laptop.

". . . few videos," Beau said.

I leaned closer to watch as Beau pressed play on the news clip he'd been watching. One of the students who organized the protest was being interviewed, along with an esteemed Deaf actress who'd received an honorary degree from Gallaudet, and then the hearing president whose election caused the initial uproar.

As we watched the rest of the interview, I had to sympathize with the student and the actress. The news anchor was making it difficult for them to get a word in edgewise even though he was the one asking all the questions about the protest and what they hoped to achieve. They looked nothing but frustrated throughout the entire interview, almost always being interrupted when they were trying to sign something. I was always annoyed by the same thing.

TOO LONG, I signed when the interview was over.

TRUE, Beau agreed. "But maybe . . . clip some . . . ?"

DON'T KNOW, I signed back. I was already worried it would be hard to keep our classmates interested for ten minutes.

"We'll make . . . work," Beau said with a firm nod.

And we did, clipping the video down to an acceptable minute and a half, mostly shots of the students marching on Capitol Hill and Gallaudet's front gates closed up. Beau worked some type of computer magic to get the clip inserted into the PowerPoint.

Then we moved into editing, revising our works-cited page at the end of the presentation, making notecards with speech cues. We'd both gotten so tangled up into the work that it came as a shock when Dana—I hadn't even realized she was still here—flipped the living room lights on, walking into our line of sight. She was speaking to Beau, so I sat back against the couch, stretching my arms above my head.

When Dana was finished speaking, whatever she'd said to Beau suddenly had him on his feet, turning toward the foyer behind us. I was so used to Beau becoming flushed all the time that it came as a surprise when his face went ashen instead. His lips formed the words *hey, Dad*, and that was the missing piece I needed.

Beau was the mirror image of the man who was removing his coat and slipping his shoes off in the foyer, maybe just thirty or so years younger. The man had an authoritative air about him, wearing nicely ironed clothes, his graying hair brushed back in a somewhat sophisticated hairstyle. He introduced himself as Doctor Watson when he approached, holding out a hand for me to shake.

"Nice to meet you," I said, this uncomfortable feeling

creeping up my spine when Doctor Watson's gaze zeroed in on my hearing aids.

"Homework?" Doctor Watson said, nodding to our mess on the coffee table.

I only saw Beau say, "Yes, we . . ." before everything else was lost on me. He had his hands raised as if he wanted to sign as he spoke with his dad, but the pained look on his face made me think he didn't know how to sign what he was saying.

I could sympathize with Beau there at least. Signing and using your voice at the same time when you were just learning to embrace sign language was difficult under the best of circumstances, but I kind of hated that I still managed to feel somewhat left out as Beau and his dad were talking.

Something Beau said made Doctor Watson raise an eyebrow and take a step forward to look more closely at our PowerPoint still pulled up on my laptop. The project was open to the slide where we listed the protestors' four demands, and either Doctor Watson had perfected the art of remaining impassive, or he wasn't impressed with what he saw.

"Interesting," Doctor Watson finally said. "But . . . think Red Scare might've . . ."

I purposely looked away so I didn't have to lipread the last of Doctor Watson's sentence. I was anticipating a lack of interest in the subject from some of my classmates, but I didn't want to witness it from Beau's dad too.

I watched Beau instead, more questions forming in my mind as I observed his behavior around his dad. He didn't seem quite as confident as he did at school, not so sure of himself. His hands were at his sides, his gaze focused on a spot on the wall above his dad's head.

Sure, Beau's dad did seem intimidating, but what was it about him that would get Beau to act like this, like he was trying to draw in on himself?

I think the constipated look on Beau's face was what made me do it, use my voice to say, "Well, we're just about finished here. Wanna take me home now, Beau?"

Beau jumped on my words like they were a lifeline, nodding eagerly, and he said, ". . . be back soon," to Dr. Watson.

". . . safe," Dr. Watson said to Beau, and I imagined his voice must've sounded cold with the suddenly austere expression on his face. Then that look was gone when Dr. Watson glanced my way and gave a short, polite nod.

Beau leapt into action, saving the presentation on my laptop, powering it down, piling our work together. I shoved everything carefully into my backpack and followed Beau back into the foyer to grab my shoes after I waved good-bye to Dana. She'd been watching the whole exchange with an expression that looked like sadness. I had a strong suspicion this wasn't the first time she'd seen something like this.

The moment we were out of the house and Beau shut the front door behind us, he turned to me, signing, SORRY, immediately. MY FATHER, HE . . .

FINE, I signed back.

"It's fine," I repeated aloud when Beau seemed unconvinced. "I get it. Your dad, he seems intense. Caught us off guard."

Beau gave a pained smile at that and nodded, signing, TRUE.

He was starting to look a little more relaxed now that there was some distance between us and his dad, his posture not so tense anymore. It had me wondering if he always reacted like that when he was around his dad, like he'd been caught red-handed doing something he shouldn't.

It's not because Beau is . . . embarrassed *by me or anything,* I thought as I settled into the passenger seat of Beau's car.

No. Nothing like that.

Right?

CHAPTER 16

FINE, Kathleen kept signing on our way to Mr. Wells' class the next day. YOU FINE. YOU BOTH FINE.

I KNOW, I signed back.

Even though he'd just come aboard yesterday with this project, Beau was prepared. He was up at the front of the classroom, hooking my laptop up to Mr. Wells' projector the second we walked in.

I set my backpack down at my desk and pulled out the stack of notecards Beau and I put together last night. Beau was adamant we include every important detail to make our case and seemed even more into it than Nina had been.

Please let this go well, I thought, notecards clutched in my grasp as I went up to join Beau.

Kathleen followed, her eager expression almost identical to Mr. Wells'. Kathleen told me she remembered seeing DPN in the news and apparently it had been a huge factor in her decision to go to school to become an interpreter. My classmates might not be interested in the presentation, but Kathleen would be, and I guess that helped, knowing she'd be there interpreting with an encouraging smile if I needed it.

READY, Beau signed, gesturing at my laptop.

COOL, I signed, sucking in a deep breath.

Mr. Wells was kind enough to flash the lights when he was ready for us to start, and I felt my stomach drop and settle somewhere around my knees.

It was now or never.

I caught Beau's arm as he was turning on the projector, our presentation flickering to life, and signed, NOT WANT USE MY VOICE.

For solidarity, I wanted to say.

Beau didn't seem surprised by this, instead signing, I UNDERSTAND.

THANK YOU, I told him, and he smiled. His dimples did nothing for my nerves.

Beau took the lead—not that I minded—and jumped into the opening spiel we practiced during our study session at his place last night. I didn't bother having Kathleen interpret this part, since I already knew what Beau was saying. He talked his way through the first slide, a compilation of pictures taken during DPN of students protesting, marching on Capitol Hill and at the closed front gates of Gallaudet.

When it was my turn, I passed the notecards off to Beau, so I'd have both hands free to sign. Looking to Kathleen, she gave me an encouraging nod and another thousand-watt smile, and my next breath came a little easier.

You can do this, I told myself confidently.

My hands were a mess of shakes through my first couple signs, but it wasn't so bad in the end. I kept looking from Kathleen to Beau, and there was something in their expressions that kept me going.

Halfway through the slide on the media's response to DPN, I was starting to wonder if all that worrying had been pointless. There were a few people leaning forward in their seats with interest, like Beau had done yesterday, but nobody was whispering behind their hands or trying to hide any laughter. Even if some people weren't paying attention, at least they weren't being snide about it.

When Beau was flipping to the next slide with the small clip he'd pieced together from the interview he found on YouTube, Jackson raised his hand and waited to be called on. I thought whatever he was going to say would be meant for Beau, but when Kathleen came a little closer to interpret, I realized it was directed toward me.

Whatever Jackson said made Kathleen hesitant. Her lips pursed, her posture going rigid. She clearly wasn't happy with what Jackson was asking, but as my interpreter, Kathleen technically had an obligation to relay the information to me, regardless of her own personal feelings.

HOW THAT IMPORTANT FOR REAL WORLD? Kathleen signed while Jackson sat there, staring at me expectantly.

REAL WORLD? I signed, and those signs felt weird on my fingers—at least in this context.

I was pretty sure I knew what Jackson was hinting at, and I didn't think I wanted Kathleen to finish interpreting what he had to say.

MOST PEOPLE NOT DEAF, Kathleen signed, and I kept my attention fixed on her and not Jackson. WHY THAT M-A-T-T-E-R FOR US?

I couldn't come up with a coherent response, so I signed to Beau, PLAY VIDEO.

Beau pressed play without hesitation.

It wasn't the interview half of the video I was interested in, but the compilation of scenes at the beginning that showed the world's reaction to DPN and all the support that came flooding into DC for Gallaudet students from *everywhere*—Deaf and hearing.

Beau hit the pause button when I signed, STOP, to him. I brushed aside Kathleen when she prepared to interpret, and I addressed Jackson myself.

"As you can see, there are more Deaf people around the world than you think. More hearing people involved with this than you think."

"Yeah, but . . ." Jackson said, going palms up.

"But what?" I said. "What, just because my world looks a little different from yours suddenly that means it's not as important? I know what it's like to be a part of the hearing world because I used to be hearing. But I also understand what it's like to be a part of the Deaf world because I am Deaf now. Not everyone gets that chance though, and that hearing president sure didn't. No matter how hard you try to understand something, sometimes there's this personal connection to the cause that you're missing, something you may not ever reach, and that can make all the difference. *That's* why this is important to the real world."

I'd never been one to give many Deaf pride speeches like this one, but in this case, I felt it was warranted. Just because you didn't understand something didn't make it any less significant.

Jackson took so long with his response I foolishly thought he was going to drop the subject, but he turned awkwardly in his seat to speak to Kathleen, leaving me unable to lip read what he was saying.

FINE, BUT THAT 3-0 YEARS PAST, Kathleen interpreted, keeping her eyes on me instead of Jackson. NOW TECHNOLOGY HELP DEAF HEAR AND PEOPLE WALK AND MORE. PAST DOESN'T M-A-T-T-E-R NOW.

"I'm pretty sure Mr. Wells would disagree with you on that one," I said, trying and failing to keep from rolling my eyes. "The past *does* matter. Deaf President Now showed the world Deaf people don't need to be coddled, but this is just a tiny part of the Disability Rights movement, you know."

I was on a roll here, ready to keep going and say what was *really* on my mind for once, and I wasn't even going to think of what all my classmates would say about this.

"Some people would even say the Disability Rights movement started over in Denver, where people in wheelchairs chained themselves to buses to protest lack of accessible transportation. But even then, it would be years before the ADA was passed. History really does involve *everyone*."

I stood there in front of the class waiting for a response from Jackson or anybody else, but it didn't come. I kept my lips pressed together to keep from letting any funny breaths escape, and my heart was still pounding uncomfortably against my chest.

I looked to Beau next and was a bit taken aback to see that he was smiling. When I signed, WHAT'S UP? at him, he just gave this casual shrug and signed back, NOTHING, and gave a cheesy thumbs-up.

I didn't get the chance to push the issue further until class was over and I was powering down my laptop. It had been difficult to sit through three more presentations while wondering if my classmates were whispering about everything I threw at Jackson.

HEY, I signed, reaching out to grab Beau's arm as he passed, backpack slung over one shoulder.

BAD PRESENTER? I signed when Beau turned to look at me, pointing back at myself.

NO, he signed quickly with a shake of his head. WONDERFUL.

SURE? I signed back, skeptical.

Beau took a step closer, and I chose to ignore the way my heart gave a stupid little stutter in my chest.

"They heard . . ." he said, pointing at me.

"They heard me?" I said, hoping I understood him correctly.

YES, Beau signed with another nod. THEY HEARD YOU.

CHAPTER 17

One week after the midterm showdown in Mr. Wells' class, Kathleen caught up to me just as Mom was pulling into the pickup loop after school, eager to tell us about this group of Deaf teens getting together at a local coffee shop. Mom hadn't hesitated telling Kathleen we'd be there, and now I wasn't sure if I was supposed to be ecstatic or terrified at the thought of meeting Deaf people my age for the first time since we moved here from New Jersey.

WHY YOU NERVOUS? Mom signed to me when she parked in front of the coffee shop where the group was supposed to be meeting. WONDERFUL YOU MEET MORE DEAF KIDS.

NOT NERVOUS, I signed back.

EXCITED? she asked next.

Mom seemed excited herself, despite the permanent look of exhaustion that had made itself at home on her pretty face since we moved here. There were a few more streaks of gray in her brown hair than I remembered too. How she'd been splitting her time working from home to be with Connor and going into her office was still unfathomable to me.

READY? Mom signed, pointing to the coffee shop.

YES, I signed, unbuckling my seatbelt.

The coffee shop was crowded for a Thursday night. The place was trendy with that locally owned feeling no Starbucks ever had, with lots of tables, couches, and old armchairs all over. If Connor were with us, he would've made straight for the giant checkers board along with the other games set on shelves in the corner.

Mom and I got in line and bought ourselves some hot tea and a cookie to share. Gathered around the one couch and the surrounding chairs by the front window were a handful of teens and two women I was willing to bet were members of this new Deaf group.

I pointed them out to Mom and she gave me a smile and an encouraging nudge to get moving. Each step toward the group felt heavier than the last.

Why was I so nervous? This was going to be exciting. Maybe I'd even make a new friend or two. Making a new friend who was Deaf was long overdue since moving to Colorado.

A woman dressed in a knit sweater with a colorful Thanksgiving turkey on it got to her feet as Mom and I approached and said, "Hi! My name . . . and you . . . ?"

Mom shook the woman's hand, smiling, saying something I didn't quite catch.

"What's . . . name?" the woman said to me next, shaking my free hand vigorously.

M-A-Y-A, I finger spelled, adding my sign name next.

The woman stared at me with her eyebrows pulled together and head tilted to the side until Mom stepped up and said my name aloud.

"Well, it's good . . . you. Why don't . . . there?" the woman said, gesturing to an empty spot on the couch next to some girl deeply engrossed in whatever was on her phone.

I guessed it wasn't that unusual the woman didn't understand what I was signing, but if she had a Deaf kid, shouldn't she know ASL? My own mother had busted her butt learning ASL with me.

WHO? I signed to Mom, wanting to know who the woman was as she sat in a nearby chair.

Sitting on the floor next to the woman's chair was a boy of probably fourteen or so, more interested in his tablet than his surroundings. His dark hair was cut short, so I could clearly see he had a cochlear implant, the one piece of assistive technology that was a hot topic of debate within the Deaf community.

Cochlear implants were kind of like hearing aids in that they worked to improve hearing, but the process of getting one involved an irreversible surgery and a lot of follow-up speech therapy if you were born Deaf and never developed oral skills. I remembered one history class back at Pratt where the girl who sat beside me had a cochlear implant, and she had it turned off a lot of the time, signing just as much as the rest of us. When I mustered up the courage to ask her why she never had her cochlear on, she told me it was because of how strange things sometimes sounded being filtered through it. Crackly, like the noise was being processed through a computer so everything sounded electronic. That's the word she used—*electronic.*

She said it made her tired sometimes too, having to

process all the extra noise she wasn't used to, and it made her head hurt occasionally. And the required speech therapy after the surgery had apparently been a pain in the butt. That in itself would be enough to turn me off from getting a CI. They did a lot of good for people, I knew that, but it just didn't seem like the right fit for me.

And I would never say—or sign—this to anyone, but I was deathly afraid of the necessary surgery to get a cochlear implant, even if the surgery was more common than it used to be. Being stuck in a hospital fighting meningitis while at the same time losing my hearing was more than enough to cause me to develop an irrational fear of hospitals. Those days had been some of the worst of my life.

Now that I was looking more closely at the handful of other teens here, I could see they all seemed to be a few years younger than me. There was only one other boy, and he too had a cochlear implant, visible as he chatted up the girl sitting next to him. Neither of them were signing.

I couldn't tell if the three other girls had cochlear implants because of their longer hair, but I was willing to bet they did. The fact that nobody was signing was a huge indicator.

Mom nudged me and pointed to the woman who got up to greet us. HER NAME J-O-A-N, she signed. SHE HERE WITH HER DAUGHTER C-A-S-E-Y.

Joan, the woman in the turkey sweater, was talking animatedly, and her daughter Casey was apparently the one with the coffee blabbing away with one of the boys.

WHO THEY? I signed, gesturing to everyone else.

It took a few minutes for Mom to introduce everyone.

THE SILENCE BETWEEN US

By the time she finished, I'd come up with a pretty good idea of what was going on. This wasn't a group of Deaf kids—it was a group of kids who could technically hear . . . just in a *very* different way. When it came to my turn to introduce myself, I refused to use my voice. I wanted to see for myself if anyone else in this group besides Mom and myself knew sign language.

MY NAME M-A-Y-A, I signed. HIGH SCHOOL SENIOR. NICE T-O MEET YOU ALL.

My suspicions were proven correct. All I got after Mom interpreted for me were a couple of confused looks and polite nods.

Joan jumped into conversation after that, and Mom started interpreting for me again. WE START GROUP, WHY? I WANT C-A-S-E-Y T-O MEET MORE KIDS WITH CI. HIGH SCHOOL SCARY, AND—

I held up a hand to stop Mom and Joan mid-sentence.

NOT HAVE CI, I signed, pointing to myself. HEARING AIDS.

Joan's eyes flicked over to Mom as she voiced for me. I watched Joan's face fall a fraction of an inch before she gave an airy wave, saying, "That's . . . okay. I just wanted to . . ."

I didn't even bother trying to lipread the rest of what Joan was saying. I looked back to Mom and signed, NOT GROUP FOR DEAF?

Mom relayed my question to the others, and Joan's daughter Casey answered, "Oh, I'm not deaf."

I was so taken aback by Casey's response that the only thing I could think of to say was, "What?"

Casey brushed back part of her hair to show off her tan

colored CI and tapped a finger to it, saying, "I'm not deaf. I hear . . . fine."

Helplessness wasn't really the right word to describe how I felt when Casey said that. It was something more than that, something distressing, and I couldn't put a name to it. Something was missing here, and I felt it almost like a physical ache.

Cochlear implants were great, sure, but take those away and you wouldn't be able to hear. It was only with the help of assistive technology that you'd be able to hear. So what was so wrong about saying you were deaf? Not big D Deaf, but *deaf*—just not being able to hear.

DON'T KNOW SIGN, I told Mom, gesturing around at the group.

She agreed with a short nod, looking just as caught off guard as I was. She leaned over to Joan to say something, and whatever she said made Joan nod.

"Didn't want . . . stuck in . . . bubble. Thought it . . . she learn . . . talk," Joan said, glancing toward Casey, who was back to talking with the boy beside her.

There was nothing wrong with having a cochlear implant. Of course there was nothing wrong with it. But there wasn't anything wrong with being Deaf either. I just couldn't believe none of these kids had been taught ASL.

What happened if their CI somehow broke and then they were left without a way to communicate because they didn't know sign? Not everybody carried around a notebook and pencil to jot down notes all the time. Wouldn't you *need* to know sign language if there was even the slightest chance of that happening?

HEY. Mom waved at me to get my attention. WHAT'S WRONG?

NOTHING, I signed back.

I had nothing left to contribute to the conversation. I felt so wildly out of place here, surrounded by these freshmen with cochlear implants who didn't know how to sign. Even at Engelmann I never felt so unsettled.

I just sat on the couch, drinking my now tepid tea, drafting a text to Melissa. She was the one person I could talk to who would actually get it. If her parents could've afforded it, I bet they would've gotten her a CI, but even then it was impossible to imagine Melissa *not* knowing sign language. ASL was as much a part of her as anything else.

Eventually I sent her a text saying, *If you had a CI . . . would you still sign?*

Melissa's reply came a few minutes later while I was finishing the rest of the cookie Mom bought for us to share.

YES! But I don't want CI, so don't matter.

That made me feel a little better.

My phone vibrated with a second text from Melissa a minute later.

Why u ask?

FaceTime later? I texted back, and Melissa's response was a big smiley face emoji.

Finally, our time at the coffee shop came to an end. It felt as if the meeting lasted a lot longer than a measly forty-five minutes, and I couldn't get out of there fast enough. I barely managed a half-hearted wave before racing for the exit.

Mom hung back to talk to Joan while the kids stood

around exchanging phone numbers. A sharp pang of jealousy twisted my gut seeing this, and it took a second to snap myself out of it. I'd exchanged phone numbers with Nina, hadn't I? Beau too, even though it was only because of that midterm project. And if the others had the same line of thinking as Casey, that they didn't even consider themselves deaf, would they even want to be friends with me? Would I get more of those weird looks I'd gotten used to at Engelmann or maybe flat out ignored?

Mom exited the coffee shop a few minutes later, and I scrambled into the passenger seat the second she unlocked the car.

Neither of us signed a single thing on the ride home.

Everything was always silent for me, but this silence was completely different. I wanted to say something to Mom, to at least attempt to tell her what I was feeling, but no words and definitely no signs came to mind.

The living room lights were on when Mom pulled the car into the driveway at home. I could see the babysitter Mom hired for the evening through the thin curtains in the front window, sitting on the couch. I wasn't sure where Connor was, but my guess was that he was sitting up close to the TV watching Spider-Man cartoons.

WHAT'S WRONG? Mom finally signed to me, tapping my knee.

I bit down on my lip, inhaling deeply. My breath must've sounded funny because Mom automatically leaned toward me, her eyes wide in concern.

DON'T UNDERSTAND, I signed with a shaky hand.

Mom sat there waiting for me to elaborate while I kept

growing more and more frustrated with myself. I couldn't figure out why that get-together had shaken me up so much. I hated that angry tears were beginning to spill down my cheeks.

DON'T UNDERSTAND, I signed again, forcing myself to get on with it. WHY GIRL SAY SHE NOT DEAF?

Mom seemed pained as she thought about how to answer. Her movements were slow as she signed, DON'T KNOW.

GIRL HAVE CI, OK, I signed. FINE. BUT WHY SHE NOT KNOW SIGN LANGUAGE? WHY THEY ALL NOT KNOW SIGN LANGUAGE?

DON'T KNOW, Mom signed again. SOME PARENTS THINK DIFFERENT.

YOU WANT CI FOR ME? I signed to Mom, the question suddenly pushing its way front and center.

YOU KNOW BEST, Mom signed, and a warm smile was taking over her face. I WANT FOR YOU WHAT YOU WANT.

She paused here, eyes fixed on the center console. Then she signed, IF YOU WANT CI, MAYBE WE—

NO, I signed quickly, stopping her before she could get too far into that sentence. I NEVER WANT CI, BEFORE AND NOW. NOTHING WRONG WITH CI, BUT THAT NOT FOR ME. I LIKE MYSELF DEAF.

GOOD, Mom signed a moment later. Her smile was wide enough to crinkle her pretty brown eyes at the corners.

It was a smile I hadn't seen much of since we moved to Colorado. Helping Connor get adjusted to this place and frequent trips to the hospital for his breathing treatments took a lot out of Mom. My poor attitude probably hadn't helped any. Seeing Mom's smile now, I realized I'd missed it.

NOTHING WRONG WITH THAT, Mom repeated, squeezing my knee again. YOU SHOULD LIKE YOURSELF DEAF.

PROMISE, I assured her.

NO WORRY ABOUT KIDS WITH CI, Mom signed to me. YOU MAKE FRIENDS, DEAF AND HEARING.

YES, I agreed after a beat.

Of course, Melissa was my closest friend despite being back in New Jersey. I sometimes even got a few random messages on Facebook from some old classmates back at Pratt. Nina was my friend. She was picking up sign so well there were times I forgot she was hearing. Spending time with her was never boring either, and she took the extra step to get to know me—me, the weird new Deaf girl with the interpreter.

And then there was Beau. Hanging out and signing with him was way more fun than that awkward meeting had just been. Even telling him about my disastrous chemistry midterm was preferable to another minute in that coffee shop. I'd been with kids that were supposed to be like me, and yet I felt ten times more comfortable with Beau, despite our occasional communication fumbles.

So far, I hadn't come across anyone else besides Nina who even put forth the amount of effort Beau did in practicing sign language. Those two were really the only reason I sometimes actually looked forward to school.

YOU OK? Mom signed to me, catching me before I could head upstairs to my room.

YES, I told her. Even though five minutes ago it felt like the last thing in the world I wanted to be doing, I felt myself beginning to smile.

CHAPTER *18*

Two weeks after the failed coffee shop meeting, Connor sat cross-legged on Mom's bed, carefully folding one of Mom's sweaters while Saturday morning cartoons played, and Mom ran around the bedroom like a chicken with its head cut off. She'd announced at dinner the night before that her company was sending her on a weekend trip to Aspen—a town about two hours from Denver. I thought the timing was perfect. Mom needed some time to relax, and even though Thanksgiving was only a few days away, I knew this would be her real vacation.

YOU SURE YOU FINE WITH CONNOR? Mom signed to me one handed, walking out of the bathroom with some toiletries.

This was probably the nineteenth time she'd asked me.

FINE, PROMISE, I signed yet again, the same response I'd given her each time she asked.

I didn't think Mom was this frantic because she didn't trust me to watch Connor. It was just that she was worried about the breathing treatments he needed regularly and that she wouldn't be here for two days to sit by Connor's side while he went through them.

She seemed to have already forgotten she spent plenty of time coaching me through each step of prepping Connor's nebulizer, how to replace his oxygen tank, what to do if he started having difficulties breathing or started coughing so hard he coughed up blood. I knew this routine of Mom's inside and out.

HEY. FINE, I signed again, catching Mom's hands while she fumbled zipping up her duffel bag. PROMISE.

Mom pulled me in for a tight hug, resting her chin on top of my head.

OK, she signed with a wobbly smile when she finally released me.

Connor and I helped Mom cart her things downstairs to the rental car her company arranged for her. We needed the van at home in case anything happened.

SEE YOU LATER, Mom signed to me after she finished hugging Connor and peppering his face with kisses. CAR KEYS IN KITCHEN. TEXT ME IF YOU NEED SOMETHING.

ALWAYS, I assured her.

Connor and I stood on the front steps and waved Mom off, waiting until she disappeared down the street before heading back inside.

"What would you like to do today, squirt?" I asked Connor as I shut the front door.

He held up one finger, signaling for me to wait, and jogged off with his oxygen tank in hand to grab our notebook. He sat himself down on the couch once he retrieved it and carefully wrote me a note on a fresh page before passing the notebook over to me.

I sat down next to him while I read his note.

Watch Spider-Man. Mac and cheese for lunch.

I laughed then went to get the first Spider-Man movie going and make us a bowl of popcorn. I'd been so busy with homework and midterms and fretting about college applications that I hadn't spent as much time with Connor as I should've. I missed my little brother, even if we did live in the same house.

We spent the afternoon and most of the evening watching Spider-Man movies and then various Marvel-themed cartoons. In between the movies and cartoons, we got out the board games and played Monopoly and Trouble, both of which I let Connor win.

As promised, we had macaroni and cheese for lunch and leftovers for dinner, finishing off with a dessert of mint chocolate chip ice cream.

A pleasant warmth had curled up inside me seeing Connor so animated and excited for the first time in what seemed like ages. Moving to Colorado had been a more difficult adjustment for him than I think we could've imagined.

Connor was passed out on the couch by the time nine o'clock rolled around, which was my cue to turn the TV off and get him up to bed. It took some serious effort to get him up the stairs, changed into his pajamas, and tucked into bed.

"Love you, squirt," I said, kissing his forehead. "See you in the morning."

I woke to someone shaking me. I quickly sat up, shoving a mess of hair out of my eyes. Connor was standing beside my bed, one hand gripping the bed for support, his fingers curled into the blankets. He was not wearing his cannula, and there was no oxygen tank in sight. In the dim light of my lamp I could see there was a bluish tint creeping its way into his face.

"What is it? What's wrong?" I demanded, all but throwing myself off the bed in my haste to get to him. "Tell me what's wrong."

I don't know how he managed to do it, but he tapped both his index fingers together, his hands trembling, the sign for *can't*, and motioned to his throat.

Connor couldn't breathe.

There are moments in your life when time speeds up instead of slowing down.

I don't know how I got Connor out to the car, how I remembered to grab the car keys and look up the address to the nearest hospital, or even how I got the car into gear and down the driveway.

Connor was up in the front seat next to me, hastily buckled in, arms wrapped around his legs with his head resting on his knees.

"Breathe, Connor, just keep breathing," I kept saying, but I couldn't be sure if he was actually listening. "We're almost to the hospital, I promise. Everything is going to be okay. The doctors there will help you and everything is going to be okay."

Everything is going to be okay.

Connor had to be getting *some* air into his lungs because he was still conscious, but I'd never seen my little brother in such a bad state. I checked him at every stoplight, squeezed his arm, told him I loved him and that everything was going to be okay, but I don't know how much of it he understood and how much was lost in the panic.

That I didn't get us into an accident on the way to the hospital was an epic feat. The steering wheel jerked wildly in my hands when I bounced up the driveway in front of the ER entrance and quickly threw the car into park, yanking my seatbelt off so fast the edge burned my hand.

I wrenched open the passenger side door and unbuckled Connor, carefully scooping him up into my arms. He was light enough for me to carry, but my knees were knocking and everything was going all topsy-turvy. I staggered a few steps before I regained my balance. When I turned around with Connor in my arms, there were people in hospital scrubs rushing toward me. Somebody was coming out the doors with a gurney, and someone else was trying to take Connor from me.

Lipreading was never the easiest under the best of circumstances, but lipreading in this moment was not even remotely possible.

"Wait, please, my brother—he's got CF, he can't—"

No one seemed to hear me.

"Please, can you tell me what's going on? I have to—"

A female nurse had a tight grip on my arm when they took Connor from me, lay him on the gurney, and slipped an oxygen mask over his face. I used the sleeve of my shirt to wipe at my eyes, trying to get rid of the tears, but it didn't work. I couldn't stop crying. I couldn't see clearly. The woman's face was blurry and kept shifting in and out of focus.

I ripped my arm from her grasp and raced after the people wheeling Connor inside the hospital. I only got a few feet inside the ER before another nurse blocked my path. I knew she was speaking, but I was looking over her shoulder, watching Connor disappear through the double doors just past the check-in desk.

"That's my brother, I need to go with him—I need to—"

I made to move around the woman to get through the doors, but she worked her way in front of me to stop me again.

That was my breaking point. I could feel the scream working its way up my throat. I don't know how the words sounded coming out of my mouth, but they made the woman look like I just slapped her across the face.

"I'M DEAF!"

She took a step back, putting a good foot of distance between us. I stood there for a few moments trying to get my breathing under control again. I was sure I did not sound calm when I said, "That's my little brother. I need to be with him!"

I was probably shrieking at this point, no doubt a spectacle to the people I could see behind the check-in station watching us. "Where's your VRI? Hospitals are supposed to have one!"

Video Remote Interpreting was a system hospitals and doctors used because it was cheaper than hiring a live interpreter. It required a video camera and a monitor, and most of the time it was on a cart wheeled around from room to room as needed. Turn the system on, an interpreter would show up on the screen and communication between the doctor and the patient was supposed to take place that way.

I don't know how long I remained in the ER waiting room while a nurse went to go track down the VRI. Once you experienced being thrown into fast forward, having time go ticking back down to a crawl was not an easy thing to adjust to.

It was a stroke of pure luck I remembered to grab my phone before racing out of the house with Connor, and I used it to text Mom the second I could. It was just after two in the morning, but Mom never had her phone more than an arm's length away when she went out of town. She was worried enough about going to Aspen; she would answer.

At hospital w/ Connor. Don't know what's wrong. They are tracking down VRI now.

I slumped down in one of the uncomfortable chairs filling the waiting room and dropped my head back, squeezing my eyes shut.

Why was this happening? *Why was this happening?*

Mom's response came a minute later.

I'm on my way.

Mom had a three-hour drive ahead of her, and three hours sounded like an eternity. I got up and did some pacing. I sat back down. I got up for a drink of water from a fountain by the bathrooms. I sat back down again.

How long did it take to track down a VRI? They couldn't possibly be *that* busy this time of night.

I leapt to my feet when I saw the same woman from earlier crossing the waiting room to me, notepad and pen in hand. The ID badge pinned to her scrubs said her name was Kelsey. When she held the notepad out to me, I made the instantaneous decision to turn my voice off and communicate strictly through this notepad.

My heart went freefalling when I read Kelsey's words:

Our VRI seems to be broken.

My hand was trembling as I carefully wrote my response of, *What?*

Kelsey took the notepad back, wrote something down, and passed it back to me.

Can't establish internet connection with interpreter.

This had to be a joke.

NOW WHAT? I wrote in capital letters, underlining the two words. *What about my brother?*

Kelsey's lips went tight when she read my note, and her eyes were narrowed when she wrote down her response on the notepad and passed it back to me again.

Do you have anyone you can call to come sign for you?

Now this was a sticky situation. Hospitals were supposed to have VRIs for this exact reason, if no live interpreter was available—and this late at night it was unlikely one could be found.

I had no idea what I was supposed to do. I didn't have Kathleen's number, and she was an educational interpreter anyway, trained to interpret in an academic setting, not one like this.

Well, there *was* maybe one person. If Nina had been farther along in learning sign, I would have texted her, but she wasn't quite as good as someone else I knew, and I *needed* to know what was happening with Connor.

It was a long shot and I didn't think he would actually answer given how late it was—and maybe there was even the chance he wouldn't want to talk to me after this, because this was *a lot* to ask of someone you were only just getting to know—but I sent the text to him anyway.

I need your help. Can you meet me at hospital?

CHAPTER 20

I t was just past three o'clock in the morning when Beau came striding into the ER. He was still in the sweatpants and T-shirt he must've fallen asleep in, his jacket and sneakers hastily thrown on, and his hair was a mess. But he was here, and his eyes found me immediately.

WHAT HAPPENED? he signed as he approached, concern etched across his face.

It took a tremendous amount of effort not to leap into his arms and beg him to tell me everything was going to be okay. I had to take a few deep breaths while I gnawed on my lip before I could sign a proper response.

MY BROTHER, I signed to Beau. CAN'T BREATHE.

YOUR BROTHER OK? WHERE INTERPRETER FOR YOU? he asked, and he jabbed a finger back at the check-in station.

I signed, DON'T KNOW, about ten times because *I didn't know*.

I didn't have an interpreter, we'd been at the hospital over an hour now, and I still had no idea what was going on with Connor. If he was even . . .

Beau took me by the hand and steered me over to the

check-in station, slapping his free hand down on the counter to get Kelsey's attention from where she sat behind her computer. Had he picked up that habit from me?

I saw Kelsey say, "Who . . . you?" to Beau and he did one spectacular job of signing and using his voice together when he signed, I SIGN FOR HER. WHAT HAPPENED WITH HER BROTHER?

Beau conveniently did not mention he wasn't a certified interpreter, just that he was here to sign for me.

Kelsey sized Beau up, looking as if she were about to object, but the next thing out of my mouth was a sigh of relief when she very clearly said, "Okay."

SEE HIM NOW? I signed to Beau, because that was the one thing that hadn't left my thoughts in the last hour.

I needed to see my little brother.

Beau relayed my question to Kelsey, and she did some tapping around on her computer before she shook her head. I felt myself deflate even more.

WHY? I signed, swallowing back a sob. WHY?

I didn't need Beau there to interpret when Kelsey said, "They need to stabilize . . . first."

I couldn't take any more. I walked back to the chairs in the waiting room and threw myself down in my seat, crumpling forward and dropping my head into my hands. My entire body was throbbing with the unfamiliar ache of heartbreak, both mental and physical. One thought zipping through my mind like lightning: *If I were hearing, could I have gone with Connor?*

It was a stupid thought, I knew it. But I couldn't get rid of it.

This had to be the first time I think I hated the fact I was Deaf. I just wanted to know what was going on without a stupid interpreter here. I just wanted to be with my little brother. And I hated this feeling of complete and total helplessness.

I forced myself to look up at the soft touch to my arm. Beau had sat down beside me, reaching out to me, and I simultaneously wanted to shove him away and pull him in close.

YOU OK? Beau signed.

I suddenly had an urge to apologize to him. Beau didn't sign up for this. It was a lot to ask of him—maybe *too* much—but the fact he was here, right beside me, his hand outstretched as if for me to take it, had to mean something. Didn't it?

NO, I signed to him honestly. NOT OK.

SORRY, Beau signed back. HARD FOR YOU, I KNOW.

I dragged my eyes over to meet Beau's gaze when he gave my hand a gentle squeeze.

HE OK, he signed to me. YOUR BROTHER.

DON'T KNOW THAT, I pointed out.

He gave a nod of agreement and signed back, MAYBE. BUT TRY NOT WORRY.

I sucked in a huge breath of air, leaning my head back to stare up at all the beige dots covering the white ceiling tiles.

Not worrying was easier said than done. It wasn't Beau's little brother in some hospital bed, struggling to breathe.

When the receptionist, Kelsey, came over to us in the waiting room, I sat upright, gripping Beau's knee so tightly I saw him wince. I hadn't kept a close watch on the clock for fear of losing my mind completely, so I wasn't sure how much time had passed since I was last told I couldn't go see Connor.

Kelsey looked to Beau when she approached and said, ". . . her you can . . . see him now."

SEE HIM NOW? I quickly signed to Beau, and he nodded, signing, YES.

I was up and on my feet, hot on Kelsey's heels as she led us to the double doors Connor disappeared through when we first got to the hospital. I wasn't sure when I laced my fingers through Beau's, holding onto his hand impossibly tight, but I didn't let go.

Kelsey led us down a long corridor full of medical equipment, people in scrubs, and beds with green privacy curtains pulled closed on either side of us. It felt like we walked the distance of a football field before Kelsey finally stopped and pulled back the curtains around a bed toward the end of the corridor.

Beau's hand slipped from mine as I took a step forward, my eyes fixed on Connor. He looked so *small* in the gigantic hospital bed, dressed in one of those oversized gowns, a breathing tube inserted carefully down his throat. I chose to focus on the fact that Connor was breathing and not the fact he looked so miserable, even unconscious.

My hand was trembling when I reached out to Beau, trying to sign, HE OK?

I must have gotten the point across because I caught

sight of Beau speaking to Kelsey, but all Beau signed in response was, DOCTOR HERE SOON, HE EXPLAIN.

Kelsey tugged the privacy curtains shut on her way out, leaving Beau and me alone with Connor. I felt rooted to the spot, my mind kicking into overdrive trying to process everything that happened in such a short amount of time. It took effort to put one foot in front of the other to go to Connor's side.

I stood there, my hand curled around Connor's tiny one, until the privacy curtains were pulled open again and a gray-haired man in one of those white doctor's coats stepped in, a chart tucked up under his arm. Beau had taken a seat in the one chair on the other side of the bed. He got to his feet as the man came forward.

He introduced himself to Beau as they shook hands, and they both came up to the bed where I stood. I saw Beau say, "Just . . . slow," and the man nodded.

DOCTOR W-E-S-L-E-Y, Beau started to sign, pointing to the man, and I nodded, stumbling my way through introducing myself in sign language.

WHAT HAPPENED? I signed, motioning to Connor.

Beau listened for a moment, then turned to me. HE HAVE . . . Beau paused as soon as he began and then said something like, "In . . . please." A second later, he started finger spelling, C-O-L-L-A-P-S-E-D L-U-N-G.

A collapsed lung was always a possibility when you had cystic fibrosis, but the fact that it happened to my little brother—when having a collapsed lung could *kill* you—was beyond my comprehension. I could've lost my brother tonight.

I curled my fingers tighter around Connor's hand, not caring that a fresh wave of tears was threatening to yank me under the surface again.

HE OK NOW? I signed with one hand, not moving my eyes from Connor's face.

Beau had to wave a hand to get me to look at him again, and he signed, OK NOW, BUT HE STAY FOR A FEW DAYS.

Beau explained a nurse would be over soon to move Connor to his new room on a different floor. I waited until Dr. Wesley left us to sign to Beau, THANK YOU FOR YOUR HELP.

NO PROBLEM, he signed back, a weak smile on his face.

YOU GO HOME NOW, I signed next.

I would be forever grateful Beau went out of his way to come down here in the middle of the night to help me, but I wanted to be left alone with my little brother now. I couldn't see myself able to stop crying anytime soon, and I hated when people saw me crying. Beau had seen me doing a whole a lot of it.

OK IF I STAY? Beau signed in response. WAIT FOR YOUR MOTHER WITH YOU, he added when I gave him a skeptical look.

I don't know why he wasn't jumping at the chance to get out of here. This had to be awkward and uncomfortable, not to mention inconvenient.

I gave up trying to deduce his reasoning and signed, OK.

FIND RESTROOM, Beau told me as he reached for the privacy curtains. COME BACK SOON.

When Beau disappeared, I carefully maneuvered myself onto the hospital bed next to Connor, making sure not to disturb any of the tubes or wires he was hooked up to. The bed was more than big enough for the both of us as I lay down beside him. He unconsciously shifted toward me in his sleep when I rested my head on the pillow beside him.

"Please be okay," I whispered. *"Please."*

CHAPTER 21

I must have fallen asleep, because I was met with a harsh, unfamiliar light when I opened my eyes again. Everything was shifting in and out of focus when I sat up, and after a few seconds I realized I wasn't in the ER with Connor anymore.

The ER had been replaced with a bland hospital room with beige walls and old green furniture. Connor was still asleep in the bed, the breathing tube still present. Mom was next to him, slumped over in the chair beside the bed, her chin in hand, eyes closed.

I stumbled my way off the cramped loveseat I'd been moved to and went over to Mom, shoving my hair out of my face as I went. Her eyes snapped open when she heard me moving and she straightened up, blinking the sleep out of her eyes.

YOU OK? was the first thing she signed to me.

FINE, I signed, even though I didn't mean it one bit. I was stiff all over and my head was throbbing painfully. YOU SHOW UP, WHEN?

EARLY MORNING, Mom answered. TIME 5:30.

177

TIME NOW? I asked, looking around the room for a clock.

Mom pulled her cell phone out of her bag and signed, TIME 8:24, MORNING.

How could I have slept for three hours?

I SHOW UP, B-E-A-U WITH YOU, Mom signed to me when she put her cell phone away.

Right. Beau.

I . . . DON'T KNOW, I started to sign to Mom, wanting to tell her everything that happened. DON'T KNOW WHAT HAPPENED, DON'T KNOW HOW HELP CONNOR, HOSPITAL V-R-I NOT WORK, I—

Mom caught my hands in hers and squeezed tight, and I knew she was just trying to comfort me, but I felt like I was going to collapse.

NOT BLAME YOU, Mom signed when she released my hands. NOT YOUR FAULT.

FEEL MY FAULT, I signed back.

Mom scooted over in the chair and gently tugged me down next to her, wrapping one arm tight around my shoulders.

YOU DO YOUR BEST, she signed to me. SCARY, I KNOW, BUT YOU HELP CONNOR. HE OK.

I dropped my head onto Mom's shoulder and shut my eyes, wishing everything around us would just fall away and disappear into nothingness. I could feel the vibrations in her throat and I knew she was talking, so I leaned up to get a better look at her.

CONNOR OK, Mom signed, her free hand pressed against my cheek. I KNOW YOU NOT THINK THAT, BUT YOU BRAVE. NOT EASY.

NOT . . . I had a hand against my chest, wanting the heavy pressure there to go away. I just wanted things to be normal again.

Mom raised an eyebrow in confusion, not understanding where I was going with this.

I DON'T KNOW IF I CAN BECOME R-T, I signed, tremors running through my hands. I DON'T KNOW IF I CAN.

Mom's expression went from confusion to shock.

WHY NOT? she quickly signed back.

BECAUSE WHY? I LOSE MY MIND WHEN CONNOR CAN'T BREATHE. HOW I HELP KIDS WITH SAME PROBLEM IF I CAN'T COMMUNICATE?

It had taken me years to get to the place where I was comfortable being Deaf, enjoyed it and embraced everything that came with it. But now it felt like it was the one thing standing in the way of the dream I'd had since I was a child.

I hadn't been able to help my brother last night. I'd been panicked and confused and unable to speak, sign, or listen. I'd cried a million times and barely held myself together. If I couldn't help Connor, how could I help anyone else?

DIFFERENT, Mom signed firmly. KIDS YOU WORK WITH NOT YOUR BROTHER. DIFFERENT EXPERIENCE.

SURE? I signed skeptically. BECAUSE I DON'T LIKE HOW I FEEL NOW.

UNDERSTAND, Mom agreed. BUT I BELIEVE I-N YOU.

I knew Mom believed in me, but why didn't that feel like enough?

YOU FEEL DIFFERENT LATER, Mom signed after a slight pause. PROMISE.

I wanted to take Mom's promise to heart, but right then it felt impossible.

When enough time had passed to where my breathing had become even again, Mom turned back to me and signed, B-E-A-U HERE STILL.

"What?" I said aloud, and signed, REALLY?

Mom nodded, taking a sip of coffee from the cup that had been on the nightstand.

WHERE? I signed, hastily pulling myself up to my feet.

WAIT ROOM, Mom answered, nodding toward the door.

I let myself out of the room as gracefully as possible and took off down the hallway at a sprint, following the signs leading to the waiting room. When I rounded the corner, I came skidding to a halt when I saw Beau.

He was standing off to the side, in conversation with a short, brown-haired woman dressed in Thanksgiving-themed scrubs. Reading his body language and seeing how relaxed he appeared to be, the polite smile on his face, Beau must know this nurse.

I was close enough to where I could catch a couple words of what he was saying, like, "school's good" and what I thought might be, "Yale." I was sure I looked ridiculous standing there, my eyes glued to Beau, but I wasn't about to waltz up to them and butt into their conversation.

Beau noticed me a moment later and was quick to wrap up with the nurse. He gave her a fast hug before moving my way.

HELLO, he signed, meeting me in the middle of the waiting room. HOW ARE YOU?

Responding with, FINE, would've been a lie, so instead I settled for signing, WHY YOU HERE?

Beau gave a blink of confusion and used his voice to say, "I wanted to make . . . you're okay."

I ended up signing, FINE, anyway.

I was trying for a calm, collected expression, but I wasn't sure how successful I was.

DON'T LIE, PLEASE, Beau signed to me, an unusually somber look on his face. YESTERDAY BAD FOR YOU.

FINE, I repeated, biting down on my lip. MY BROTHER OK NOW. YOU LOOK TIRED. GO HOME.

He winced once he understood what I was saying to him after I had to repeat myself, and he very hesitantly signed back, I WAIT FOR YOU.

WHY? I signed.

Beau took his time responding to my question. Splotches of color dotted his cheeks, and I saw him swallow hard.

I . . . WORRY FOR YOU, he signed after a long pause. DON'T LIKE YOU SAD. I WANT YOU OK.

I ignored the way my heart stuttered in my chest at Beau's confession, and I shook my head, insistent when I signed, FINE. REALLY.

Beau very much looked like he wasn't buying it, but he relented in the end, giving a one shouldered shrug. IF YOU SURE, he signed with a weak smile.

I had no rational explanation for why I did it, but I took a step closer and wrapped Beau up in a hug. He didn't waste any time sliding his arms around me in return. I scrunched my eyes closed, ignoring everything else around us, and for a split second it felt like I didn't have a rough few days ahead of me while Connor recovered. Eventually I had to tell myself it was time to let Beau go.

GO HOME, I signed to Beau, taking a step back. TIME FOR SLEEP.

Beau did another one of those shrugs of his and signed, OK. YOU TEXT ME LATER?

YES, I signed back. I TEXT YOU LATER.

did not text Beau later, purposefully ignoring all the messages he sent my way. I didn't text anyone, save for the random ones to Nina and Melissa to let them know I was still alive.

I spent Thanksgiving in the hospital with Connor, where cell phone reception was shoddy to begin with, but that wasn't really the reason behind the radio silence on my end.

I was afraid to talk to Beau again. The communication barrier between us, no matter how hard Beau was working to pick up sign language, was even more evident now than before. I would forever be thankful for Beau and what he did in the hospital that night, but it had been a struggle for both of us.

And there were little things too, like his dad. Obviously, Beau was intimidated by his father, so I could only imagine what Dr. Watson thought of Beau skipping out in the middle of the night to come to my rescue at the hospital.

There were serious differences in our two worlds. I didn't know if he would think bridging that gap was worth it. *I* didn't even know if I wanted to bridge that gap myself.

So I chose to focus on homework and being with my family instead, responding to Melissa and Nina's messages just enough to let it be known I was alive and—relatively—okay. Everything else could wait.

⁀

Returning to school the Monday after Thanksgiving break came with a massive load of butterflies in my stomach I couldn't get rid of. My palms were sweaty at the thought of walking into AP Statistics and seeing Beau for the first time since that night in the hospital. But I shoved back the apprehension I felt—pushing it to the place where I could now stow away my new fears about becoming a respiratory therapist.

I kept the events of Thanksgiving break to myself, not filling Kathleen in on anything that happened, pretending like everything was normal. It felt a little like lying, telling Kathleen I was just fine, but as it was going to be my scripted response to anyone else that asked, I might as well get used to it.

Most everyone was seated in AP Statistics when Kathleen and I entered the classroom. I took my regular seat in front of Beau like nothing had changed over break, pulling out my textbook and homework assignments.

The tap on my shoulder came shortly before Mrs. Richardson began the day's lesson.

I felt something suspiciously like guilt when I turned around to look at Beau and saw the concern etched across his face. I'd ignored him all break when I knew he only wanted to see if I was doing all right.

WHAT'S UP? I signed nervously.

". . . okay?" Beau said, and he leaned toward me, his hand outstretched as if to touch my hand. I might've wanted him to.

FINE, I signed back quickly. SORRY. TIRED.

Beau nodded, but it didn't seem like he was buying my excuse. I suspected it wouldn't be too long before he was asking me that question again.

And it came when we were sitting across from each other at our normal table in the cafeteria at lunch, another simple, YOU OK?

YES, FINE, I signed back for what seemed to be the thousandth time.

Both Nina and Kathleen asked me the same thing.

YOUR BROTHER? Beau signed to me next.

I hesitantly signed, BETTER.

That was the truth at least. Connor still needed more time before he would bounce back completely, and there was no question of his going back to school until next semester. A home health care provider would start coming over sometime this week to help out around the house. Mom was already investigating home school programs, but I wasn't sure how well that was going to work out with how demanding her job could be. They moved her halfway across the country for a reason—and that meant more work than before.

I was starting to think that if I got a job to help bring in some money maybe Mom might have less to worry about with everything else going on, that it wouldn't matter so much if her paychecks were a little short because she left work early to come home every now and then. Thanks to the move, I wasn't going to be taking Pratt's graduation seminar class, part of which required students to build resumes and learn how to write cover letters, but I was thinking my guidance counselor Mrs. Stephens should probably be the first person to speak to about the whole process of finding a job.

Under normal circumstances I would never think of abandoning Mom at home while Connor needed the extra care, but with the home health care provider coming she would be getting a little reprieve. There was temporary relief on the horizon, and I hoped I could improve that with a little extra income.

GOOD, Beau signed with a nod. HAPPY.

SAME, I replied.

Nina chose to cut in at that moment, leaning toward us to say, ". . . everything okay?"

"Fine," I said immediately, and Beau gave a nod of agreement.

I thought there might have been a suspicious gleam in Nina's eyes, but she let it go with a shrug.

"So . . . was thinking," she said, resting her chin in her hands. ". . . some homework . . . for finals?"

It was an automatic response to look at Beau when I did not understand what Nina was saying, and he already seemed prepared, signing, HOMEWORK AND STUDY FOR F-I-N-A-L-S.

I felt myself release a sigh. The last thing I wanted to do was study. I would rather set up camp at the mailbox in thirty-degree weather to wait for any news from

Cartwright or spend as much time as I could keeping Connor company.

"Okay," I said. "When and where?"

We decided to start the studying after school at a local coffee shop. It was called The Steaming Bean, and according to Nina, it was a popular place come finals time for high school and college students. On the way over, Nina wound up in the backseat of Beau's car with a stack of books in her lap from his traveling library.

The place was empty for a Monday afternoon, so finding a table to unload our books and homework things wasn't difficult. The atmosphere was calming, smelling of chocolate and espresso, and there was a cozy little fireplace tucked away in the corner. Beau took it upon himself to buy us all a round of peppermint mochas even though Nina and I insisted we could buy our own drinks, and then we got to work.

First up was prepping for our Historical Literature class. Our teacher told us beforehand that our final was going to be an eight- to ten-page essay over the two major works we'd covered this semester—*Beowulf* and *Canterbury Tales*. I wasn't much of a writer and would take numbers over words any day of the week, but it was impossible to miss the way Beau's face lit up when we started talking about the essay.

I sat back in my chair and sipped at my mocha as Beau launched into a longwinded critique of *Beowulf*. Before long he dragged Nina into it. Every so often I would see a flash of his dimples when he would smile at something Nina would say. He seemed genuinely enthusiastic about *Beowulf,* which I didn't understand *at all* because it had been an immense struggle not to fall asleep during most of the lectures over that text.

I gave a startled jerk when Nina waved a hand at me, signing, HEY, and I had to wonder how long I'd been spaced out, looking at Beau. I felt a little creepy.

WHAT'S UP? I signed, setting my empty mocha cup down.

YOU OK? Nina said, one eyebrow raised.

"Fine," I said, really wishing people would quit asking me that. "Just . . . thinking about the essay and all."

Beau grinned and gave me a dorky thumbs-up. "You'll . . . fine," he said. "Promise."

He signed, RESTROOM, to us and got to his feet, heading off to where the bathrooms were at the back of the coffee shop.

He got two steps away before he was suddenly down on one knee. He probably would've fallen flat on his face if he hadn't thrown out an arm to grab at the nearest table to keep himself upright.

I rushed to his side without thinking, dropping to my knees in front of him. Nina was there too, saying something, offering a hand to help Beau regain his balance.

"Hey, what's wrong?" I said aloud, not thinking to sign.

Beau waved away Nina's hand and winced when he pushed up on the table and very carefully got to his feet. I could see his knees knocking as we both stood up.

My hands hung in mid-air, not sure if I wanted to sign or say something to Beau. He was still clutching at the table, and his eyes were shut tight, lips a thin line.

I felt helpless when I looked to Nina, and I was taken aback to see an expression of exasperation on her face instead of concern for Beau. It looked like she was annoyed with him.

"Did . . . take . . . ?"

The last word Nina said to Beau involved a lot of syllables, so there was no way was I going to be able to figure out what she was saying.

Beau shook his head when he opened his eyes again, but there was an undeniably soft look on his face when he said, "Thanks for . . ." to Nina.

She gave him a tiny smile while she rolled her eyes in response and nudged Beau with her shoulder.

It wasn't until Beau was off in the bathroom and Nina and I were sitting back down at our table that I realized the hot feeling working its way through me was jealousy. Beau never looked at me the way he'd just looked at Nina, but I had no idea why that should bother me.

"What's wrong with Beau?" I blurted out.

Nina wiped her mouth with a napkin after taking a sip of her mocha before she answered my question. "Beau . . . okay," she said. "He's . . ."

She put her hand up to her temple and made a flapping gesture, the sign for *stubborn*—also conveniently the sign for donkey.

"Beau's stubborn," I said with a frown, and Nina nodded.

What was that supposed to mean? What did Beau being stubborn have to do with anything?

"What do you mean by that?" I said when a minute had passed, and Nina still hadn't elaborated.

HE SHOULD TELL YOU, was her careful reply in sign language.

Well, that sure cleared things up.

"And are you two . . . um . . ." I went sinking down in my chair, trying not to cover my face with my hands out of embarrassment. "I mean, you and Beau . . . ?"

Nina arched one eyebrow as she reached for her mocha again, and she gave this kind of sly smile I'd never seen from her before. I had the feeling Nina knew exactly what was floating across my brain at the moment.

"Me . . . Beau? No . . ." She shook her head. "We're . . . friends. Nothing there . . ."

PROMISE, she added in sign, and I believed her.

Nina leaned forward with interest, a curious expression taking over her face. Instantly I dreaded what she was about to say.

"Now you . . . Beau . . . ?"

I was blissfully saved from answering by Beau's return from the restroom. I gave him the once-over as inconspicuously as I could, and it was a relief he didn't seem to be in as much pain as a few minutes ago. He had a look of discomfort as he sat down, stretching his right leg out in front of him at an awkward angle. Not so much a cool guy thing this time; he had to be in pain.

That was the leg with the massive scar I'd seen briefly the day before midterms.

YOU OK? I signed to Beau when he glanced up from his copy of *Beowulf.*

He signed back, YES, way too quickly, but I wasn't buying his answer.

Promising myself I'd get to the bottom of this soon was a lot easier than everything else had felt lately.

sat on the floor behind the kitchen table with Connor, his face squished against the back door as he watched the snow falling outside. Really, he should've been resting after his breathing treatment, but the second I'd signed, SNOW, he'd looked like he was about to burst with excitement and he rolled off the couch with more energy than I expected from him.

This wasn't the first snowfall he'd ever seen, but this snow in Colorado looked a little different from snow in New Jersey. The porch light was on, illuminating the backyard in a gentle glow. The more snow that began to cover the ground, the more sparkles came dancing off the snow in the light.

"Can . . . go outside?" Connor asked me, tapping a finger on the back door.

"Not a chance," I answered. "Let's just enjoy it from here."

Connor's face twisted down in a pout, but he was back to looking enchanted by the snow a few seconds later.

I felt footsteps from where I sat on the floor by the back door and knew it could only be Mom coming toward us. When I moved myself around to get to my feet, she came walking into the kitchen with a couple grocery bags in both arms, and there was an unbelievably happy smile on her face.

"What's wrong?" I said suspiciously, grabbing two grocery bags from her. "Why do you look like that?"

Mom couldn't sign with the way her hands were occupied, so I leaned in to watch her say, ". . . have mail."

Mail?

I hoped whatever was in the grocery bags I took from Mom wasn't breakable because I dropped them and snatched at the pile of mail tucked up under her arm. I went straight for the largest envelope, tossing the rest of the mail on the nearby counter. I think I gave a sob when I saw Cartwright's crest on the envelope, addressed to Maya N. Harris.

"Open . . . !" Mom said, rocking back on her heels with her hands clasped before her after she set her grocery bags down.

My fingers were trembling while I attempted to tear open the envelope as neatly as possible. Mom came closer to peer over my shoulder, and even Connor joined us as I carefully pulled out the first sheet of paper in the envelope. The words seemed to dance across the page, making it difficult to comprehend.

A slow minute passed before the words fell into place.

Mom gripped me by the shoulders, and when I finally looked up at her she had her eyebrows raised expectantly at me.

I didn't think I was capable of forming any words to speak, so I signed, YES.

THE SILENCE BETWEEN US

YES? Mom repeated, her eyebrows now disappearing up into her hair.

YES!

I couldn't believe it. I *could not believe it*.

I got into Cartwright.

Kathleen stood there in the middle of Mrs. Richardson's classroom reading and rereading my acceptance letter from Cartwright. Each time she got through it and went back to the beginning, her smile grew even bigger.

When she carefully set my letter on my desk, she signed, CONGRATULATIONS! before pulling me in for a hug.

WONDERFUL, WONDERFUL, Kathleen signed when she let me go.

I probably signed, HAPPY, a few too many times, but I doubted she'd hold it against me.

A FEW MONTHS, GRADUATION, AND COLLEGE! Kathleen signed with her brilliant smile.

This time her enthusiasm was contagious. I couldn't remember the last time I smiled so much.

I looked around when Kathleen paused mid-sentence to sign HELLO to someone behind me. I wasn't surprised it was Beau walking into class. I was surprised it was his name that came flying from my lips, and that my first reaction was to grab my acceptance letter and literally go running to him.

"Beau!"

I felt the ecstatic smile slip from my face when Beau

stopped dead in his tracks, staring down at me with a mixture of confusion and surprise.

SORRY, I immediately signed, now fully aware of the curious stares from our few classmates already seated.

"No," Beau said quickly, shaking his head. "I've never . . . say my name . . ."

AGAIN? I signed in confusion.

It took Beau a moment to sign, I NEVER HEAR YOU SAY MY NAME BEFORE. But he was smiling now instead of looking like a deer caught in the headlights. So, did that mean he was . . . *happy* too?

Beau gestured to my acceptance letter clutched tight in my grasp, and I suddenly remembered what I'd gone running to him for in the first place.

Wordlessly, I passed the letter over to Beau. If it was possible, he looked even more thrilled than Kathleen. I let out a yelp when he suddenly had his arms around me in a hug that was not totally unwelcome. A little alarming, sure, but once I hugged him back, I had no desire to let him go.

I felt like dissolving into giggles instead of tears like the first time I'd hugged him while in the hospital. I was starting to feel a little lightheaded catching that scent of his—cinnamon spice.

When the lights flashed to start class, Beau and I quickly took our seats, and I folded my acceptance letter and tucked it safely into my backpack. There was a tap on my shoulder when Mrs. Richardson was occupied with her computer, trying to pull up today's notes on the projector.

Beau signed, CONGRATULATIONS! when I twisted around in my seat to face him.

THANK YOU! I signed back, trying to suppress more giggles. LETTER FROM Y-A-L-E? I signed to him next.

Beau was even more anxious to get into his first-choice college than I was, so for his sake I sure hoped he'd gotten some similar mail.

He made a sour face and shook his head, signing, NOT YET.

SOON, I assured him, and reached over to give his hand a comforting squeeze.

Beau smiled, and before I could get totally lost in his dimples, he nodded up at Mrs. Richardson. I quickly faced forward but couldn't quite wipe the smile off my face.

My excitement at my acceptance from Cartwright still hadn't faded one bit by the time lunch rolled around. It turned into a struggle trying to communicate with Nina because I couldn't choose between using my voice or signing and everything was coming out a jumbled mess. Kathleen had to step in to tell her the news before excusing herself to go to lunch off campus, and then I gave Nina my acceptance letter to read.

CONGRATULATIONS! Nina signed, throwing an arm around my shoulders for a hug. WONDERFUL!

I KNOW, I signed back happily.

"Did . . . tell Beau?" Nina asked after I'd tucked the acceptance letter into my backpack.

My gaze automatically flicked over to where Beau sat at our regular table next to Jackson. I quickly looked away when Jackson caught sight of me staring and he gave me one of those unsettling winks of his.

"Um, yeah," I answered Nina's question. "He's happy for me too."

Nina and I bought sandwiches from the food line and a tray of fries to share and took our seats at the lunch table. I wound up sitting across from Beau—somehow I was always sitting across from or near Beau—and was taken aback to see the cross look that was beginning to creep over his face.

I got a few bites into my sandwich when Jackson leaned closer to Beau and started to say something that only made Beau's frown deepen. I was only able to make out Jackson saying, ". . . don't mind if . . ." before I had to give up trying to lipread.

I fixated on my sandwich instead, picking at a wilted piece of lettuce. I wanted to know what Jackson was saying because Beau was obviously getting a little worked up about it, but it really was none of my business. Sometimes I was too nosy for my own good.

When I was halfway through my sandwich, Jackson was suddenly leaning toward me waving a hello, and immediately I became suspicious.

"Can I help you?" I said once I was finished chewing my food.

". . . sure can," Jackson said with what I think was supposed to be a dazzling smile. ". . . was wondering . . ."

He didn't even get the chance to finish his sentence before Beau cut in, signing so quickly I did a double take.

AGAIN? I signed. It was a reflex—I couldn't possibly have understood him correctly.

Beau's cheeks went from bright pink to flaming red as he repeated himself, signing what I thought he had the first time around.

YOU ASK ME IF I WANT DATE? I signed next, the words tumbling off my fingers.

Beau nodded, a look of relief flashing across his face. I felt myself giving a sigh of relief too.

GOOD, I signed. BEFORE YOU ASK IF I WANT DIVORCE.

Beau understood after I finger spelled the word for him, and I watched his eyes go wide as he quickly signed, NO! NOT THAT. I WANT . . .

I leaned across the table to take Beau's hands in mine, prompting him to make the letter *d* with his fingers. When he did, I brought his two hands together, so the tips of his fingers were touching, rather than moving them apart like he'd been doing.

"That's how you sign it," I told him. "You come together, not break apart."

"Okay," he said with a timid smile.

When he slipped his hands out from mine—I suddenly didn't want to let them go—he signed, HAVE DATE WITH ME?

I didn't even stop to think about it before I signed, YES.

It was after we'd been smiling at each other like loons for one long moment that I remembered Nina was sitting right next to me. Nina, who knew enough sign language that I was pretty sure she knew exactly what just happened. Jackson on the other hand probably figured this was all something good by the dopey looks Beau and I were sharing.

When I looked over at Nina, kind of like a kid who just got caught with their hand in a cookie jar, she was smirking.

She just signed, FINALLY.

CHAPTER 24

Melissa's chipper smile was plastered across the screen of my iPad while I sat in the middle of my bedroom floor amongst a mess of clothes.

DOESN'T MATTER, I kept signing to Melissa, throwing aside a blouse my aunt Caroline got me for my sixteenth birthday that I never wore. DOESN'T MATTER WHAT I WEAR.

Melissa was shaking her head in disagreement and signed, YES! again.

I held up a sweater in a pretty gold color for Melissa to see and she made a face, scrunching her nose up.

COLD HERE, I reminded her.

I'd already sent her a picture of the mountain of snow in our backyard.

OK, Melissa finally signed. FINE. NEED COLOR.

I got up and yanked open the top drawer of my dresser, rummaging around a bit until I found what I was looking for. It was a soft red winter hat with a flower knitted onto the side. I thought it was cute but never had much occasion to wear it.

Melissa gave a thumbs-up and signed, PERFECT, when I showed her the hat.

NEED CHANGE, I signed, grabbing my iPad off the floor. HE SHOW UP SOON.

Melissa waved frantically at me so I wouldn't end the call after I signed my good-bye, and she signed, NO KISS FIRST DATE.

My jaw dropped, and the first thing I thought to sign was, NEVER!

I ended the call with Melissa after promising to send her updates via text on how the date was going. After I got changed, stuffed my feet into my boots, and got my hat on as nicely as possible, I dashed off to the bathroom to brush my teeth. No way was I walking into my first date with bad breath.

The lights in the hallway started flashing on and off when my mouth was still full of toothpaste, so I figured Beau must have just arrived. I finished up in the bathroom as quickly as possible and barely remembered to take my hearing aids out and put them back in their case on my dresser before sprinting downstairs. Any time wet stuff started falling from the sky I did not wear my hearing aids.

I was short of breath when I made it to the bottom of the stairs, grabbing at the handrail. Beau was here on time like I knew he would be, but I was taken aback to see him on the couch next to Connor, Spider-Man action figure in hand, looking like he'd been at play with my little brother for ages. Beau was a nice guy, but it was just . . . not what I expected, seeing him with Connor like this.

I couldn't think of a time when I hadn't felt fiercely

THE SILENCE BETWEEN US

protective of Connor, wanting to shield him from every-thing I possibly could out there in the world, but this, unbelievably, was not one of those times. I stood there at the bottom of the stairs watching my little brother laughing and playing with Beau, and the only thing I could think of to do was smile.

This was genuine—there was no mistaking any smile of Beau's where you could see his dimples—and I wasn't sure how to handle the variety of emotions bouncing around inside me.

Mom looked just as surprised as I felt when she came walking out of the kitchen with a cup of coffee in hand and saw Beau and Connor together.

B-E-A-U YOUR DATE? she signed to me with one hand, nodding toward the couch.

Connor had a bad habit of answering the door and letting in whoever was on the porch, so it wasn't shocking he'd beaten Mom to the punch this time either.

YES, I signed back. HEARING BOY, I KNOW, BUT . . .

My sentence fell short when Beau noticed me and got to his feet, returning Spider-Man to Connor.

HELLO, he signed, coming over to me and Mom. READY?

YES, I signed quickly, ready to grab Beau by the arm and drag him out the door before Mom got going on whatever parental embarrassment she was getting ready to inflict.

WHERE YOU GO? Mom signed before I could make my escape.

SURPRISE, was Beau's answer, making my stomach do that freefalling thing again.

READY? I signed, pointing toward the front door.

Beau nodded, sending a grin my way, and of course my mother didn't miss that.

CAREFUL, she signed, following us to the front door. NEED YOU HOME IF SNOW BAD.

PROMISE, I signed.

Beau had left the car running, the heat going full blast, so it was like slipping under a blanket fresh out of the dryer when I buckled myself in his car.

We were a couple blocks away when I finally asked, "So can you tell me where we're going now?"

I was sure whatever Beau had in store for our date had to be something indoors with all this snow, but I still wanted to know what it was.

"I said . . . surprise," Beau said with a pretend stern look on his face.

"And?" I said. "I'm not one for surprises."

WAIT, Beau signed to me at a stoplight. OUR DATE FUN, PROMISE.

There wasn't much conversation to be had on the way to wherever Beau was taking me. He couldn't face me while driving so I could lipread, and he couldn't exactly sign with me with his hands occupied on the steering wheel. The longer we were in the car, though, the easier it became to relax. Beau had this calming presence whenever I was around him that was hard to ignore.

We left Denver behind after about twenty minutes, getting on the I-70 heading west. I still wasn't too familiar with Colorado, but I noticed we were going into a more mountainous area. Everything was covered in snow, the sky a smooth white, and I had the thought that we might currently be on our way to Narnia.

I sat up in my seat when Beau took an exit with signs pointing toward a place called Georgetown.

"What's Georgetown?" I asked with interest.

It was impossible to tell what Beau was thinking as he carefully navigated the ice-covered streets, not answering my question. It took another ten minutes before we passed under a large sign that said, "Welcome to Georgetown!"

It was a small town tucked away in the mountains that couldn't have had more than a thousand or so residents. There were a bunch of older style houses right out of another century, a handful of shops, and maybe a restaurant or two in the downtown area. It was cute and scenic with all the snow, but what on earth were we doing here?

Beau parked the car in a dirt lot behind an ancient hotel and turned to face me.

"What are we doing here?" I asked.

Beau had this smile on his face as he got unbuckled, opening the car door.

"You like Christmas, right?"

B eau had taken us to an old-fashioned Christmas market.

Georgetown's downtown was apparently where this Christmas market had taken place for the past few decades, and it was not difficult to see why the streets were packed with people of all sorts bundled up in jackets, hats, and scarves.

The main street was right out of a Hallmark Christmas card. There were lights, garlands, and wreaths, as well as a roaring bonfire up the street in the middle of a series of market stalls where people were selling homemade goods, woodwork, and cinnamon-roasted almonds.

The piles of snow up on the sidewalks and a man dressed up in old-fashioned clothing as Saint Nicholas gave the atmosphere even more Christmas spirit. I did a double take when I saw carolers in Victorian garb, songbooks in hand, a small crowd gathered around them.

Beau placed a hand on my arm as we stood there on the sidewalk beside the visitor center. YOU LIKE? he signed.

YES, I signed back honestly. DIFFERENT, BUT . . . BEAUTIFUL. I LIKE.

Beau visibly relaxed. GOOD, he signed. HAPPY.

"I like it," I said aloud. "But why did you bring us here?"

I'd never been on a date before, but I was fairly certain this wasn't the type of date other seniors in high school would go on. Not that I was complaining, but . . .

Beau scrunched up his face as he thought about how to respond, stuffing his hands in his pockets. I perked up, ready to lipread what he had to say.

"This . . . what me . . . my mom . . . used . . . long time ago," he finally said, nodding toward the market up the street. ". . . special, right? . . . thought you might like . . . not school-related."

The only thing I could think of to say was, "Oh."

Oh.

This was only the second time Beau had mentioned his mom. I knew talking about her wasn't an easy thing for him to do, and yet he was sharing something like this with me? Something he genuinely enjoyed and wasn't worrying about how goofy or un-date-like it might be.

THANK YOU, I signed to him.

I THINK MAYBE HERE BEST, Beau signed, still looking anxious. N-I-N-A TELL ME MOVIE, BUT . . .

Knowing exactly where he was going with this, I held up a hand to stop him.

"I like going to the movies too. I just need closed captioning. But seriously, Beau, this is wonderful. I'm excited."

SAME, Beau agreed, a smile breaking out across his face

"Let's get started then."

We started up the left side of Main Street first, browsing through the cute, old-fashioned shops that sold Christmas-themed items and antiques. There were a couple galleries full of nature photography, clothes shops, bookstores, and an old general store still standing in all its original glory. Georgetown's Christmas market had perfected the art of making you feel like you were stepping back in time.

Beau paid for us to go on a carriage ride around town, which seemed to increase the holiday cheer even more. A young girl wearing a bright pink coat and hat stood up and started telling us about Georgetown's history as two Clydesdales pulled us through town—or at least that's what Beau told me. He tried to interpret what she was saying, but she was speaking too quickly for him to keep up.

FINE, I signed, not even thinking about it when I gave his hand a squeeze.

Beau did not let go of my hand.

His fingers were long and thin, warm beneath the woolen blanket tossed over our laps as he traced a random pattern across the back of my hand. My heart gave a few erratic beats and breathing properly was suddenly a struggle.

My hands were probably the most important part of myself because I used them every day to communicate. But it was strange thinking that no person ever seemed to give that any attention, focusing more on the signs I made rather than what I used to make those signs.

I flipped my hand over, letting Beau's fingers move to my palm. My skin felt hot pressed against his. Just like with that hug during class, releasing his hand and breaking contact was the last thing I wanted to do.

I think I stopped breathing when Beau laced his fingers through mine. Peeking up at him took some effort, and I saw Beau was staring straight ahead like he was merely watching all the houses go by, but there was no mistaking that smile of his.

The carriage ride ended when we returned to the giant pine tree covered in Christmas lights next to the marketplace. There were a few brief seconds when Beau released my hand to help me down from the carriage, but once my feet were carefully on the snow-covered ground, my hand was back in his. Now I couldn't keep from smiling too.

We wandered over to the marketplace where we tried on a few different hats and scarves and Beau bought us hot cider and a bag of cinnamon-roasted almonds as a treat. It started snowing as we stood huddled together by the bonfire, sipping our hot cider, almonds stuffed in our jacket pockets.

BEAUTIFUL, I signed again, pointing up at the sky.

Beau tried to hide his grin as he sipped his hot cider.

"What?" I said. "What's that look for?"

"Nothing," he said. "Just . . ."

He finished his sentence by signing, HAPPY.

SAME, I signed back. HAPPY.

Thanks to the shorter days this time of year, night started to fall and the market began closing up. Beau led me across the street to a restaurant called Troia's Café and we wound up having an early dinner of pasta and meatballs.

I had a mouthful of noodles when Beau signed, TRAIN NEXT.

AGAIN? I signed. What did he mean, train?

"Train . . ." Beau repeated. "Up . . . mountain. Christmas lights . . ."

He stuck a hand in his jacket pocket and came up with a folded piece of paper. He slid it across the small table to me. It was a ticket he'd printed off the computer, brightly colored and advertising the Georgetown Loop Railroad and their Santa's Train & Lighted Forest event for the holiday season.

"This is for kids, isn't it?" I said to Beau, handing the ticket back.

Beau surprisingly nodded. AGE EIGHTEEN, he signed, pointing back at himself with a grin. BUT I FEEL LIKE KID.

SAME, I signed, pleased by his playfulness. I didn't get to see this side of him at school, and I liked it.

Holding Beau's hand again on our way back to his car after dinner wasn't as much of a surprise this time around, but I still felt like dissolving into a giddy mess. Strange what a boy could do to you.

Driving through the rest of Georgetown—which was only a few more streets—was necessary to get to the Loop Railroad. All the lights in town were flickering on as Beau drove us up a small hillside. I stayed turned around in my seat to memorize the sight. Everything about this old mining town hidden in the mountains was enchanting.

The Railroad Loop was just as crowded as the Christmas market had been, although this time with a bunch of kids hyped up on hot cocoa and sugar cookies. I snagged a couple cookies from the table set out for paying visitors and slid my arm through Beau's as we got in line to get on the train.

A man dressed in a conductor's uniform took our tickets when we reached the front of the line. We found a spot in the train's second car and took seats by the back window. The car was heated, but I sat close to Beau anyway, so I could pretend we needed to huddle together for warmth.

I watched all the snow-covered pine trees zoom past outside as Santa's train traveled the loop, and I even found the dim glow coming from the moon hidden behind a layer of clouds. The kids in the car had a blast once Santa showed up in his red suit and hat and started handing out treats from the bag he carried with him.

"Did you ride the train with your mom too?" I blurted out.

YES, Beau signed back. ALWAYS FUN.

COOL, I signed with a grin.

There was a moment of chaos when the lights in the car suddenly went out, but only because we'd reached the main event with all the Christmas lights. I moved up even closer to the window to get a better look at the elaborate scenes of Santa's workshop, a gingerbread house, and even a few Star Wars characters, all made entirely of lights. The lights bathed the surrounding snow in a variety of colors—a spectacle in itself.

I ended up being so pulled in by all the lights, wanting to see more, I barely realized Beau was tapping me on the knee to get my attention.

"Sorry, what?" I said, turning to him.

The only source of illumination in the car was coming

from the lights we were passing outside, far too dim for me to get a good look at Beau's face to lipread what he was saying to me.

I signed, DON'T UNDERSTAND, as I shook my head, but Beau didn't seem to be able to see me all that well either.

I leaned away from the window and scooted closer to Beau, my annoyance with this suddenly challenging conversation growing. Couldn't they have kept at least *one* light on in this car?

"I don't understand what you're saying," I told Beau apologetically.

I saw Beau raise a hand and I thought he was about to try and sign to me, but he put a finger to his lips instead, the universal sign for *shhh*. I must've been talking too loudly then, something I did a lot, because how was I supposed to know how loud I was being?

"Beau, what . . ."

Beau was leaning closer like he was attempting to lipread himself, but there was something different about his expression this time. I kept waiting for him to try to speak to me again or maybe even sign something, but that never came. There was only a breath of space between us left, and for whatever reason I didn't make the connection that Beau was going to kiss me until his lips were actually pressed against mine.

For one second I sat there like a fish out of water with no idea what I was supposed to do. This was my first kiss, here in the middle of a darkened train car with Christmas lights outside. What was I supposed to do with my hands? With my face?

Then my brain started melting and thinking became impossible as Beau's fingers skimmed across my cheek and around the back of my neck to tilt my face up toward his. On instinct, I curled my fingers into his jacket to tug him closer.

I felt his breathless laughter against my lips, and I wanted to laugh too, wondering how we even ended up here in the first place. If somebody asked me months ago what my thoughts on Beau were, I would've said I wanted nothing to do with him or his stacks of books. And now I was thinking Beau should've kissed me a really long time ago.

When we finally broke apart, the lights in the train had come back on. I could see Beau clearly now, and I wanted to memorize his unbelievably slaphappy look.

I was the first to speak, or rather sign. The only thing I could manage to sign was a shaky, WHY?

Beau pointed to the ceiling of the train car with a finger, and I looked up to see a little sprig of mistletoe dangling above us. How cliché.

"Lame!" I said with a gasp.

MAYBE, Beau signed, flashing a cheeky grin. "But . . . needed . . . encouragement."

WHY? I signed again.

I LIKE YOU, Beau signed to me then with practiced ease.

Just three simple words, and he signed them like he'd never been more confident in himself.

SAME, I signed back, no hesitation on my part either.

I didn't know where or how or even why it all started, but a hearing boy liked me. Even weirder was that I liked him too.

M y foot barely crossed over the threshold into the house Tuesday afternoon, three days after my date with Beau, when my phone started vibrating in my jacket pocket, the LED light flashing along with it.

I was expecting it to be a text, not a FaceTime call, and I definitely wasn't expecting to see the words: INCOMING CALL—BEAU WATSON across the screen. Mostly we'd stuck to texting in the few days since our date, but we'd literally said good-bye to each other not fifteen minutes ago.

WHO? Mom signed to me on her way into the kitchen, pointing back at my phone.

Instead of responding, I pushed the green ACCEPT button, and Beau popped up into view a second later. I opened my mouth to say *hello*, but the word fell short when I took in his face and saw that he looked completely freaked out, his expression taut and his posture rigid.

WHAT'S WRONG? I signed immediately.

Rather than sign his answer, Beau held up a large cream-colored envelope for me to see, Yale University's impressive crest stamped on the top left. No wonder Beau looked like he was about to be sick. This was the response he'd been waiting on practically for *years*. What Beau considered to be the key to his future was right there in his hands.

"Holy crap," I blurted. "Why haven't you opened it yet?!"

WAIT FOR YOU, Beau signed with one hand, setting the envelope down.

"That's nice, really, but *open it!*"

Beau's shoulders rose and fell as he took deep breaths, reaching for the envelope again. His hands were shaking while he tore open the envelope and shook out the contents. A couple brochures fell onto the counter along with a thick, official looking paper.

"What's it say?" I asked when the silence started to stretch on.

Beau's eyes were moving back and forth rapidly as he read the letter, but I had no idea what he was thinking because of the blank look stretched across his face. My heart started to sink the longer he went without answering.

"... got ..." Beau said finally, looking up from the paper.

AGAIN? I signed, frowning.

My guess was Beau had no idea how to sign whatever was on the letter, so he just signed, YES.

"You got in?" I said aloud, loud enough to make Mom pop her head into the living room with an alarmed look.

YES, Beau signed again, his movement sluggish.

"Beau, that's awesome!" I said, signing, YAY! at the same time. "Aren't you happy? Be happy!"

Beau's lips twitched with a small smile, but he still didn't sign anything.

"You ... I mean, you are happy, right?"

Somehow, I didn't believe him when he signed, YES, again.

"Hey," I said, and when he looked up at me from the letter, I signed, PROUD, and pointed back at him.

That got a full-on smile from him, and I felt myself start to relax a little. Maybe Beau just processed things differently. He must have been excited about getting into Yale, he just didn't know how to express it yet. This *was* major news for him.

THANK YOU, Beau signed, his smile growing. I . . .

Beau suddenly stopped mid-sign and straightened up as a man came walking into view on the screen. I immediately recognized Dr. Watson. He didn't seem to notice me on the phone, reaching for the mess of Yale stuff on the counter instead.

YOU OK? I signed to Beau, pointing a finger at Dr. Watson.

Beau nodded quickly, signing, SEE YOU LATER, and the FaceTime call went dead.

I wandered into the kitchen still in a slight daze, casting my phone aside on the counter to go help Mom with dinner.

OK? Mom signed when I joined her at the sink as she washed some vegetables.

GOOD, I signed back. "That was Beau. He just got his acceptance letter from Yale."

WOW, Mom signed one handed. COOL.

Her focus was on the vegetables, her shoulders tense, her movements short and jerky. It didn't take more than a mere second to tell that Mom was seriously *stressed*. And she didn't get like this often, only when things were really overwhelming. Immediately I wanted to berate myself for not doing more to help out.

Mom always said my main focus should be on school, but I couldn't just ignore everything else going on at home. Connor was still on the mend and he needed more attention and care than usual, and Mom and I had been working extra to make sure that happened—or at least I hope I'd been working extra.

I was still contemplating this all when Mom asked me to get the bell peppers she forgot to pull out from the fridge. What was even more glaringly obvious than Mom's stress was that there wasn't as much food in the fridge as there usually was. The more I thought about it, the more I couldn't remember the last time Mom had been grocery shopping.

I snatched some bell peppers from the crisper, went to the sink to rinse them, then grabbed a cutting board to do some chopping. I had to shove a stack of mail off the counter to make room for the cutting board and paused when I saw the bill laying open on top, from Spring Meadows Home Health Care. The amount listed beside the due date next week made my jaw drop.

That's almost the same as a hospital *bill*, I thought, my mind buzzing as I started carefully slicing into the pepper. The kind of hospital bill that took *months* to pay off.

We got plenty of those thanks to the extended hospital stays Connor seemed to have every few months or so. And Mom worked for a good company and had decent health insurance, but even as a seventeen-year-old I knew a bill like *that* was just outrageous.

I needed to start applying for jobs. Now was as good a time as any to start pulling my weight around here.

When I walked into AP Statistics the next morning, I saw Beau sitting in his regular spot with his sunshine smile in place. I gave him the once over as I crossed the room to my seat, trying to decide for myself if his smile was genuine or not.

He perked up more when I took my seat and he signed, GOOD MORNING.

HELLO, I signed back. YOU OK? YESTERDAY—

Beau started signing before I could even finish my sentence, saying, NO, FINE.

SURE? I signed skeptically.

PROMISE.

I gave in with a shrug and pulled out my homework, ready to get on with class. Finals were next week, and we were blissfully reviewing past lessons instead of covering new content. I was having enough difficulty focusing as it was with Beau sitting right behind me.

Later, Nina came rushing up to us out in the hallway when we were shuffling off to AP US History and grabbed Beau by the arm, talking about a mile a minute. I stood there watching her back and forth with Beau, catching the word "Yale" more than once.

Beau finally turned to me and said, "We're having . . . party . . . my house tonight."

OK, I signed, giving a small smile.

YOU COME? Beau signed with hopeful eyes.

PROMISE, I assured him.

Nina had that knowing look in her eyes as we continued on our way to class, and I had this sinking feeling it would only be a matter of time before she started pestering me and Beau about the nature of our relationship.

Maybe that wouldn't be such a bad thing, seeing as I had no idea where Beau and I currently stood either, and I would actually very much appreciate knowing what he thought about the nature of our relationship now.

When I parked the Caravan at the curb outside Beau's house, I sat there for a couple moments, trying to get a grip on myself. There were a lot of cars lining the curb and filling the driveway, which made me think this was not some casual get-together.

But I'd told Beau I would come tonight, and I meant it. Even if whatever we were didn't have a name, he'd still been over the moon with my college acceptance letter, and the least I could do was show the same amount of enthusiasm for him. And regardless of how Beau felt, this was Yale we were talking about, an Ivy League institution. This kind of thing deserved to be celebrated.

I shoved my hands into my pockets and kept my head down against the cold on my way up to the house. When

I reached the front door, I didn't even get the chance to knock before it swung open and Beau was standing there in the doorway, something like relief flashing across his face when he ushered me inside.

WHAT'S WRONG? I signed automatically, but he waved away my question and signed, NOTHING.

I had to take my shoes off and hang up my jacket in the hall closet before following Beau into the living room where the party was taking place. The house hadn't changed much since my visit at midterms, but my guess was that Dana had put some elbow grease into making everything have an extra clean shine to it.

Taking in the amount of people in the living room had me fighting the urge to duck behind Beau to shield myself from view. This scene of Beau's guests conversing by the fireplace, those who weren't in high school chatting over glasses of wine, the delectable appetizers spread out on the coffee table, probably would've made the perfect stock photo for fancy living.

I felt very underdressed in my jeans and T-shirt when I saw the skirt and blouse get-up two girls I knew from the student council were wearing. The only redeeming thing about this—apart from getting to stand so close to Beau— was that Nina was here. Yeah, she was currently talking to Jackson of all people, but at least she was here.

DON'T WORRY, Beau signed to me when he saw me gnawing on my lip. NICE PEOPLE.

Nice of him to try to reassure me, but I had my doubts about that, catching sight of the look Dr. Watson sent our way when he saw Beau sign to me.

A man came wandering over to us while I was debating pulling Nina away from Jackson to chat with her myself. He looked pretty similar to Dr. Watson actually, save for the graying hair, so my bet was that this was one of Beau's relatives.

MY UNCLE, Beau signed as I shook the man's hand. E-D-D-I-E.

"Nice to meet you," I said, hoping he wouldn't notice how clammy my palm was.

Beau's Uncle Eddie pointed to his ear and said, ". . . deaf?"

I nodded, forcing myself to keep meeting his gaze and not go scampering off from the intensity of Dr. Watson's stare. What was his deal?

"Cool," Eddie said with a grin, and he left it at that.

I appreciated that.

Beau introduced two more family members next. There was his aunt Paula, Eddie's wife, who seemed nice as she smiled and shook my hand. Then there was their daughter, Lacey, who did not bother with a *hello* and just gave a limp wave.

Everyone else I knew were friends or student council members from Engelmann, so any further introductions were unnecessary. But tonight was about Beau, so it was no surprise most eyes were on him. This wasn't so different than standing next to him at school.

FOOD? Beau signed, nodding toward the appetizers on the coffee table.

SURE, THANK YOU, I signed.

I decided to stuff my face while the socializing continued. I didn't really notice what I was eating, but I was relishing the distraction. Guests were itching to talk to Beau and congratulate him on his acceptance from Yale. That wasn't the type of conversation I wanted to be lipreading.

Beau barely registered my signing, DRINK, to him, pointing toward the kitchen, while a colleague of Dr. Watson blabbed away at him. I slipped away before he could respond.

It was a pleasant surprise to come across Dana in the kitchen preparing more appetizers for the guests, and I said, "Hello," aloud in greeting.

Dana did a double take when she saw me and dropped the bagel chips she'd been sorting, wiping her hands off on her apron before she came over to give me a hug. A little startling, but I didn't mind so much.

"Good . . . see you," Dana said when she let me go, patting my cheek, and then she signed, HOW ARE YOU?

"Has Beau been teaching you sign language?" I asked with a small smile.

YES, Dana signed back, and she laughed. "Beau sure . . . talk . . . you . . . lot."

It wasn't a stretch to fill in the blanks of what Dana was saying. It also wasn't easy to keep myself from getting hot in the face. How often *did* Beau talk about me when I wasn't around? (Really, anytime I wasn't looking at him he could be talking about me, because I never heard anything he said.)

Dana understood me when I signed, WATER, PLEASE, and went to the fridge to grab me a bottle of water. I twisted the cap off and took a few swigs, watching the party going on in the living room. Nina had teamed up with Beau and a few other student council members, and when Nina noticed me a second later she sent me a smile and motioned for me to come join them.

HELP HER, I signed, pointing to Dana.

Maybe that was a tiny fib, but Dana did look like she could use some help getting another tray of food together.

I kept one eye on the party while I helped Dana arrange some vegetables, hummus, and other dips. It was impossible to miss the way Dr. Watson was hovering a few feet from Beau, puffed up like a rooster. Anytime someone looked their way, Dr. Watson would clap Beau on the shoulder in an 'atta boy gesture.

Beau definitely was aware of his dad's behavior, with the way his lips would tighten and his eyes would narrow when he looked over at Dr. Watson. It made me wonder why no one else seemed to have caught on to how uncomfortable Beau was starting to appear, but then I realized that nobody paid attention to Beau the way I did.

"Do you think he's happy?" I blurted out, looking to Dana.

Dana paused as she doled out some hummus into a fancy serving bowl and looked back at me in confusion. "Who?"

"Beau," I said, nodding toward the living room. "I mean, do you think he's actually happy about getting into Yale?"

This wasn't the first time that thought crossed my mind, but it was the first time I'd ever said it aloud. This was supposed to be a party celebrating Beau's grand achievement and yet now he was looking like he'd rather be anywhere else.

Dana's perpetual smile seemed to droop as she looked over at Beau. I think she'd already come to the same conclusion I had.

". . . don't know," she finally said when she glanced my way again. ". . . hope so."

Me too, I thought.

When we finished arranging the extra trays of appetizers and brought them out into the living room, Dr. Watson took this as his cue to call everyone to attention, a fresh glass of wine in hand—clearly about to give some sort of toast.

I slid into a spot next to Nina, which also gave me the perfect opportunity to lipread whatever Dr. Watson was going to say. I threw all my focus into it, and it was only because Dr. Watson seemed to be a grand public speaker that I was able to make out the gist of what he was saying. I wasn't able to split my attention between lipreading and watching Beau for his reaction, but I certainly didn't miss the look on Beau's face when Dr. Watson said that Beau was going to do his father proud by following his footsteps and going into medicine.

I did everything I could not to do a double take at this.

Beau going into medicine? No way.

I mean, Beau was so personable he'd probably make a great pediatric surgeon like his dad, but that didn't seem like the right path for him. I'd always imagined Beau going to college to do anything and everything he could with books.

But Beau was forcing a smile while people applauded him, and thirty seconds later he excused himself, signing, RESTROOM, when I caught his eye.

Nina pulled me into conversation then, so I didn't have the opportunity to do much else besides wonder what on Earth was going on with Beau.

CHAPTER

S lipping away from the party when Beau didn't reappear after ten minutes was simple after I signed to
Nina that I was going to the restroom. It was a little
strange no one else seemed to be wondering where Beau
was, but I was more than happy to go look for him.

There wasn't much else on the first floor of the house
besides what looked like Dr. Watson's study, a guest bedroom, and a bathroom, and Beau was in none of those
places. I felt marginally creepy tiptoeing my way upstairs,
but the desire to locate Beau and make sure he was okay
won out.

Upstairs there were more bedrooms and bathrooms,
decorated in the same style as the rest of the house, and
one of these rooms had to belong to Beau. Rather than go
around calling out his name, I took a chance on the closest
bedroom to the stairs and peeked inside.

This was definitely Beau's room, and almost exactly
how I imagined. Two pristine bookcases that looked as if
they'd come right out of a university library took up most
of the space in the room. Books were strewn all over the
bed, this time mostly school texts instead of novels. Next

to the bed was a neatly organized desk with an open laptop and various homework assignments.

Beau was sitting at the desk, leaning over with his chin in hand, and I could see his acceptance packet from Yale spread out in front of him. I could only see part of his face from where I stood in the doorway, but I was pretty sure he was frowning.

I rapped my knuckles on the doorjamb, and Beau quickly spun around in his desk chair, looking surprised when he saw me standing there.

SORRY, he signed quickly.

FINE, I signed back, then said, "Is it okay if I come in?"

Beau nodded, motioning for me to enter, and I took a seat across from him on the bed.

"So," I said after a beat of tense silence. "When are you going to tell your dad you don't want to go to Yale?"

The flush I was expecting to come rushing into Beau's cheeks didn't show up. He raised an eyebrow, a rather wry smile pulling at his lips.

". . . that obvious?" he said.

EASY READ, I signed, pointing a finger at him.

Beau's smile widened for one second before it disappeared completely. He leaned back in his chair, running his fingers through his hair. It was strange to see him looking so crestfallen. He never let anyone see him that way at school. But he didn't have to put on a show for anybody here.

FINE WITH Y-A-L-E, Beau signed suddenly, his shoulders rising and falling with a heavy sigh. GOOD SCHOOL. Then he said aloud, "But . . . don't want . . . medicine."

"Yeah, I figured," I said. "So, what do you want to do?"

Beau gestured to something behind me, and I glanced over my shoulder at his bookcases. When I looked to Beau again, he said, ". . . study . . ." and followed up by finger spelling, L-I-T-E-R-A-T-U-R-E.

That response was so classically Beau it made me smile.

YOU MAKE GOOD TEACHER, I signed to him.

MAYBE, Beau signed. DON'T KNOW. He made a sweeping gesture around the room and said, "But . . . don't want . . . trade my books for . . ."

"Med school?" I supplied, and Beau signed back, YES.

I could understand that, even if med school was my end goal.

YOU TELL YOUR FATHER? I signed to Beau curiously.

He winced at this and quickly shook his head. He looked repulsed by that idea.

I didn't say or sign anything, waiting for Beau to respond in his own time. There was obviously something else behind his not wanting to be upfront with his father.

". . . can't," Beau finally said, and before I could even ask why, he was suddenly on his feet, his walk uneven as he went over to his bookcase.

When he sat down on the bed beside me, he was holding out a small picture frame for me to take. Carefully holding the frame, I bit down on my lip to keep from smiling as I looked over the photo. It was of Beau, maybe seven or eight years old, and a woman who was obviously his mother. She was very pretty with a bright smile, her long brown hair falling around her face in pretty waves. Beau had clearly gotten his brilliant green eyes from her.

YOUR MOTHER? I signed, passing the picture back to Beau.

YES, Beau signed back. His eyes were a little brighter than normal as he set the picture face down on his pillow. ". . . my fault she died."

My mind went blank at Beau's words. I couldn't even come up with anything to sign or say. Even if I was having difficulty stringing words together, Beau wasn't. He was in the middle of something here, and I wasn't about to stop him.

Beau held up a finger, signaling me to wait a second, and bent over, carefully rolling up his right pant leg. I leaned over to see that scar of his up close, and then I sort of wished I hadn't.

He started signing once his pant leg was carefully rolled up to his knee. His first sign was, CAR, followed by finger spelling, C-R-A-S-H.

BROKE, he added, tapping the side of his leg. TIME THREE. BAD. A LOT . . . S-U-R-G-E-R-I-E-S. "Spent . . . time . . . hospital," he finished aloud.

My mind zipped back to that day when Connor was in the hospital and I'd found Beau in the waiting room chatting with a nurse. He must've spent a fair amount of time in the hospital if he was still friendly with the nurses.

When Beau signed, MY MOTHER, next and a tremor ran through his hand, my breath caught. I really hoped I was wrong about what his next sign was going to be. I knew it was coming, but a wave of sadness still threatened to suffocate me when Beau signed, DIE.

Beau and his mother had been in a car crash. Apart from his leg, Beau apparently made it out relatively unscathed. His mother hadn't.

It was good my preferred method of communication was sign language, because I couldn't trust myself to speak. But just signing, SORRY, didn't seem like enough.

It clearly was not fine when Beau signed back, FINE.

REALLY, I signed next.

What else could I say?

"Is that why you, um . . . I mean, in the cold, you have trouble walking? Because of your leg. You sit with your leg all stretched out in front of you too."

Mom broke her wrist one time in a tennis match during a company barbeque back in New Jersey, and she always complained about the tight pain in her wrist the cold caused. If Beau had surgeries on top of the breaks, that probably didn't help at all.

Beau nodded, signing, YES, then said, ". . . have rod . . . my shin. Nina . . . tells me . . . take medicine for . . . but . . . never remember."

There's the reason Nina was so annoyed that day we studied at the café, I thought distractedly.

"Okay," I said. "But I don't see how this makes it your fault your mom died."

Beau waved away my words like they were nothing and went on signing, HAD S-O-C-C-E-R PRACTICE. LATE. WANT MOTHER DRIVE ME . . .

I held up a hand to stop Beau before he could finish signing. I didn't need him to finish. I knew exactly where this was going.

"No. No way. No way is that your fault, Beau."

"But—"

"If you think your father blames you for the car accident and this is the way you have to make it up to him, stop right there."

Beau's face slipped, and he paused with his lips parted, taken aback. "But . . . don't . . ."

"Remember the first day of school when you were so surprised I can talk?" I said, choosing to use my voice.

Beau didn't seem so happy recalling that particular memory as he gave a short nod.

"Well, I can speak fine because I wasn't born deaf. I became deaf when I was thirteen because I got sick."

This wasn't a sad story to tell anymore. These were just the facts, and even now I didn't think I'd go back and make any changes. Everything had a way of working out in the end.

WHAT HAPPENED? Beau signed curiously.

"Meningitis," I told him. "Came down with it when I was visiting my grandma in Louisiana. Could've happened to anyone, and I'm actually really lucky I came out of it just having lost my hearing. It could've been a lot worse. But you know what? My mom blamed herself. She thought it was all her fault because she was the one who let me go on that trip and I ended up getting sick."

It was interesting seeing the emotions flashing across Beau's face as he took in my story. I think he knew the direction this was headed, and it was fairly obvious he didn't want to hear the rest of what I had to say.

"But it wasn't really my mom's fault, was it?" I said.

Beau shook his head, signing, NO.

RIGHT, I signed back at him. "That car accident wasn't your fault, Beau. And you've got nothing to make up to your dad. So why are you going to make yourself miserable becoming a doctor?"

As good as I was at reading faces, I couldn't get a read on Beau after that. He was deep in thought, maybe about Yale or his parents or maybe what I'd just said. Whatever it was, though, he didn't say or sign anything.

OK? I signed shakily when this silence stretched on between us.

Beau didn't respond. He kissed me instead.

The first feather-light brush of his lips against mine had every little thought or worry I had rapidly slipping out the back of my head. I wasn't sure where this was coming from, especially right now, but Beau was kissing me, and it was hard to think about anything else.

I had my fingers laced in his hair and he had his arms around my waist and then suddenly he was jerking away from me, leaping to his feet and moving away.

I would've fallen flat on my face if I hadn't thrown out an arm to grab at the bed to keep myself upright. I was about to ask Beau why he'd jumped away from me like he'd been electrocuted—when I was pretty sure neither of us wanted that kiss to end anytime soon—but the reason became obvious when I saw Nina standing in the doorway.

Her arms were crossed, and she had this bemused expression on her face as she looked back and forth between the two of us.

NOT MY FAULT, I signed to Beau, hopefully too quickly for Nina to understand. YOU START KISS, NOT ME.

Beau scrubbed his face with his hands, his shoulders slumping with one of his regular sighs. He must have been saying something to Nina because her amused smile was turning into a full-blown smirk. She looked like she was about to start laughing. She did the palms up gesture and said something like, ". . . your . . . business."

". . . want . . . ?" Beau started to say, then pointed downstairs.

I didn't even think twice about signing, NO. NEED STUDY, I added when Beau's face fell in disappointment. BUT I SEE YOU TOMORROW.

RIGHT, Beau signed with a nod. TOMORROW.

I kept my head down on my way out of the room, a little afraid to meet Nina's gaze, because I knew an interrogation was waiting for me as soon as Nina got the chance.

Everyone was still assembled in the living room over drinks and food, so there weren't many eyes on us as we came down the stairs. I only stopped to wave good-bye to Dana, who smiled back from where she stood in conversation with someone who looked like a colleague of Dr. Watson's.

Beau put on shoes and a jacket and followed me outside to walk me to my car, though I was pretty certain it wasn't for another kiss.

"Thanks . . . coming," Beau said, pulling open the driver's side door for me.

"Sure," I said. "Congratulations on Yale. If it's really what you want."

Beau stood there in the driveway and waved me off. The conflicted expression on his face was impossible to miss when I peeked at him in the rearview mirror.

CHAPTER  28

Winter break probably should've been called spring break in the end. Once finals were over and school was out for two weeks, unseasonably warm weather arrived out of nowhere, melting the snow and bringing almost seventy degrees every day. Whenever I would marvel about this, Nina would sign, HAHAHA, and tell me to get used to it, because this apparently wasn't anything out of the ordinary for Colorado.

I got two days into the new semester before I finally broke down and told Mom, "I want to get a job."

She did a double take, looking up from her dinner plate like I'd grown another head.

REALLY? she signed.

YES, I signed back. I THINK GOOD FOR ME.

YES, Mom agreed quickly. BUT . . . SCHOOL IMPORTANT.

I KNOW, I signed. BUT JOB IMPORTANT, SAME.

It wasn't like I wanted to pick up full-time work at a credit union or a department store, but something simpler, like a cashier or hostess at a restaurant. Nina worked part-time at a nearby Target, and she had at least double the workload at school.

The more time I spent with my hearing friends, the more I realized I needed to be out in the hearing world—even if it made me uncomfortable—so I could get used to communicating and handling certain situations. I needed to be ready for anything college and beyond might throw my way. I knew being Deaf wasn't going to hold me back, and I was ready to prove that, even if it wasn't in a hospital just yet.

OK, Mom signed hesitantly. YOU WANT JOB, I SUPPORT YOU.

The expression on her face was a little less than pleased, but she knew as well as I did that sooner or later I was going to have to get a job. We both knew that just because I was Deaf did not mean I couldn't work. I didn't just want to sign up for social security payments after graduation and call it good. I wanted more than that.

THANK YOU, I signed.

Connor cut in right after Mom signed, WHERE? and tapped the table, wanting to know what we were signing about.

"Later, squirt," I said. "Finish your dinner."

I pulled out my laptop after I helped Mom clean up the dinner dishes, got Google up, and dove right into my job search. Chances were a lot of businesses might be letting their holiday workers go now that we were a couple weeks into the new year, so I didn't know how many job openings I might find. The sooner I got applications out there, the better off I'd be.

Browsing through the Google results of my "Parker, CO jobs" search, I found a site with job listings and started doing some clicking around. Concessions clerk at the movie theater in town was an idea and so was part-time stocker at the King Soopers grocery store.

I was onto the third page of job listings when another promising one caught my eye. The opening was for a part-time barista position at the Steaming Bean Café, that cute little place where Beau, Nina, and I had gone to study before finals. The café had been cozy and welcoming. I didn't know much about making coffee, but it seemed like the perfect place for a first job.

Mom came wandering into the living room from the kitchen and set a cup of hot tea on the end table beside the couch where I sat working.

APPLY FOR JOB? she signed, tapping the lid of my laptop.

I nodded, signing, FOR COFFEE STORE.

The spark of excitement that lit up Mom's eyes seemed genuine as she signed, YAY!

YOU WONDERFUL. She took a seat next to me on the couch. LUCK.

THANK YOU, I signed back. Probably I would need all the luck I could get.

REMEMBER SCHOOL IMPORTANT, Mom added as she glanced over the job listings pulled up on my laptop.

I KNOW, I agreed. PROMISE.

Mom's brows pinched together. WHY YOU WANT JOB?

THINK . . . MAYBE TIME FOR NEW THINGS, I told her.

GOOD, Mom signed, giving me a nudge with her shoulder. PROUD, she added, squeezing my hand.

THANK YOU, I told her.

ALWAYS, she signed back.

⌁

The email came three days later. I'd been obsessively checking my email ever since I submitted those job applications and was hit with disappointment every time I saw there were no new messages in my inbox.

Beau had offered to drive me home from school, but I'd declined thanks to an after school doctor's appointment with my new ENT, so we were waiting outside in the cold by the pickup loop. I think I let out a shriek when I saw I'd gotten a response from the Steaming Bean.

WHAT'S WRONG? Beau signed in alarm while I stood there, gaping at my phone.

HEY. Beau waved a hand near my face when I didn't answer.

I didn't think I *could* answer. I was suddenly terrified to open the email and see some kind of politely worded rejection there, something Mom told me I should prepare for just in case.

WHAT'S WRONG? Beau signed again.

NOTHING, I signed automatically. I . . . APPLY FOR JOB. THEY EMAIL ME.

He looked taken aback by the unexpected news, but he was smiling a second later and signing, READ!

I took in several deep breaths as I forced myself to click on the email. Once the words settled the right way on the screen, I carefully read and reread the email. I started mouthing the words as I read, trying to process the information.

"Well?" Beau said when I finally tore my gaze from my phone.

"They want to interview me."

Even if I were able to hear my own voice, I know my words would've sounded funny coming out of my mouth. That was a sentence I'd never said or signed before. My first round of filling out job applications, and already I got a response asking for an interview.

WONDERFUL, Beau signed to me, followed by a, YAY!

When I didn't sign anything back, Beau's excited face became concerned, and he reached over to curl his hand around my own, signing, YOU OK?

SURPRISE, I signed honestly. DON'T KNOW IF I . . .

When I just lamely gestured to my left ear, Beau caught on to my line of thinking and signed, DOESN'T MATTER.

Actually, in some cases being Deaf kind of *did* matter.

EMAIL THEM, Beau signed, gesturing to my phone. SAY YES.

I WILL, I signed, and because it was going to be impossible to hide, I added, NERVOUS.

WHY? Beau signed, looking confused.

"Sometimes it can be hard getting an interpreter on short notice," I said. "And they can be kind of expensive too."

NO WORRY, Beau assured me without missing a beat.

THANK YOU, I signed back as I chewed on my lip.

"Interviews . . . not . . . big deal," Beau said, using his voice. "You'll . . . fine. They'll find . . . interpreter too."

I hope, I thought, as I started tapping out my reply to the

Steaming Bean. As long as they were willing to meet with me in the afternoon once I was finished with school, there shouldn't be a problem.

On the other hand, I knew there was no possibility of my getting through this interview without an interpreter. And I doubted Kathleen would be willing to spend her evenings and weekends with me too. Interpreting a job interview wasn't exactly a part of her job description.

My fingers faltered as I started to worry that I hadn't thought this through.

At a few weeks shy of eighteen, I'd sat through so many hearing tests over the past nearly five years as doctors tried to determine the severity of my hearing loss, I could almost administer one to myself.

You spend fifteen minutes in a soundproof booth with a clicker you'd press anytime you heard any of the range of sounds the audiologist looped into the ear pieces plugged up to both your ears. If there wasn't a clicker, you got to raise your hand instead.

We were in a new state with a new doctor at a new hospital, and I was desperately hoping we weren't about to start this whole process over again. I tried not to pout like a little kid the entire way to Children's Hospital, but I'd always dreaded these ear, nose, and throat appointments. Nobody liked being poked and prodded in the ears or having your hearing tested when it was pretty obvious you had none.

NERVOUS? Mom signed to me when I happened to glance her way.

FOR JOB INTERVIEW, YES, I signed. FOR DOCTOR APPOINTMENT, NO.

FINE FOR BOTH, Mom signed, then tossed an arm around my shoulders to give me a squeeze.

A handful of minutes later, a chipper nurse came up front to retrieve us and take us to the back where the exam rooms were. Not a surprise, a small flat-screen TV on a cart with wheels sat waiting for me in the purple room the nurse led us to. This nurse—Mom signed to me that her name was Wendy—seemed to know what she was doing and got the VRI booted up in a matter of moments.

The interpreter on screen was a kind, elderly gentleman who had no problem jumping right into the appointment. Once Wendy took down my height and weight, we had about a ten-minute wait before the doctor actually arrived, which was a bit awkward with the interpreter just sitting there on screen waiting along with us.

When the door opened, a short woman with graying blonde hair falling out of its bun came walking in. She looked tired, but she still greeted us with a smile. I thought my last doctor, Dr. Hartwood, was a bit of an old grump, so it was nice to see a happy face in the office.

The interpreter finger spelled that the woman's name was Dr. Porter, and she got right down to business after the introductions were over. She took a peek down my throat, up my nose, and spent the most time looking in my ears.

More than one doctor told Mom and me that my ears were in good shape. Very minimal damage to my eardrums thanks to two rounds of ear tubes as a kid—not an uncommon thing—but otherwise perfectly fine. I just couldn't hear. The interpreter on screen signed the same thing— *your ears look fine*—and it just made me think even more

239

that this whole appointment was totally unnecessary. But Mom had always been a big fan of the saying *better safe than sorry*, which I guessed was true.

Dr. Porter finished up by cleaning out my ears with this weird, pick-like tool, and took a seat on one of the nearby chairs after she washed her hands at the sink. As nice as Dr. Porter seemed, this was just about identical to every other ENT appointment I'd had over the years. I wanted to go home and dive into some homework or find some articles on how to ace job interviews, not sit around in a doctor's office bored out of my mind.

I wasn't sure how long Mom had been tapping my knee when I finally snapped back to attention. She was giving me a disapproving glare and nodded at the interpreter on screen, signing, AGAIN PLEASE.

The interpreter pointed at Dr. Porter and signed, SHE ASK IF YOU CURIOUS ABOUT CI.

This again?

I shrugged in response, signing, NEVER WANT CI. STILL NOT WANT CI.

Dr. Porter listened to the interpreter voice what I signed, nodding along in understanding. I watched her say, "Well . . . have many benefits. There . . ."

I definitely stopped paying attention while Dr. Porter went on to list all the pros of getting a cochlear implant, how it could improve my future, how I was a good potential candidate for one. Dr. Porter probably gave the same talk to all the parents of Deaf kids; she was just doing her job.

I genuinely did not see anything wrong with my future or how a cochlear implant might make it better. And why would I voluntarily agree to a surgery I'd be just fine without?

More to the point—and what people didn't seem to understand—I *liked* being Deaf. Some of the best things in my life happened without my being able to hear, like excelling in my studies at Pratt, meeting Melissa, meeting Nina and Beau . . .

The appointment wrapped up sooner than expected and with no hearing test either. I made sure to thank the interpreter for his time before ending the call, grateful we hadn't had a repeat of our visit to the ER with Connor.

I shook Dr. Porter's hand on the way out, and she waved us off with another tired but cheerful smile. Mom fell into step beside me as we made our way back through the waiting room toward the elevators. I noticed she had a couple sheets of paper in one hand.

WHAT'S UP? I signed, nudging her and pointing to the papers.

FROM DOCTOR, Mom signed, holding the papers just so to prevent me from seeing any of the writing on them.

ABOUT? I signed, pushing the issue.

We were in the elevators on our way down into the parking garage when Mom finally handed the papers over to me. As expected, the papers contained facts about cochlear implants, which insurances typically covered the surgery—if at all—and what the follow-up therapy would look like.

Mom didn't stop me when I crumpled up the papers and tossed them in a trashcan as soon as we reached the parking garage. We were buckled in the car, sitting there with the engine idling, when Mom signed, WHAT'S WRONG?

I wasn't angry because cochlear implants had been invented or that a lot of people chose to undergo the surgery to get them. CIs were a cool piece of technology. I was angry because it was only when I started attending a hearing school that cochlear implants entered the conversation. A year ago, CIs weren't on Mom's radar, and suddenly she was all interested in me getting the procedure, or at least that's what it felt like.

I answered Mom's question by signing, NOTHING.

SURE? she signed back, looking unconvinced.

MY FRIENDS LIKE ME DEAF, I signed slowly, thinking about my response as carefully as possible. LIKE MYSELF DEAF, I added, placing a hand against my chest. WHY I NEED CI NOW?

YOU NOT NEED CI, Mom signed to me quickly. BUT CHOICE HERE IF YOU WANT.

DON'T WANT, I signed back, and I *meant* it. Why would I suddenly change my mind? ALL DONE NOW?

SURE, Mom signed, putting the car into gear.

We drove home in silence.

CHAPTER 30

was checking my email religiously after that first message from the Steaming Bean. My reply had included an
enthusiastic *Yes, I'd love an interview!* and some resources
for local interpreting agencies after my short explanation of
my hearing loss and using sign language. I had high hopes
for another quick response, but each time I refreshed my
email with no new message waiting in my inbox, my frus-
tration began increasing at an alarming rate.

AGAIN? Kathleen signed to me when I snuck a peek
at my phone under the worktable in Ms. Phillips' art class.
WHAT'S UP?

SORRY, I signed quickly, dropping my phone into my
backpack. WAIT FOR EMAIL.

ABOUT INTERVIEW? Kathleen signed, looking almost
as thrilled as she had when I'd shown her my acceptance
letter from Cartwright.

It wasn't so easy to return her smile this time around.

Kathleen knew about my interview with the Steaming
Bean because she was the one to refer me to a handful
of interpreting agencies in Denver. It was my potential
employer's responsibility to supply the interpreter, not

243

mine, which is why I hadn't asked Kathleen to do it, and she hadn't offered. This was an entirely new process for me, but I figured it was better that I do it the right way the first time around.

But the more time that passed without a second email from the Steaming Bean, the more paranoia started making itself at home in the back of my mind.

Scheduling an interpreter for some event or doctor's appointment usually wasn't that big of a deal because the law required it. Same with any employer, but this was different. I hadn't been hired yet. They could just as easily pass me over because I was Deaf and use the excuse that they'd already filled the position because they didn't want to pay for an interpreter, and that would be the end of it. Nobody would ever be able to prove anything like *discrimination*.

So probably this obsessive worrying was a bit premature, but it was a little difficult to just brush it all under a rug and forget about it. I wasn't oblivious to my mother's increasing financial struggles. The sooner I got a job, the better off we'd be.

PATIENT, Kathleen signed when she caught me sneaking another peek at my phone in my backpack instead of focusing on my charcoal sketches.

I KNOW, I signed back, pressing down hard on the paper with my charcoal pencil. NERVOUS.

YOU FINE, Kathleen told me, and I wished I could be as confident as she looked. DON'T WORRY.

HAHAHA, was my response.

As hard as I may have tried to follow Kathleen's advice and just be *patient*, I trudged my way through another twenty-four hours of a grueling wait before the email came. I had my phone out beneath the lab table in chemistry class yet again and only had the chance to see that I had a new email in my inbox before Kathleen sent a disapproving look my way and nodded pointedly up at the whiteboard where Mr. Burke was working on a set of formulas.

It took an insane amount of self-control to keep my phone tucked away in my backpack for the rest of class. It was a good thing this was a class I didn't share with Nina or Beau. I wouldn't have been able to keep the email to myself.

OK, NOW LOOK, Kathleen signed, an excited smile in place again when we were standing by my locker after the final bell.

The thudding of my heart against my chest felt painful as I pulled my phone out of my backpack. A tremor shot through my hand while I tapped open my email and clicked on the response from the Steaming Bean.

Each word I read in the email came like a sharp jab that made my breath get stuck in my throat.

Dear Ms. Harris,

Unfortunately, the position was recently filled, but we thank you for your interest and encourage you to apply again at a later date.

Sincerely,
The Staff at Steaming
Bean

I gave a start when Kathleen squeezed my shoulder, snapping me away from the disastrous email now burning up a hole in my inbox.

Kathleen didn't sign anything, just looked at me expectantly with raised eyebrows.

NOTHING, I signed to her once it seemed as if the non-existent ringing in my ears was gone. ALL DONE.

Kathleen's hopeful expression slipped, and she signed, NO INTERVIEW?

I shook my head, biting down on my lip and shoving my phone into my back pocket.

"They found someone else. But it's okay," I said aloud. "There'll be more interviews."

The words were a downright lie flying past my lips— this didn't feel *okay*. But they made Kathleen's smile reappear, so that was something at least.

TRUE, she signed back, along with a few more signs of encouragement for me before we parted ways.

I was proud of myself for not letting any hurt, angry tears escape as I made my way to the student parking lot where I knew Beau would be waiting for me. He'd been driving me home for the past few weeks, which certainly made things easier on Mom.

Beau was already in his car when I found him, some book propped up against the steering wheel which he tossed into the backseat as I opened the passenger side door and slipped in.

I thought I might find a little sliver of relief seeing Beau and his quirky smile, but that didn't happen when he signed, HELLO. EMAIL?

There was no point in hiding it, so I told him, "Yes."

That was all Beau needed before he rapidly started firing questions at me in sign.

I signed, WAIT, at him and took a minute to get a grip on myself, yanking my fingers through my hair and pulling it up into a messy ponytail.

Something on my face definitely must've given away that I wasn't okay. When I finally turned to Beau, he signed, WHAT'S WRONG?

"No interview," I settled on saying. "They've already filled the position."

I could almost see his brain whirring, filling in the missing pieces of what I wasn't telling him, what he might've been reading from the look on my face.

WHY? Beau finally signed. When I didn't answer, he signed, YOU THINK BECAUSE YOU DEAF? next.

My lack of response seemed to confirm something for Beau.

Beau wasn't facing me straight on so I couldn't be exactly sure of what he was saying—it was kind of like a little rant actually. But I caught the two important things—"Not hire" and "deaf."

"What? Are you going to bully them into hiring me?"

I definitely remembered making it clear to him back at the beginning of the school year that I could handle myself.

NO, Beau signed, snapping his index and middle fingers to his thumb. BUT IF THEY NOT HIRE YOU BECAUSE—

BECAUSE WHY? DEAF? I signed, pointing back at myself.

Beau didn't sign *yes* or *no*, but it was obvious by the

expression on his face that was exactly what he was thinking.

"Beau, this isn't . . . look," I said, struggling to string together a coherent thought. "You think this is something I wasn't expecting? Something I haven't ever experienced before?"

This had to be the first time I'd ever seen a flash of genuine anger cross Beau's face.

"Maya, not hiring . . . because . . . deaf . . . that's . . ."

"Discrimination? Welcome to my world."

I was not oblivious to the way some teachers, like Mr. Wells, rarely called on me when posing questions to the class, even though there was no reason to think I wouldn't give the same thought-provoking response any of my classmates might. You could definitely write off my fully participating in Socratic seminars, a real favorite classroom activity in Historical Literature class.

And all this was just in high school. In college and out in the real world, things were going to be vastly different, and I was by no means eager to face it. I wanted to believe for just a little bit longer that the world was a nice place and people who were "different" were still treated kindly.

"This doesn't . . ." Now Beau was struggling to come up with something to say and finished his thought by signing, BOTHER YOU?

"Of course this bothers me," I answered. I could feel my voice trembling as I spoke. "To tell you the truth, this kind of thing will probably always bother me."

"Then . . . should go . . ." Beau was saying. "Make them . . ."

STOP, PLEASE, I signed.

A feeling of defeat was quickly replacing my anger that had started brewing when I read that email from the Steaming Bean.

WHY? Beau demanded in sign.

He seemed to be absorbing all the anger I felt dissipating inside me.

"You have to pick and choose your battles, right?" I said. "This one just isn't worth it to me right now."

SURE? Beau signed.

Actually, I was sure I'd never been more unsure of anything in my life. But what could I possibly do now? It's not like I had the time or money to take this coffee shop to court, and even if I did, lawsuits like this were an uphill battle.

As irksome as it was, wouldn't it just be better to brush this incident off and keep looking for another job? Maybe one where I wouldn't have to interact with people, like at the local humane society. I could work in the kennels. Dogs were never judgmental, and all the loud barking would hardly bother me.

NO, I signed to Beau, at a loss for words.

We did not sign or speak to each other again until Beau was pulling up into my driveway.

He turned to me, and I felt my stomach start twisting into knots with dread at what he might be about to say to me.

"Have . . . ever thought . . . ?" he said, then tapped a finger to his head, a couple inches behind his ear.

It wasn't technically the correct sign, but I knew well enough what he meant.

"A cochlear implant isn't a cure-all, you know," I said,

maybe a little too harshly. "It's an expensive and irreversible surgery with a lot of follow-up therapy. And even if I wanted one, it wouldn't mean my life would automatically get better."

Beau's cheeks filled with color, maybe out of embarrassment or shame, I couldn't tell, and he gave a short nod. He signed, SORRY, followed by, CURIOUS.

"They work for a lot of people, but it's not for me," I said firmly. "Trust me."

Beau gave another quick nod, signing, OK.

"Maybe they were jerks anyway," I said, my hand on the door handle as I prepared to step out of the car. "I think my hearing aids are cool."

A smile took over Beau's face as he signed, YES.

"Connor thinks they make me look like a top-secret spy."

". . . correct," Beau said before he started laughing.

"And you know what? I got into my dream college. So *there.*"

I wasn't going to give up on my job search after one failed near-interview, but this wasn't a very encouraging start. And seeing how angry Beau got when he'd put two and two together and realized what I was pretty sure went down, I wasn't too eager to repeat the experience. The chances of something like this happening again weren't exactly impossible.

It didn't always look the same way, but this was pretty much an everyday occurrence for me, someone getting weirded out for some reason or another because of my lack of hearing. Most people never said *hello* or *good morning* to me in the hallways at school, and some still stared whenever

I started fiddling with my hearing aids or changed their batteries, even though my first day at Engelmann had been months ago.

Outside of school was even worse. Anywhere I went I almost always received *the look*, that pitying one I hated so much, even if I was doing something as simple as helping Mom grocery shop. And nobody needed that.

So, what was the future going to look like for me and Beau if he got upset and angry over something like this anytime it happened? Beau worked hard for the things he achieved, and I knew that, but he'd never have to work the way I did just to get the simple things some people were handed on a silver platter.

On my way up the driveway after saying good-bye to Beau, I started to wonder if it was finally time to start addressing the differences between our two worlds.

S omething in Mrs. Stephens' expression seemed a tad bit more shrewd than normal. Our biweekly appointments after school to stay current with everything college usually went off without a hitch. We got into a routine of getting right down to business, Kathleen interpreting as she stood behind Mrs. Stephens' desk while we discussed my current grades, filled out the necessary forms to register for orientation, and the like.

But maybe there was just something off about my face today that made Mrs. Stephens brush aside the packet I got in the mail about freshman orientation and ask, ". . . there something wrong?"

I looked to Kathleen while she finished interpreting what Mrs. Stephens was saying. Kathleen was signing, YOU LOOK UPSET.

I'd done my best to put the Steaming Bean incident from my mind. I got through another round of job applications and was currently waiting for any response before Mom told me I needed to hit the pavement and do some "face time" with potential employers.

As discouraging as the whole Steaming Bean thing had

been, and even if Mom had already told me when I'd hinted that our finances might be rough that we were doing all right, I still needed to get a job.

But no matter how many times I would deny it to Beau and Mom, the Steaming Bean incident had thrown me off. I spent more time thinking about it than I should have, wondering if they really had filled the position or if they just said that because they didn't want to pay for an interpreter. I was pretty sure if I put this out there to my friends back at Pratt, they'd probably be able to share similar experiences.

FINE, I signed, looking back and forth between Kathleen and Mrs. Stephens. BUSY A LOT.

Mrs. Stephens nodded as she listened to Kathleen speak and said, "Senior year . . . busy. . . . anything . . . bothering . . . ?"

"I'm fine," I said aloud this time.

There was this moment when I thought Mrs. Stephens wasn't about to let subject drop, but she relented after a couple of tense beats.

I looked back to Kathleen as she jumped into interpreting again while Mrs. Stephens started shuffling things around on her desk.

GOOD IDEA IF WE CONTACT C-A-R-T-W-R-I-G-H-T FOR APPOINTMENT, Kathleen was signing.

FOR? I signed in confusion. DORM? CLASS?

Mrs. Stephens shook her head and Kathleen signed, FOR INTERPRETER.

I grudgingly had to accept she had a point. Mrs. Stephens admitted she'd never worked with a Deaf student before and was unsure how long it would take to arrange for an interpreter to accompany me to all my classes and labs during my time at Cartwright.

By the time I left Mrs. Stephens' office, we'd been able to schedule an appointment with the Disability Resource Office on Cartwright's campus for next Tuesday afternoon.

NO WORRY, Kathleen signed to me in the hallway outside Mrs. Stephens' office. NO PROBLEM WITH INTERPRETER. PROMISE.

I HOPE, I signed back.

A miniscule drop of doubt had settled into the back of my mind at the thought of not being able to get an interpreter for my college classes. I waved good-bye to Kathleen and backtracked to my locker on the other side of the school.

Ever since Beau and I had become whatever we were now, he'd been perfectly happy to drive me home after school. Getting the ten extra minutes with him each day was fantastic. But there had been a quiet tension between us since the Steaming Bean. I knew exactly what it was and what caused it—that talk about cochlear implants and how he'd seemed to think things would magically become easier for me if I got one.

I just wasn't ready to face it with everything else on my plate. If Beau and I kept on the way we were going, it'd come out soon enough.

I checked my phone after I grabbed everything I'd need for homework from my locker and saw that I had a text from Beau, letting me know he was waiting for me in the library. I found him at one of the tables across from the librarian's desk, deeply engrossed in AP Statistics homework.

He looked up when I took a seat across the table from

him and gave me a smile. No matter how weird it sometimes seemed like things had become between us because of the Steaming Bean incident, being on the receiving end of one of Beau's smiles still got me feeling warm in some funny places.

"How was . . . appointment?" he asked, flipping his textbook shut.

FINE, I signed to him. SET UP MEETING FOR INTERPRETER.

A look of confusion crossed Beau's face and he signed, WHY?

"It'll be the same as Kathleen," I said with my voice. "I'll need an interpreter going with me to each of my classes every day."

Beau nodded and signed, TRUE.

I sat there waiting while he gathered up his homework things and shoved it all in his backpack, and we left the library together. The ride home was uneventful, and my thoughts were tangled up with what Mrs. Stephens said about arranging an interpreter for my first year of college.

College was going to look a lot different for me and chances were I wasn't going to get lucky twice and wind up with a great interpreter like Kathleen. But I'd made friends with Nina and Beau at Engelmann. It shouldn't be too much to hope that the same would happen at Cartwright on the friendship front.

THANK YOU, I signed to Mom as she parked in the lot

just outside Cartwright's administration building. I KNOW YOU BUSY, BUT—

Mom waved a hand to cut me off, signing, FINE, with an exasperated smile. COLLEGE IMPORTANT, she added, yanking the keys from the ignition.

I KNOW, I signed in agreement.

That still didn't make me feel any less guilty for pulling Mom away for a few hours to take me to meet with the Disability Resource Office in the middle of a school and work day.

DON'T WORRY, Mom signed to me on our trek through the parking lot up to the building's entrance. THEY FIND YOU INTERPRETER, EASY.

I did my best to muster up a smile, not sure what to sign or say.

The Disability Resource Office was on the building's fourth floor, and it was a tense ride up in the elevator even though Mom kept giving me comforting squeezes and signing, YOU FINE, multiple times.

There was determination in my step on my way down the hallway to the office. I held myself with as much dignity as I could muster, pressing the office's doorbell and waiting to get buzzed in. Mom stuck close to my side on the way over to the front desk where the receptionist sat, and I said, "We're here to see Nadine Frederickson."

The receptionist nodded with a polite smile and reached for her desk phone to make a call. A moment later, Mom tapped on my arm and pointed to the other side of the miniscule waiting room where a woman was opening a door. The woman seemed pleasant enough as she came forward to introduce herself and shake our hands. She was wearing a nametag with Cartwright's logo on it that said her name was Nadine Frederickson, Director of Disability Resources.

"Nice to meet . . ." Nadine said, then gestured behind her. ". . . my office?"

We followed her back to her office, a tiny space barely bigger than a closet and yet still equipped with a full-size desk, computer, filing cabinet, and two chairs for guests. I took a seat while Mom remained standing, moving over to stay in my line of sight to interpret.

There were a couple moments where Nadine shuffled things around on her desk and typed some stuff into her computer, not saying anything. I looked to Mom for an indication of what was going on, and she just shrugged. When Nadine finally turned in her chair to address us, the corners of her mouth were tucked into a frown.

WHAT'S WRONG? I signed to Mom immediately.

There was a slight pause as Mom listened to what Nadine began to say, and then her face started to fall too.

WHAT'S WRONG? I signed again, leaning forward in my seat.

When Nadine was finished speaking—speaking only to Mom, ugh—Mom finally started signing to me, and she didn't seem all that thrilled.

COLLEGE NEED PROOF YOU DEAF, was the first thing she signed to me.

I slipped both my hearing aids off and set them on Nadine's desk, signing, HERE.

". . . need . . . hearing . . ." Nadine said with a wince, purposefully not looking at my hearing aids.

TEST, Mom signed to me when I looked back at her. A-U-D-I-O-G-R-A-M. Getting a copy of my last test from years ago was no big deal. It would just take a day or two.

Mom kept her attention fixed on Nadine while she spoke before signing to me. What she signed just about knocked the air out of my lungs and made me grab at the arms of my chair for support.

"There's a wait list for interpreters?" I said out loud.

A LOT O-F DEAF STUDENTS APPLY RECENTLY, Mom signed to me while Nadine started talking a mile a minute. THAT GOOD, BUT NOT A LOT O-F INTERPRETER HERE FOR EDUCATION RIGHT NOW, AND—

I stopped Mom mid-sign, holding up a hand. "Wait a minute. If there's a wait list for interpreters, how long will it take me to get one?"

My brain was firing off questions faster than I could get my hands to sign, so I was stuck using my voice.

Nadine went palms up, a bit anxious now as she looked back and forth between me and Mom. "Maybe . . . ?"

Mom's eyes widened at whatever Nadine told her, and she both said and signed, REALLY?

HOW LONG? I signed to Mom, my nerves jangling.

Mom signed back, DON'T KNOW. I HOPE SOON.

"So . . . so . . ." I licked my lips a few times, my mouth uncomfortably dry now. "What does that . . . ?"

Nothing was happening the way it was supposed to. Not having an interpreter available right this instant wasn't the end of the world because fall semester didn't start until the end of this coming August. But I didn't want to wait a whole semester to start college.

HEY, Mom signed at me. YOU OK?

FINE, I signed. ALL DONE NOW?

Mom signed, WAIT. She spent a few more minutes talking with Nadine before she signed, OK, ALL DONE.

Nadine escorted us out of her office and waved us off with a courteous smile, but I chose to ignore that. Mom started signing to me again on our way back to the car, but I couldn't pay attention. What if I had to withdraw my application from Cartwright because there was no available interpreter for me? What if I had to wait *years*?

Anger didn't really seem like the right word to describe what I was currently feeling. This was a lot more complex than that.

There were thousands of Deaf people out there like me wanting to get into college and expand their education. Yet suddenly there weren't enough interpreters to go around? This wasn't sitting right with me. Chances were I was just jumping to conclusions here, but I had this unsettling thought that maybe it was because nobody expected Deaf people to actually go to college.

Mom got the car unlocked and climbed in the driver's seat, but I just stood there, resting my forehead against the window, begging my brain to quiet down. I wasn't sure how much time passed before I felt Mom's hand on my shoulder, gently urging me to turn around and face her.

WHAT'S WRONG? Mom signed, keeping one hand tight on my shoulder.

WHAT HAPPEN IF COLLEGE CAN'T FIND ME INTERPRETER? I signed as I sucked in a shaky breath of air.

THEY WILL, Mom signed, pointing back at the

administration building. PATIENT, she added, tapping a finger to my forehead.

I tried to keep signing, but my hands seemed incapable of cooperating the way I wanted. "I thought I'd tackled the hardest part," I told Mom. "Getting into college and all that. But now this? I know you say they'll get me an interpreter eventually, but . . . what if this is a sign I'm not supposed to go into respiratory therapy?"

Mom took my face in her hands and very clearly said, "Adjust . . . expectations."

She pressed a kiss to my forehead before she let me go and took a step back, and then she signed, LIFE NOT WORK HOW WE THINK.

I KNOW, I signed back quickly. BUT—

NO, YOU DON'T KNOW, Mom signed in disagreement. YOU YOUNG. NEED TIME.

I tried to respond, but Mom kept cutting me off before I could get more than a few signs in.

YOU SAD NOW, I UNDERSTAND, she signed, her movements very firm. BUT YOU NEED FOCUS. THINGS WILL IMPROVE.

She finished making her point by signing, PATIENT, again.

Unfortunately, patience had never been my strong suit.

t wasn't the warmest day outside, but I thought I could use a change of scenery during lunch. After the events of yesterday, I wasn't up for much talk today, and I knew Nina and Beau would want every detail of my visit to Cartwright.

There were a bunch of picnic tables set up in the small courtyard outside the cafeteria, and I had my pick since almost no one was going to venture out into the cold to enjoy their sandwiches. I dropped my backpack onto the ground next to the table on the far side of the courtyard and sat down. Wallowing had never been my favorite pastime, but I couldn't snap myself out of it.

I just about jumped out of my skin when a hand came down on my shoulder, and the breath I'd sucked in came out in a rush when I saw Beau and Nina standing there behind me, looking as shocked as I felt at their sudden appearance. They both signed, SORRY, while I worked to breathe properly again.

FINE, I signed back, one hand still at my chest.

SURE? Nina signed, taking a spot at the picnic table across from me. YOU LOOK . . .

Apparently, she couldn't come up with the appropriate sign to describe what I looked like, so she settled for saying, ". . . off."

I looked back and forth between Nina and Beau as Beau took a seat across the table from me too, debating telling them what happened yesterday. I mean, they *were* my friends. Okay, maybe Beau was a little more than *just* a friend. But they still might not understand exactly how devastating the news was, and I wasn't in the mood for false cheer. In the end, I explained what happened at the Disability Resource Office yesterday, trying not to get emotional about it all over again.

SORRY, Beau and Nina signed in unison when I finished my story.

". . . seems like they . . . find . . . interpreter," Nina continued, resting her chin in her hands. ". . . just take time."

I KNOW, I signed, exhaling heavily. "But . . . is it so bad that for once in my life I just want things to work out?"

"What do . . . mean?" Beau asked with a frown.

I started tapping out a beat on the tabletop with my fingers, trying to formulate my thoughts into something that would make sense.

"Ever since I lost my hearing I've had to put in ten times the amount of effort just to keep on top of things, you know? Like in school and pretty much every other aspect of my life. I mean, I honestly worried I wasn't going to get into college because I'm Deaf. And now this? I mean, I wouldn't change *anything* about my life, but can't I just have this one simple thing?"

I THINK . . . Beau started to sign hesitantly, UNDERSTAND.

"You do?" I said, feeling a bit skeptical. Wasn't like he'd run into this situation before.

Beau signed, YES, and glanced over at Nina for backup.

Nina took her time responding.

". . . think . . . will . . . worth . . . wait," she said, putting on a smile. "Hard work pays . . ."

"Yeah, maybe," I said, that feeling of defeat working its way through me again. I cared about my friends, I really did, and I knew they cared about me too, but they weren't helping right now.

HEY, Beau signed to get my attention. OK?

The earnest and concerned look on his face was so endearing I couldn't keep the tiny smile from tugging at my lips.

FINE, I signed, and this time I kind of meant it.

Beau broke out into a grin too and reached across the table to curl his hand around my own.

". . . know . . . adore each other," Nina said with a pretend-exasperated expression. "But let's . . . about something happier . . . like Maya's . . ."

"My what?" I said in confusion.

BIRTHDAY, Beau signed for me. SOON, RIGHT?

I felt caught off guard at the mention of my birthday because I'd honestly forgotten it was coming up. There were a few more important things on my plate at the moment besides my eighteenth birthday.

But it was touching that Nina and Beau had remembered my birthday when I'd completely spaced on it. They paid more attention to some things about myself than I did. I was just beginning to dread whatever was about to come out of Nina's mouth because I *knew* that calculating look in her eyes.

"And?" I said, deciding to play it cool so Beau and Nina would see that I did not want to make a big deal out of my birthday.

YOUR BIRTHDAY! Nina signed, giving me this look that clearly said, *duh!*

"Yes, well, I'm choosing to ignore my birthday this year," I said, slapping a hand down on the table. "It's not a big deal."

"No way," Beau said with an incredulous look. ". . . turning eighteen."

"So?"

IMPORTANT, Nina signed, practically squirming with glee. WE NEED CELEBRATE.

"Oh, come on. Really?" I said, trying not to grimace.

YES! Nina signed back excitedly.

I looked to Beau for backup, but all he did was go palms up as if to say, *This is Nina's show here.*

REALLY? I signed with an involuntary wince.

"Yes!" Nina said at the same time Beau signed, YOU WILL HAVE FUN.

WANT SMALL, I signed to Nina, and she nodded quickly, signing back, UNDERSTAND.

Hoping the birthday thing would be put to rest, I unwrapped my sandwich and took a bite. Beau and Nina started in on their own lunches, and for a moment I started to temporarily forget everything that had been going wrong lately. I had two people here that I was pretty sure would support me no matter what happened.

As much as I wanted to ignore the whole interpreter situation with Cartwright and focus on more important things immediately at hand, I was telling Kathleen what happened before the day was out.

NORMAL? I signed to her as we stood beside my locker after the last bell. I FEEL COLLEGE SHOULD HAVE MANY INTERPRETER.

Kathleen was nodding along with an inquisitive look on her face. NOT STRANGE, she signed. SOMETIMES THAT HAPPEN. BUT . . .

I felt my breath catch waiting for what she would sign next. Kathleen mentioned a while back that she'd been an educational interpreter for a *long* time. She had to be in the know where education was concerned, right?

Please don't let her deliver any more depressing news, I thought uneasily.

I MAKE CALL, Kathleen finally signed, a confident smile taking over her face. I KNOW SOME PEOPLE. I TELL YOU LATER INFORMATION I FIND.

THANK YOU, THANK YOU, I signed quickly, and before I could think twice I threw my arms around her in a hug.

I could feel Kathleen laughing by the vibrations in her chest, and she was still smiling when I let her go and took a step back.

This didn't mean Kathleen was offering a solution by any means, but she seemed like the type of person to get things done. If there was anybody to put my trust in, it was Kathleen.

TRY NOT T-O WORRY, Kathleen signed, then chucked me under the chin. ALL OK.

It'll all be okay, I told myself as Kathleen and I parted ways and I went outside to find Beau.

I sure hoped so at least. Thinking about whatever Nina was going to throw together for my birthday had me feeling queasy, but putting on a happy face and going along with it was the least I could do. Without Nina, I wasn't so sure where I would be in the tangled web that was Engelmann.

I had to throw Beau into that equation too when I saw him outside, leaning against his car with a book in hand, like always. My heart did this stupid little jump when he looked up as I approached and smiled warmly.

FEEL BETTER? he signed when I stopped in front of him, tossing his book on the roof of his car.

I was going to answer his question honestly, but there was something else I'd rather do first.

I curled my fingers around Beau's collar and tugged him down to my level so I could kiss him, because why not? Didn't seem like Beau minded either since he was kissing me back.

BETTER NOW, I signed once I let him go.

CHAPTER 33

*C*an't *do birthday stuff today*, I texted Nina late Saturday morning, curled up on the couch in the living room with Connor beside me. *Little bro not feeling well*.

Connor had a rough go of it this morning, hacking up more mucus and fluid than usual, and his discomfort was evident. There wasn't much I could actually do to help him except stick close and watch Spider-Man cartoons—his go-to when he wasn't feeling well.

Nina texted back almost immediately, wanting to know if Connor was okay and if there was anything she could do to help. I assured her everything was fine, just that we would have to reschedule the birthday stuff for later. I still wasn't feeling super celebratory, even though I appreciated her enthusiasm for making my day memorable.

Don't worry, said Nina's next text. *We'll bring the party to u*.

Repeatedly texting Nina from there on, telling her how unnecessary it was to bring the party to me, was pointless.

The doorbell rang a little over an hour later, the lighting in the living room flashing on and off for a couple seconds. When I opened the door, Beau and Nina were standing there on the front porch, holding a stack of pizzas, a happy birthday balloon, and what looked suspiciously like a few presents.

They both said, "Happy birthday!" rather than signing it, their arms full of birthday paraphernalia.

"What's all this?" I asked, holding tight to the door handle. I was torn between gratefulness that I had such awesome friends and embarrassment over being the center of attention. Especially since I was still wearing sweats, an oversized baseball T-shirt, and hadn't showered yet.

"Come on . . . just . . . two . . ." Nina said, nodding at Beau. ". . . brother . . . have fun!"

Connor was already off the couch and standing next to me in the doorway, eyeing the balloon Nina had wrapped around her wrist. Mom joined us next, putting a hand to my shoulder, signing, HAPPY BIRTHDAY, when I looked at her.

FUN, Mom signed, doing that thing where she wiggled her eyebrows to make me laugh.

Yeah, my mother was so in on this whole thing.

"Mother, I am in my pajamas!"

"So?" Mom said with a shrug, then pointed to the stairs. "Go change."

ONE SECOND, I signed to Mom as Beau took the pizzas into the dining room and Nina gave Connor the balloon.

I sprinted up the stairs to my bedroom and threw on the first pair of jeans and clean T-shirt I could get my hands on. I yanked a brush through my knotted hair and pulled it up into something resembling a ponytail, then got my hearing aids in and ran back downstairs.

Everyone was gathered around the dining table with the pizza, the handful of presents, and a small cake with blue frosting and sprinkles. I got another round of them signing HAPPY BIRTHDAY to me and somehow I managed to respond with a feeble, THANK YOU.

In the grand scheme of things, I guessed letting Nina have her fun with this was the least I could do. She was the first hearing friend I'd made at Engelmann, and it was hard not to think that I would always be thankful for her.

Connor sat with us at the table while we grabbed slices of pizza, but he got bored pretty quickly with the conversation and went back to the cartoons in the living room. Mom seemed the happiest I'd seen her in a while, talking and signing with Beau and Nina, and I started to think that maybe this whole thing wasn't such a bad idea after all.

I got through two slices of pepperoni with extra cheese before I gave into the laughter. Watching Beau attempt to sign and eat at the same time was far more amusing to me than it should have been.

"How do . . . sign with . . . hand?" Beau asked with a deep scowl. "When . . . eat?"

After a while signing and eating at the same time became second nature to Deaf people.

I bit down on my lip to smother the giggles, but I think one or two escaped. "Practice."

Nina insisted on opening presents next before doing the whole cake thing, and I was happy I only had three items to unwrap. The first present was from Nina—a lotion and body soap set that smelled like vanilla sugar from some fancy store. Next was a joint gift from Nina and Beau, a gift certificate to Cartwright's bookstore, which they claimed was very important thanks to all the overpriced textbooks I'd need.

Mom had included her own handful of presents for me in the gift exchange—a birthday card along with a gift certificate to a clothing store for my new college wardrobe and the boxed set of all the seasons of my favorite TV show. Even more touching was that Connor had pooled together his allowance to buy us a new notebook and a booklet of Marvel stickers to decorate it with.

My last present was a book that was not surprisingly from Beau, and I had the feeling it was from his personal collection. I was by no means the avid reader Beau was, and yet I was still very touched by the battered copy of *Jane Eyre* I now held in my hands.

I inspected the old book, flipping through the yellowing pages. This wasn't a first edition, but it was definitely dated, with old-fashioned illustrations depicting scenes from the novel.

Tucked between the first few pages was an envelope that held a simple blue card with the words *Happy Birthday* written across the front in Beau's untidy handwriting. Inside there was a small note addressed to me that read:

I haven't seen you with many books before, but you'll have to tell me what you think of this one. You might find you have a thing or two in common with the main character.

Written underneath that was a quote from the novel.

"I am no bird, and no net ensnares me."

I tucked the card back into its envelope, slid it back between the pages, and carefully set the book on the table.

When I finally turned to look at Beau I wasn't surprised to see him watching me intently, trying to gauge my reaction to his present.

It seemed ridiculous to only sign, THANK YOU, but that was all I could manage in that moment with Beau's green eyes fixed on me the way they were.

YOU LIKE? he signed quickly.

LOVE, I signed back honestly, resting my hand on the book.

Beau gave a tiny sigh of relief and signed, GOOD. HAPPY.

If it weren't for Nina stepping in, signing that it was time for cake now, I think Beau and I might've sunk even further into the moment.

I kept repeating those words from the book to myself as I cut into my slice of cake.

I am no bird, and no net ensnares me.

Birthday celebrating wasn't really so bad. There was a bunch of laughter and stories from school being traded back and forth, with Mom and sometimes Connor in on the fun too. I was a little surprised by how much I was enjoying this and how it wasn't awkward having my friends and my mom together in the same vicinity, which usually left the door wide open for embarrassment.

Nina got to wrapping things up later in the afternoon thanks to an evening shift she had at Target, and since she'd carpooled with Beau, he had to leave as well. I was a little sad to see them go, but I figured Beau probably had a mountain of homework to get through before Monday.

THANK YOU, I signed to Nina and Beau while I walked them outside after they said their good-byes to Mom and Connor. FUN.

SAME, Nina signed, tossing an arm around my shoulders to pull me in for a side-hug. HAPPY BIRTHDAY.

Beau hung back while Nina went down the driveway to his car, keys in hand, so I signed, WHAT'S UP?

I watched him suck in some air before he finally signed, HAVE GIFT FOR YOU.

"What?" I said, frowning. "I thought the book was my present."

"Yeah, but . . ." Beau said, then pulled out an envelope from his jacket pocket that he then thrust at me.

I felt my frown deepening as I took the envelope, turning it over in my hands. Nothing on the outside of the envelope gave any indication as to where it could've come from. I carefully tore open the envelope and peeked inside, confused at the sight of some papers, a brochure, and a business card.

I yanked the contents of the envelope out to give them a closer look. My hands started to shake as I rifled through the papers, hardly able to believe Beau was the one to give me all this.

The brochure slipped from my grasp and fluttered to the ground as I turned my attention to the business card for a Dr. Janet Porter at Children's Hospital in Aurora.

"What is this?"

Even if I couldn't hear them, the words felt sharp flying from my mouth.

Beau went from looking hopeful to taken aback in half a second, and he signed, INFORMATION FOR—

"What part of *I don't want a cochlear implant* did you not understand?"

I gave Beau the moment he obviously needed to collect his thoughts, because this clearly wasn't the response he was anticipating. When he couldn't come up with any signs, he started talking, saying, "I was thinking about . . . job interview and college . . . how upset . . . were. I did research . . . cochlear implants . . . and . . . thought maybe . . . want . . . look . . ."

"Stop. Just stop please."

Beau pressed his lips tightly together and nodded.

My vision got a little blurry as I reached down to grab the brochure I dropped. Hot, angry tears were threatening to escape now.

It'd taken a long while, but somehow, I'd developed genuine feelings for the hearing boy standing right in front of me. He was learning my language and was nothing but encouraging when it came to my dreams—he'd probably been the most excited about my acceptance letter from Cartwright.

I didn't want to think I'd been wrong and that maybe Beau didn't actually like the fact I was Deaf at all. Except what else was I supposed to think when I was holding all this information about cochlear implants and a doctor's business card?

Why would Beau ever want me to change this quintessential part of myself?

"I don't want this," I said as calmly as I could manage. "I don't need it."

Beau went from looking confused to gobsmacked in a heartbeat and started to speak, but I tried to raise my voice to cover his.

"Why can't you understand I'm happy being Deaf?"

". . . understand, but . . . thought . . ."

"No, I really believe you weren't thinking."

I wanted to throw the stupid envelope with all that CI information at Beau and storm back inside. It took real effort to stay put and speak my mind, even if this was about to ruin whatever had been developing between me and Beau for months now.

"I don't want your pity, Beau. I'm not some poor, helpless little girl who needs to be saved. So if that's all you have for me, please just go now."

It was impossible to tell how much time passed while I stood there by the front steps outside my house waiting for some kind of a response from Beau. He looked like he was stuck between a rock and a hard place, unsure of what to say to me.

When the moment stretched on between us with seemingly no end in sight, I gave up.

FINE, I signed, then followed up with an, ALL DONE.

I had no idea what I was *all done* with, but I was choosing to leave it at that.

Beau didn't stop me when I turned on my heel and went up the front steps back into the house, leaving him and his birthday "gift" behind.

CHAPTER 34

I was kind of surprised it took Mom as long as it did to come creeping into my room when I didn't surface after my alarm went off Sunday morning. I had my blankets pulled up high over my head and didn't budge until Mom put her hand to my side and squeezed.

WHAT HAPPENED? she signed when I ripped the blankets back and gave her a look.

She'd turned the lights on so I got a good view of the expression on her face, which was somehow both concern and exasperation.

"I don't know what you mean," I finally said.

YESTERDAY, she signed in explanation. BIRTHDAY. WHAT HAPPENED?

NOTHING, I signed as I sat up and scooted up the bed until my back was against the wall.

Mom's eyes narrowed, and she sat there waiting for a better explanation. I gave in with a huff, dropping my head into my hands so I didn't have to look at her while I spoke.

I used my voice because I didn't think I could muster up any other signs besides *stupid* or *frustrated* to describe what happened or how I currently felt.

"Beau's second birthday present for me was a bunch of information about CIs and a doctor in the area I can contact about possibly getting one. Dr. Porter, as luck would have it."

Mom's grip on my knee tightened almost painfully.

HE KNOW YOU DON'T WANT CI? she asked me slowly.

YES, I signed back. HE KNOW, AND HE GIVE ME THAT. BEFORE I THINK B-E-A-U LIKE ME, I kept on signing, focusing on signing rather than the uncomfortable feeling stirring in the pit of my stomach. AND I THINK HE LIKE ME DEAF. BUT NOW . . . DON'T KNOW.

Mom signed, OH I SEE, once I was done with my story. She seemed just as lost as I did at that moment, unsure of what to think about the whole thing.

I THINK HE WANT HELP YOU, she signed eventually. I THINK SOME HEARING PEOPLE BELIEVE ALL DEAF SAD BECAUSE THEY CAN'T HEAR.

NOT TRUE, I signed, sitting upright. NOT SAD I DEAF. SAD BECAUSE B-E-A-U WANT ME . . .

". . . to change myself," I said, finishing my train of thought with my voice. "I'm happy being Deaf. Why is that so hard to believe?"

Mom winced as she shrugged, signing, DON'T KNOW. I BELIEVE YOU.

It usually took a herculean amount of effort on my part to be honest when it came to touchy feely stuff like this, but since I'd already told Mom everything else, I might as well come right out with the rest of it.

"Mom, I really like Beau," I said. I wouldn't—*couldn't*—deny that anymore. "And just when I finally convince myself it doesn't matter he's hearing, this happens?"

"Honey, relationships . . . never easy," Mom said with a sad little smile. "But . . . doesn't have . . . end. Not if . . . don't want."

"I don't know what I want anymore."

I think I groaned as I scrubbed my hands over my face.

Mom gave my knee another squeeze to get me to look at her, and when I did, she signed, FINE. YOU YOUNG. HAVE TIME.

I guessed that was true, but what good was that going to do me, at least where Beau was concerned?

It didn't help so much with the guilt thing when she signed, SORRY, next.

"No, I'm sorry," I said, taking in a deep breath. "I guess things just got . . . weird when we moved here. I've been having a hard time figuring out who I am."

I KNOW, Mom signed with a wry smile. ART TELL ME THAT.

I nodded in agreement. My self-portrait from Ms. Phillip's art class, still hanging in the living room, was pretty much the perfect example of how I'd been seeing myself ever since we moved to Colorado. Probably I wasn't the only high school student that felt this way, Deaf or hearing.

NOW? I signed, grimacing.

Mom shrugged, signing, DON'T KNOW. YOU DECIDE.

Well, wasn't that easier said than done?

Mom gave me a comforting pat on the leg and stood up, moving toward the door.

WANT BREAKFAST? she signed one-handed as she opened the door.

"No," I said. "I want to go back to sleep."

Mom gave me an understanding smile and left the room, shutting the door behind her.

I rolled over and yanked my blankets up and over me again, squeezing my eyes shut tight. Thoughts of Beau wouldn't quit dancing across my mind, images of his smile with the dimples, the way he looked when he laughed.

Perhaps Mom was right and Beau really did just want to do what he could to help. But why couldn't he have asked me about this himself instead of assuming I wanted a cochlear implant and needed help getting it to begin with? Who even made snap judgments like that?

You did, I thought suddenly, when I was seconds away from falling asleep again.

Hadn't I thought for months that Beau was just some popular snob out to get brownie points for making friends with the new Deaf girl? Despite what happened, I still had to believe that was wrong and Beau genuinely did feel *something* for me.

I stuck a hand out from underneath my mountain of blankets and slapped around on my nightstand until I found my cell phone. I closed out all the text messages from Nina and one from Beau—*Can we talk, please?*—and typed up a text message to Melissa. This was one of those situations where you had to consult your best friend first before making any rash decisions.

Everything ok?? she texted alongside a frowny face emoji when she responded.

Not really, I texted back.

It took a few minutes to type up everything that had happened in the past few days. By the time I sent the message off to Melissa I had a short novella written, but it was the only way to get everything out and she wouldn't mind anyway. The more details, the better for Melissa.

OMG was her response that came more quickly than I would've expected.

That was it. Just the three letters. Not really the help I was looking for.

Bad?? I texted back frantically.

It . . . something else, she responded. *But how you feel?*

Hurt, I texted her, needing no time at all to answer. *Upset. I thought he liked me for ME.*

Tell him that, Melissa texted back almost immediately. *Don't settle.*

What would you do? I asked her next.

Melissa's response didn't come for some time, and it was just a short, *Don't know*, followed by, *We don't need to be fixed. He can't see that, not worth your time.*

She was right. There was one thing I knew for certain. I was happy being Deaf, and I was not about to change that just because a cochlear implant *might* make my life easier. Just because Beau thought he was doing me a favor didn't mean he actually was.

Beau was supposed to be a smart guy. He wouldn't have gotten into Yale if he wasn't. Why he wasn't getting this was just baffling to me. And if he couldn't understand this one thing I was so adamant about, then was it even worth it, trying to develop some kind of relationship when we both were just too *different?*

CHAPTER 35

Walking into AP Statistics Monday morning, I made it very clear I was not ready to talk to Beau. Not once did I make eye contact with him as I took my regular seat and pulled out my homework and textbook. I could feel the tension coming off him in waves, and five minutes into the lesson I started to imagine I could hear him squirming in his seat.

Class was fifty-five minutes of torment, and I wasn't sure how much of Mrs. Richardson's lesson I actually absorbed. My mind would veer off every few minutes and I would start to think of everything I wanted to say to Beau, how badly I wanted him to understand that I did *not* need this kind of "help" from him. I didn't need him to be my able-bodied savior.

I was up and out of my seat, shoving my things into my backpack, the moment Kathleen motioned to me that the bell had rung. I got about two steps toward the door when Beau's hand came down on my shoulder.

CAN WE TALK? he signed when I finally brought myself to look at him.

NO, I signed back immediately, but had to follow it up with, NOT YET.

There was no way this whole thing could be put to rest without talking it through, but I wasn't quite ready for it yet. And why not let him fret about it for a little bit longer? Maybe he'd start to feel the way I did.

I turned on my heel and left without waiting for Beau's response, only stopping outside in the hallway for Kathleen to catch up to me.

WHAT'S WRONG? she signed when we rounded the corner into the next hallway.

I didn't have the energy to give Kathleen a play-by-play of everything that happened over the weekend, so I gave her the condensed version.

B-E-A-U GIVE ME INFORMATION ABOUT CI FOR MY BIRTHDAY, I signed, my movements jerky. HE THINK I WANT ONE.

Kathleen's eyebrows shot up, and her mouth got all tight like it did any time she disapproved of something.

HOW YOU FEEL? she signed after a moment.

SAD, I signed back immediately. ANGRY.

And a whole list of other emotions too, but Kathleen could get the picture without my going into detail.

I was sort of expecting Kathleen to come up with a solution, like she did when I told her about the situation with Cartwright and the interpreter, but she was still silent when we reached Mr. Wells' history class.

I was prepared to go through another round of questioning when I took my seat next to Nina, but I figured by the tiny smile she gave me, and the understanding look in her eyes, that she already knew everything that had happened.

YOU OK? was all she signed right when Beau walked into class and sat down in the seat beside me.

I went with total honesty here.

"No, I'm not," I said aloud.

Mr. Wells jumped right into class the second after the bell rang, but I was still far from being grounded in the lesson. I ended up doodling all over the page in my notebook instead of taking notes. I snapped back to reality when Nina started tapping on my desk to get my attention and noticed that I'd drawn a whole page of boxes and frowny faces.

GROUP DISCUSSION TIME, Nina signed to me when I glanced her way.

YAY, I signed with an eye roll.

I turned my back to Beau and faced Nina. I didn't want to talk to him about history either.

Nina started signing and using her voice to talk about something to do with the Cuban Missile Crisis, but my attention wandered once I caught on to the looks Jackson kept shooting my way. He was sitting two rows back, leaning toward a guy I knew to be on the baseball team too. They were clearly not talking about anything related to the Cuban Missile Crisis.

It was a mixture of curiosity and determination that had me focusing on Jackson's big mouth, lipreading what he was saying. His gaze kept darting back and forth between me and Beau, so he was apparently talking about us, and he was starting to smirk.

"*Excuse me,*" I blurted out loud enough to catch the

attention of a few classmates. "You really didn't just say that, did you?"

I'd made it a point to have as little interaction with Jackson as possible, but there was no chance I wasn't going to call him out on what he'd just said.

Jackson shot upright in his seat, eyes going wide. ". . . heard me?"

"Of course I didn't. But did you forget this *disabled chick* can lipread?"

A bright red flush started to creep up Jackson's neck and into his face as everyone stared at us—Beau and Nina included. This wasn't the kind of attention he was used to.

"Sorry . . ." Jackson started to say, not even meeting my gaze. "Just thought . . ."

"No, I don't want your apology," I snapped. "I want you to understand I'm *not* disabled. Literally the only thing I can't do that you can is hear."

Jackson shifted awkwardly in his seat, pointedly staring at a spot above my head. All he said in response was, "Okay."

"And I'd appreciate it if you'd quit talking about me and Beau," I added, on a roll here and ready to keep going just to make sure Jackson *really* understood. "Whatever's going on between us is none of your business."

I refused to believe the utter crap Jackson just spouted off, that Beau was only pursuing something with me to get brownie points for dating a *disabled chick*. No matter this rut we were in, Beau would never be that cruel. He had too much heart for that.

I twisted around in my seat to face forward, crossing my arms tightly over my chest.

"What . . . that about?" Nina asked, putting a hand to my forearm as she leaned toward me.

NOTHING, I signed back. FINE.

Sneaking a glance over at Beau—he was pretending to be engrossed in his textbook, but I knew his mind was far from here—I realized I wasn't fine. I wouldn't be fine until we talked.

CHAPTER 36

Tuesday morning, Kathleen was running late and wasn't waiting by the front office like she normally did each morning. This worked perfectly for me. All I needed was a handful of minutes alone with Beau so we could talk. It would have been too awkward to have this kind of conversation in front of an interpreter.

Beau was shoving things into his backpack at his locker just like I knew he would be. His movements were sluggish, like he was running on no sleep or was completely distracted. He looked how I'd felt.

When I approached, I rapped my knuckles on the locker beside him to get his attention. I wasn't going to be using my voice for this.

Beau's green eyes went wide when he slammed his locker shut and saw me standing there. He blurted out, "You're here."

HELLO, I signed back. READY T-O TALK.

That's all I could think of to say. I was already having trouble recalling all the signs I had planned by being this close to him.

Beau's lips were parted and one hand was raised like he

was about to start signing, which I was convinced would be an apology, but it wasn't. Instead he said, "I got . . . boulder."

DON'T UNDERSTAND? I signed after a failed attempt at piecing together what he just said.

I had no idea what a boulder had to do with anything.

Beau stuck a hand in his backpack, did some rummaging around, and came up with a folded letter. I did a quick scan of the letter, a formal document from a college in Boulder. I recognized it as the same college Nina applied to. It wasn't a surprise Beau was accepted, but I wasn't sure why he felt this was the appropriate moment to share the news with me.

OK, I signed when I passed the letter back to him. GOOD FOR YOU.

I could see Beau must've been short of breath with the heavy rise and fall of his chest. He shoved the letter back in his backpack. When his gaze met mine again, he said, ". . . applied after . . . talk that night . . . wanted . . . know . . . could do something else."

WHAT? I signed, so taken aback by that statement I felt my eyebrows shooting up my forehead in surprise.

Beau settled for signing, I TELL MY FATHER I DON'T WANT MEDICINE DEGREE.

". . . not what . . . want," he said aloud, resting a hand against his chest. ". . . want English degree."

I said, "Oh," instead of keeping my voice turned off like I'd intended.

I was still angry and hurt about Saturday's events with the cochlear implant brochure and I couldn't see myself getting over that anytime soon. But I couldn't help but feel proud of Beau anyway.

"Where is this coming from?" I said, knowing I wouldn't be able to come up with any signs on the spot. "Why are you telling me this?"

Then I shook my head. I did want to know what was going on with Beau, but first I needed to tell him what was going on with me.

WAIT, PLEASE, I signed, holding up one finger. BEFORE YOU START, I WANT . . .

What did I want exactly?

I NOT CHANGE MYSELF, I signed after a moment's hesitation. NO CI. HAVE ME DEAF . . .

"Or not at all," I finished.

It didn't matter so much to me anymore that Beau was hearing. That wasn't the problem here. The problem was that he'd thought I wanted a CI just because I had one bad interview experience and some complications with finding an interpreter for college. That did not mean I needed to give up. If Beau somehow thought I couldn't do that or that a CI was the answer to all my problems—to be hearing again—then I was prepared to walk away right now and not look back. It would be painful, but I couldn't betray myself like that.

And Beau had this awkward smile breaking out across his face by the time I finished speaking, and that was even more confusing than the whole Boulder thing a minute ago. He seemed . . . almost *calm*. Like that was what he'd been expecting me to say.

I KNOW, he signed. AND I SORRY.

". . . shouldn't . . . done that," he continued using his voice. ". . . thought . . ."

I SEE NOW YOU NOT NEED MY HELP, he finished in sign with a shrug.

NO, I agreed in sign. BUT . . . WANT YOU.

That I could at least be honest about.

Beau started getting pink in the face as he began to sign in a rush, something like, BEFORE I THINK WE NOT . . . BECAUSE YOU DEAF AND . . .

I stared at him blankly while he struggled to find the words he was looking for. It looked like he was giving some huff as he threw up his hands and settled for signing, HEARING LIFE NOT PERFECT.

SAME WITH DEAF, I signed, nodding along.

YOU CONTINUE SUPPORT ME, Beau signed next. I SHOULD, SAME.

I felt myself begin to smile despite wanting to keep my cool and collected façade going.

WHO TELL YOU THAT? I signed, but I had this feeling I already knew who was responsible.

N-I-N-A, Beau answered, and I had to smother a laugh.

Thanks for the help, Nina, I thought.

HAPPY YOU UNDERSTAND NOW, I signed to Beau.

YES, Beau signed in agreement. SORRY, AGAIN. I . . .

It took him a moment before he signed, CAN WE START NEW?

"Sorry, what?"

Beau turned on his heel and walked down the hallway, disappeared around the corner, and then came walking back toward me. When he reached me, he held out a hand for me to shake, a pleasant smile on his face.

"Hello," he said. "I'm Beau . . . hearing, but . . . learning."

I shook his hand, finding it impossible not to smile now.

NICE T-O MEET YOU, I signed. MY NAME M-A-Y-A. DEAF AND HAPPY.

This was *weird*, but I got it. A fresh start here wasn't such a bad idea. Time to throw out all the misconceptions about hearing and Deaf people and start over.

"Walk . . . to class?" Beau asked, offering me a hand.

"Sure," I said, lacing my fingers through his and holding on tight. "Tell me about this English degree you want."

Beau began to sign with one hand as we set off down the hallway, telling me about the literature program he was interested in and how he'd been thinking more and more about becoming a teacher since I'd told him he'd make a good one the night of his party for his acceptance into Yale.

GOOD, I signed to him. YOU SMART. MAKE WONDERFUL TEACHER.

Beau grinned, showing off the dimples again. THANK YOU, he signed back, and then a sudden grimace tugged at his face. "My dad . . . not . . . understanding."

"Yeah, well, you've got this," I said. "It might not be easy, but not much is."

TRUE, Beau signed. BUT EASY IF I HAVE YOU.

SAME, I signed after a second of thought.

My life definitely wasn't easy, but it *was* significantly better when I had Beau next to me.

ONE YEAR LATER

I dropped the bag of soiled towels into the laundry chute and slammed the lid shut, feeling rather proud of myself.

I'd gotten through the first day of my internship at Mountain View Rehabilitation Clinic with little to no difficulty despite the worrying I'd done leading up to it. There had been an interpreter this morning to walk me through orientation, and right after lunch I got to go on my first rounds through the clinic.

It helped that all the staff here were incredibly kind, excited to have a new face around. One of the older nurses—her name was Liz—had already started carrying around a little notebook she kept tucked in the pocket of her scrubs so she could write notes to me. She'd already filled about three pages asking me questions over lunch.

This internship wasn't respiratory therapy, but I would be getting six months of experience in a medical setting, which my college guidance counselor assured me would look fantastic on my resume. I was already into my second semester of college and I was miles ahead of where I'd been this time last year. High school was long behind me and I had no desire to look back, even if what was currently ahead of me were exams and more exams for the next couple years.

"Done for . . . day?" Liz asked as I walked out of the laundry room.

I peeked at my cell phone in the pocket of my scrubs to check the time—almost five in the evening.

"Think so," I said. "Thanks for all your help today. This has been great so far."

Liz gave me a perky smile and thumbs up, setting off down the hallway with me. "How . . . think . . . went?"

"Good," I said once I'd pieced together her question. "A lot to take in, but . . ."

"Good," Liz repeated, and then she signed, YAY!

I had to laugh at this and signed, YAY! back at her.

Probably the next time I came in for a shift, Liz would have a few more signs in her arsenal. I was looking forward to it.

"Walk . . . out?" Liz said, nodding toward the clinic entrance.

"Sure, thanks."

Liz leaned over to the receptionist still at her post and said something that made the receptionist give an eye roll, and then we were off.

The sun was shining when we stepped outside, a pleasant breeze rustling the trees that lined the parking lot. Not a day you'd want to spend cooped up inside, but there was still plenty of daylight left to enjoy.

Liz put a hand to my shoulder, and when I looked her way she said, "Do . . . have ride?"

"Yeah, my mom is supposed to . . ."

I felt my voice trail off at the sight of a familiar car zipping into the parking lot, bouncing over one of the speed bumps as it parked haphazardly in the closest spot to the clinic.

". . . know them?" Liz said, pointing toward the car.

"Actually, I do."

It was Nina leaping out of the driver's seat, waving enthusiastically over the roof of the car, and then—

"*Beau!*"

COME HERE! my boyfriend was signing at me, and I think my smile was just as loony as his was.

I took off running across the parking lot without a second thought and threw my arms around Beau once I reached him.

Maybe a little too dramatic of a reunion, but I hadn't seen Beau since Christmas a few months ago. I had been under the impression he wasn't coming home for spring break. Beau was currently neck deep in Yale's esteemed literature program—much to his dad's annoyance, but Dr. Watson was steadily coming around.

I was just as busy with my classes at Cartwright and now my internship here at the clinic, so opportunities to FaceTime with Beau were not as frequent as I would've liked. Anytime I got to see him in person was reason enough to celebrate.

Nina was a little easier to keep in touch with and visit often, since she was going to CU Boulder, only a little over an hour away.

"What are you doing here?" I blurted out once Beau finally let me go, keeping one arm wrapped around my waist.

Beau started talking, something about wanting to surprise me, but I wasn't really processing what he was saying standing so close to him. I signed, KISS, instead, because that was pretty much all I needed.

I would've been quite happy to keep standing there in that parking lot kissing Beau, but only a few seconds of his lips against mine passed before there was rapid tapping on my shoulder. I pulled away from Beau with a start and my jaw dropped.

Standing in front of me, looking exasperated and amused, was *Melissa*. Melissa, who I hadn't seen in over a year and a half since we moved to Colorado. The only difference in her appearance was that she had bright blue highlights in her black hair.

I think I started sputtering like a fool, stuck between using my voice and signing at her. The only thing I managed to get out that actually made sense was to sign, WHY?

SURPRISE! Melissa signed back, and she pulled me in for a hug even more bone crushing than Beau's had been.

HAPPY BIRTHDAY! Melissa signed when she let me go.

BIRTHDAY TWO MONTHS PAST, I pointed out, and Melissa just shrugged and waved an airy hand.

"We know . . . birthday . . . few months, but . . . mom . . ." Nina was saying as she came around to join our little huddle. ". . . wanted to . . ."

My mind was still whirring, trying to process everything, so a lot of what Nina was trying to tell me was completely flying over my head. But *of course* Mom was somehow involved with this belated birthday present.

DON'T UNDERSTAND, I signed, and Melissa just

signed back, HAPPY! and jabbed a finger at me as if to say *just go with it!*

That was something I could definitely do, because it didn't really matter in the end, did it? Two of my best friends were here with me, and so was my boyfriend. I was going to have to soak up as much time with them as I possibly could.

When I looked over at Beau he was smiling, dimples flashing, and I felt my stomach do one of those stupid flips. Funny that we'd been together a year now and his smile still got to me.

"Are . . . happy?" he asked, tucking a strand of my hair carefully behind my ear, making sure not to get it tangled around my hearing aid.

"Well, duh!" I said, fighting the urge to pull all three of them in for a lame group hug.

WE THINK BETTER BIRTHDAY GIFT, Beau signed to me, and immediately I knew what he was getting at.

Last year's birthday "gift" didn't even come close to this one. This one was *much* better. After that little heart-to-heart we had in the hallway at Engelmann, Beau and I hadn't once discussed cochlear implants, and I think we both wanted to keep it that way. We were on equal footing now, no matter my deafness or his hearing.

YES, I agreed, breaking into a smile of my own.

Nina stepped up and signed to us that we were supposed to be meeting my mom and Connor at the nearby Cheesecake Factory for dinner. I wound up squished between Melissa and Beau in the backseat of the car after I jogged back up to the clinic to say good-bye to Liz.

I kept one hand curled around Beau's as Nina pulled out of the parking lot, but I couldn't stop looking at him or Melissa. Two of my most important people had just met, and knowing their lively personalities, they'd be friends as well in no time.

And now two different parts of my life—Deaf and hearing—were connecting even more.

CUTE, Melissa was signing to me, nodding toward Beau. He was purposefully looking out the window, but I caught him grinning. SIGN GOOD.

GOOD TEACHER, I signed, gesturing at myself.

Melissa cracked a smirk and I knew she was starting to giggle. MAYBE FIND HEARING BOY MYSELF, she signed, and she pretended to give Beau a longing look as she batted her eyelashes.

MINE, I signed with a huff, though I knew she was just teasing.

I KNOW, Melissa signed, giving me a playful nudge. HAPPY FOR YOU.

SAME, I signed back to her while squeezing Beau's hand impossibly tight.

A year and a half ago I couldn't have felt more terrible about moving out here to Colorado, but it hadn't turned out so bad in the end. I'd found Beau and Nina and now Melissa was here, and it didn't even matter who was Deaf or hearing.

We just were.

ACKNOWLEDGMENTS

This entire project wouldn't have been possible without Jillian Manning, who believed in me, or my dear friend Staci Nichols, who gave me the encouragement I needed to start telling Maya's story.

A million thanks are also due to the folks over at Blink, including but not limited to: Hannah VanVels, Sara Bierling, Jennifer Hoff, Annette Bourland, and too many others to name. I'm very fortunate to have a strong publishing team to work with. And of course, I must thank my amazing literary agent, Shannon Hassan, for taking Maya's story and running with it.

I want to thank the Deaf community as well, for helping me along as I figure out my place in both worlds and learn their beautiful language, and everyone else I've had the pleasure of working with in my time as a Deaf Services Specialist. It truly has been a life changing experience.

As always, I also have to thank my parents, Sharon and Tony, for their continued support, and all the members of my family. You know who you are.

I'd be lost without the support of all my fellow authors too, such as Christina June, McCall Hoyle, and Kelly Anne

Blount. They are far more knowledgeable than I am and more than willing to help out a newbie like me.

And a special thanks must go to my husband Tyler. I'm not sure what I would've done if I didn't have you to hold my hand through all my breakdowns during the whole writing process—and all while we were planning our wedding too. You're a champ.

AN INTERVIEW WITH AUTHOR
ALISON GERVAIS

**What inspired you to write *The Silence Between Us*?
Have you always known your characters' arcs or were
there some surprises along the way?**

The inspiration behind *The Silence Between Us* came
from my ongoing work with the Deaf community where
I live and the desire to portray a nontraditional character
in YA lit. You don't see many Deaf characters in books out
there on the shelves today.

I'm also Hard of Hearing myself, so I'm very familiar with
some of the frustrations Maya experiences with her hearing
loss throughout the novel. I had a basic outline to work off
when I began writing the story, but Maya's story unfolded in
its own way as I worked through the manuscript. I'm a little
surprised at how sort of spunky she turned out!

**What do you hope readers take away from *The Silence
Between Us*?**

I hope readers understand that just because someone's
world may look a little different from their own it doesn't
mean it's a bad thing. Just because someone may have a
"disability" doesn't mean that someone needs to be pitied or

ridiculed. Everyone is capable of reaching their own goals, even if it's not what you may have imagined for yourself.

Tell us more about your main characters Maya and Beau.

Maya was a personal favorite of mine to write; she says what she's thinking, she's not afraid to call people out on their biases, and she's far more confident in herself than I was in high school.

Beau is a little more reserved and self-conscious about how he is seen by the rest of the world. He tries to always appear as if he has everything together, but really, he's just as uncertain of the future and what he wants to do as every teenager is.

Do you feel like your characters are your friends or extensions of yourself? Which character do you feel resembles you the most? Which character do you wish you were more like?

Sometimes I catch a few similarities between myself and my characters, but I think every author can say that. I feel Maya resembles part of myself the most because we both have hearing loss and struggled in school because of it, but she's much more self-assured and unafraid to speak her mind. I wish I could say the same!

The friendship between Maya and Nina and Maya and Melissa is a major theme in this story. How is Maya's connection different with Nina than it is with Melissa? What makes each of their friendships unique? Are there any real-life or fictional relationships that have inspired these friendships?

The major difference between Maya's friendship with Nina and her friendship with Melissa is of course that Melissa is Deaf—like Maya—and Nina isn't. Despite how understanding Nina is of this and how much she likes Maya, that's something Nina can never relate to in the way that Melissa can. Maya and Melissa belong to the same community and share the same language and culture, whereas Nina is just starting to experience that for the first time. Maya's friendship with Nina is unique in that they are beginning to bridge the gap between the Deaf and hearing worlds, and I think knowledge of both is very important.

Your debut novel, *In 27 Days*, is quite different from *The Silence Between Us*. How was the experience of writing *The Silence Between Us* different from writing *In 27 Days*?

I had a lot more time to write *In 27 Days* than I did *The Silence Between Us*, and I'm six years older as well. A lot of changes have occurred during that time, and I'm hoping I've had more life experiences to further my writing. With *In 27 Days* I got to let my imagination run rampant, whereas *The Silence Between Us* has more of a realistic setting. It was a bit of a challenge to write *The Silence Between Us*, to be honest, because I'm still learning more and more about the Deaf community, Deaf culture, and American Sign Language, and I don't have too much experience writing without some kind of supernatural twist!

Which part of *The Silence Between Us* was the most challenging to write? What was your favorite scene to write?

I think one of the most challenging scenes to write was Maya's birthday. I don't want to give too much away, but it was tough. At the time Maya is hoping she's headed toward something real with Beau, only to have it sort of backfire. My favorite scene to write was probably when Beau and Maya are working on a school project together. It's the first time Maya really lets her guard down around Beau.

Why do you think it's important for YA readers to meet characters like Maya, Beau, Nina, Jackson, and Melissa?

I think the chance to experience someone else's world through literature can be invaluable. There aren't too many YA books out there with Deaf main characters, and I think it's time they get their chance to shine.

If you could tell your teen self anything, what would it be?

I would tell my teen self that high school isn't forever. The time will come when you get to take control of your life, and it'll be worth the wait.

What is the best piece of writing advice that you have ever received?

My favorite piece of writing advice I was never directly told but is actually a quote by F. Scott Fitzgerald: "You don't write because you want to say something, you write because you have something to say." It's important to write what you feel compelled to, not what you think will sell.

A NOTE ABOUT COCHLEAR IMPLANTS AND DIFFERING OPINIONS IN THE DEAF COMMUNITY

An estimated 48 million Americans experience some degree of hearing loss, regardless of their background. It's said to be an "invisible disability" that touches more lives than we realize. There are several different ways we can choose to treat hearing loss, and one very common way is to undergo surgery to receive a cochlear implant.

According to the National Institute on Deafness and Other Communication Disorders, cochlear implants are classified as "a small, complex device that can help to provide a sense of sound to a person who is profoundly deaf or hard-of-hearing." Cochlear implants differ from hearing aids in that they "bypass damaged portions of the ear and directly simulate the auditory nerve."

Since being introduced in the 1980s, the U.S. Food & Drug Administration estimates the number of adults and children fitted for cochlear implants to be in the hundreds of thousands. However accessible cochlear implants currently may be, they are a hot topic of debate within the Deaf community. Some believe that it is cruel to have a young child fit for a cochlear implant and to endure every-thing that follows—speech therapy, for example—and some believe it is a personal choice that only the individual can make.

Decades ago, many people adopted what is referred to as the *oralist approach*, where medical professionals and parents of deaf children believed it best to restrict the child from learning sign language so that the child master spoken English as well as lipreading to develop as much language skill as possible. Deaf children in school are said to have been reprimanded by having their wrists bound or being forced to sit on their hands to keep from using sign language and focus on English instead.

The attitude toward an oralist approach for a deaf child's education may be changing; some linguistic studies have shown there may be harm in restricting a deaf child's acquisition of sign language in favor of spoken English. Despite this, the oralist approach still seems to maintain some popularity as well as the rise of people being fitted with cochlear implants.

So you will find differing opinions concerning cochlear implants and the view the Deaf community holds, and responses will vary depending on who you speak with.

Hearing aids, on the other hand, are not quite so contested. They come in a variety of colors and fits—my own hearing aid is neon purple—and are used to amplify sound for individuals experiencing hearing loss. As helpful as hearing aids have proven to be, in most cases they do not clarify the noise being amplified, so you may still have difficulty understanding conversation, like I do. As Maya pointed out in *The Silence Between Us*, hearing aids are a temporary solution to a permanent problem.

However we may view hearing loss, the fact remains that there is an entire community and culture shared by Deaf people becoming more prominent in society thanks to TV shows like *Switched at Birth*, movies like *A Quiet Place*, and Deaf activists such as actress Marlee Matlin and model Nyle DiMarco.

Part of my job as a Deaf Services Specialist at an Independent Living Center in Colorado is to address the needs of the Deaf or Hard of Hearing consumers I work with, but also to inform the community about the issues facing the Deaf community, how we may better work alongside each other, and how people who are Deaf are perfectly capable of living independent, successful lives.

In *The Silence Between Us*, Maya makes it known that she does not consider herself disabled because of her hearing loss, and that same belief is held by many in the Deaf community. There is *nothing* wrong with having difficulty hearing, and that's something I struggled to accept while I was in school. I used to be teased and picked on because I'm Hard of Hearing. This continued well into college, and I even got in trouble at work because I tried to hide the fact that I wear a hearing aid. Even now I still sometimes get people poking or touching my hearing aid or getting angry with me because I can't understand what they're saying.

Hearing loss doesn't make you any less of a person though, and it shouldn't be something to fear, however scary it might seem. It's something that can be embraced as simply as anything else in life. All it really takes is an open mind and the notion that people who may seem "different" aren't so different at all.

There is a gap between the Deaf and hearing worlds, but there doesn't have to be. The Deaf have a community, culture, and language—just like you.

In 27 Days

From wattpad sensation @honorintherain
Alison Gervais

"A twist on Groundhog's Day meets Death, this paranormal tale [*In 27 Days*] will have readers turning the pages to see if Hadley stops Archer from making a tragic mistake." —YA Books Central

Hadley Jamison is shocked when she hears that her classmate, Archer Morales, has committed suicide. She didn't know the quiet, reserved guy very well, but that doesn't stop her from feeling there was something she could have done to help him.

Hoping to find some sense of closure, Hadley attends Archer's funeral. There, she is approached by a man who calls himself Death and offers her a deal. If Hadley accepts, she will be sent back twenty-seven days in time to prevent Archer from killing himself. But when Hadley agrees to Death's terms and goes back to right the past, she quickly learns her mission is harder than she ever could have known.

Time ticks away as Hadley looks for ways to not only talk to Archer but to know him on a deeper level. But just as she and Archer connect, a series of dangerous accidents starts pushing them apart. Hadley must decide whether she is ready to risk everything—including her life—to keep Archer alive.

In 27 Days:
• Written by award-winning Wattpad sensation Alison Gervais
• Over 25 million reads on Wattpad
• Achieved a #1 ranking in the Adventure category, and has won the hearts of millions of readers around the world
• A story of redemption, first love, and the strength it takes to change the future
• Addresses tough but true topics and problems facing readers ages 13 and up, such as suicide and family issues

Available in stores and online!

BLINK®

Enjoy a chapter from *In 27 Days*,
another great novel by Alison Gervais!

IN 27
DAYS

ALISON GERVAIS

BLINK

The Day Of

There was something *off*. I couldn't put my finger on what exactly it was, but it was definitely there.

Yes, something was out of balance, I decided as I stepped off the bus and onto the sidewalk outside John F. Kennedy Prep. The place looked like it did almost every other day, with its red bricks, bright-colored banners strung up everywhere, and the jumble of students lingering around outside the front doors. The school had been around for more than a century, and it had that Old New York feel. Nothing was ever out of the ordinary.

Yet the gray clouds rolling in across the sky felt smothering, bringing with them a feeling of suspicion and . . . sadness. An almost suffocating sadness. New York was the city that never slept, the place that had a thousand different attitudes. But I'd never felt one like this before.

"C'mon, Hadley, you're in the way."

I quickly moved to the side as Taylor Lewis, my best friend, sauntered off the bus.

I first met Taylor during freshman orientation, when I'd been wandering the halls alone while looking for my classes. From that moment onward, she'd decided to take me under her wing because we were both wearing the same shirt from

American Apparel, and decided to teach me everything she already knew about the social scene at JFK. Without her, I would have been totally lost—literally, figuratively, and most certainly socially. Now, more than two years later, we were still best friends, and I was still content to hang out in Taylor's social-butterfly shadow.

"Why do you have that weird look on your face?" Taylor asked as we followed the throng of people through the front doors.

I glanced away from a group of teachers huddled together in the hallway by the front office, their heads together, whispering, and frowned at Taylor. "What look?"

She rolled her eyes and gave me a nudge with her elbow. "Never mind. Are you ready for that test in American Government today? I can barely understand what Monroe's talking about half the time, and I swear, it's totally pointless that we even know how many cabinet members there are or whatever, and I— Hadley, are you even listening to me?"

My focus was drawn to the pair of uniformed police officers located down the hallway from my locker, standing with the principal, Ms. Greene. By the stiff, grim expressions on their faces, I guessed they must have been talking about something highly unpleasant. But what would have brought the police to our high school?

"I'm sorry, Taylor, I'm just . . ." I couldn't come up with a word to describe how off I felt. "I don't know, just worried about the test too, I guess."

Taylor snorted out a laugh as I rummaged around in my locker for my chemistry textbook. "Why are you worried, Hadley? You're, like, the only one who actually manages to stay awake in Monroe's class."

"Guess I'm just lucky." That, or I had a lawyer for a dad who would flip if I didn't keep a decent grade in Government.

I left Taylor and made for homeroom, now feeling as though someone was following close behind me, breathing down my neck. I dropped into a seat toward the front of the class and focused on keeping my breathing in a steady pattern, succeeding until the first bell rang and our teacher didn't appear.

Mrs. Anderson, the German teacher who ran our homeroom, was probably the nicest person I'd ever met. She was almost always humming under her breath, and had a thousand-watt smile for every person who just happened to look her way. I didn't have the patience to learn German—I'd barely made it through my two required years of Spanish—but Mrs. Anderson seemed like a hoot, and she made homeroom bearable despite it being so ridiculously early in the morning.

The fact that Mrs. Anderson was late just added to my increasing unease. My friend Chelsea was convinced the teacher lived at JFK because she was always somewhere in the building with coffee and a sprinkled doughnut and attended every school function and football game. So where was she? It wasn't like Mrs. Anderson to be tardy.

More than five minutes passed before the door swung open and Mrs. Anderson came walking in. There was a coffee stain on the front of her sweater, and her glasses were slightly askew as she dumped a stack of folders on her desk, saying, "Sorry I'm late, class, sorry, there was a bit of a . . ." Her voice trailed off as she bit her lip, scrubbing at the stain on her sweater with a napkin. "Something rather . . . unfortunate happened."

In the seconds between her words, my heart picked up pace and beat an unsteady rhythm against my chest. I had no way of knowing what "unfortunate" thing happened, but a gut-wrenching feeling told me that whatever it was, it was *bad*.

Mrs. Anderson sighed as she tossed the napkin into the trash and leaned against her desk, crossing her arms over her chest. "Last night, one of our students here at JFK Prep committed suicide."

I sat back in my seat, feeling deflated as I let out a sharp gasp. *What?*

I'd known the moment I stepped off the bus not twenty minutes ago that something was wrong. But *this?* I wanted to ask who had so abruptly ended their life, but I found that I couldn't force myself to speak. My mouth was suddenly as dry as the Sahara Desert, and my tongue felt like sandpaper.

"Who was it?" a kid sitting a few rows behind me asked after the first few moments of tense silence.

Mrs. Anderson fiddled with the edge of her sweater. "Archer Morales."

That name was . . . very familiar. I'd heard it before, but I couldn't put a face to a name.

Wait a minute, a small voice in my mind reminded me. *Freshman English.*

That's right. Freshman English with Mrs. Casey. Archer Morales was the boy I'd sat next to first semester. I didn't make the instant connection when Mrs. Anderson had said his name because Archer had only spoken about three words the entire year.

Mrs. Anderson's voice faded into the background as she mentioned that school counselors would be available for the rest of the week at any time to talk about what happened. Soon, I couldn't hear her at all, too preoccupied with trying to remember anything I could about Archer Morales.

He'd been very quiet and kept his head down most of the time, diligently following along in whatever text we happened to be reading. The one and only time I'd really gotten a good look at his face was when we'd been forced to answer a set of questions on *Frankenstein*.

It might have been easy to forget a guy who rarely ever spoke, but this guy happened to be the most distracting person I'd ever met. I'd become tongue-tied almost the second he'd looked at me with these bright hazel eyes that made me feel like I was being X-rayed.

Looking back on that class now, I realized I'd done my best to forget the whole experience because of the annoyed expression on that attractive face the entire time we'd worked together. What girl wanted to remember the moment a guy made it clear he'd rather be doing anything else *but* look at you?

Come to think of it, that had seemed to be Archer Morales's attitude toward everything. JFK Prep was a big school, but I'd seen him in the hallways from time to time, easy to spot because of his height and tousled dark hair, but he'd always managed to be on his own, and everyone had always given him a wide berth.

Archer Morales was—*had been*—one of JFK Prep's outcasts. And now he was gone.

I bolted upright in my seat when the first period bell rang overhead, pulling me out of my reverie. The rest of the class was already on their feet and filing from the room, talking quietly with one another instead of chatting and laughing like normal. It was even more obvious now, the change in the atmosphere. I trudged my way through the halls to chemistry class in a daze, unable to wrap my mind around the fact that one of my classmates was dead.

It wasn't as if I'd really known Archer Morales. We couldn't even have been called friends on any sort of level. He'd been all but a perfect stranger to me. So why did I feel like I was about to fall apart?

By the time school let out, the temperature had dropped outside, making the air chilly and uncomfortable as I headed for one of the buses at the curb. What I really needed was to curl up in bed and forget this day ever happened.

I took an empty seat toward the back and leaned my head against the window, closing my eyes, for once thankful Taylor had decided to ditch early to spend time with her latest beau-du-jour. None of the other girls we hung out with rode the same bus, so I was able to think in silence. The rocking of the vehicle was soothing, almost providing a distraction from the thoughts swarming around my brain like hurricane, but all too soon, the ride was over.

I pulled up the collar of my coat and crossed my arms over my chest, beginning the walk to the apartment building I'd lived in for almost my entire life. The complex was right on the edge of the Upper East Side, so it was a little more ostentatious than other buildings in Manhattan.

I often thought it was lonely, being shut up in the apartment while my parents worked impossible business hours, but I couldn't have been more thrilled I was going home to an empty apartment that afternoon. The familiarity of my messy bedroom and the comfy sheets on my bed had never seemed so appealing.

"Evening, Hadley," Hanson, the doorman, said as I approached the gray glass building. "Good day at school?"

I briefly considered telling Hanson what had happened. He was a nice man, and always seemed to be genuinely interested in how my day went. But I didn't want to say the words aloud, that one of my classmates had killed himself, because I still didn't want to believe that it had actually happened.

"Fantastic," I finally said as he held open the door for me.

"I remember what high school was like," Hanson said as I passed over the threshold. "As soon as you get out of there, the world's a much better place."

I had my doubts, but it was nice to hear Hanson say so anyway.

I crossed the marble-tiled, fountain-decked lobby to the elevators and rode up to the seventh floor. Heading down the lavishly decorated hallway, I pulled my set of keys out of my bag and unlocked the door to 7E.

My parents had never been what you could exactly call *humble*.

Our apartment was filled with pristine leather furniture, cream-colored carpets, and tasteful photos of the city hanging on the walls, which complemented the floor-to-ceiling windows that lined the living room and dining room. And the state-of-the-art, chrome appliance kitchen was almost another art piece in itself. My mother spent so little time here, it was amazing she'd even found the time to decorate the place to begin with.

A lawyer and an assistant CFO, my parents had intense work schedules, and they rarely gave me a second thought when they left the city on work trips leaving me behind for sometimes a week or longer. When that happened, my eighty-seven-year-old neighbor Mrs. Ellis would check in on me every other day or so to make sure I was doing all right, but that wasn't exactly the same thing as having a mom or dad around.

I knew I was extremely lucky to live in such a nice place and have so much money at my disposal, but the whole "rich" thing honestly made me a little uncomfortable, even if it was something I'd known for most of my life. My parents hadn't always made stellar paychecks. Sometimes I missed the simple little townhouse we'd lived in over in Chelsea before my mom was promoted and my dad took over his firm. At least then we'd actually spent time as a family and had dinner together every night.

I breathed a sigh of relief once I shut the door to my bedroom and locked it.

My bedroom was my happy place. The Christmas lights strung up above the balcony window, the Broadway playbills and pictures of Taylor and our group tacked up on the corkboard above my desk, the rows and rows of DVDs and CDs I'd collected over the years—all of it was the perfect escape from the stuffy leather furniture and the professional photographs of the city from some art gallery in SoHo that hung in the living room.

I half-heartedly attempted to memorize some formulas for chemistry, but five minutes later I gave up, chucked my textbook at the wall, and flopped facedown on my bed.

It felt as if there was some part of myself that was missing, now that Archer Morales wasn't alive and walking this earth anymore. It made me desperately wish that he were still here, despite the fact that he and I had only exchanged a few words.

Somehow I couldn't make sense of the fact that he was here yesterday, and now he was gone . . . permanently. Then again, I wasn't all that familiar with death. I'd gone to my great-grandma Louise's funeral when I was six, but that was the only time I'd ever experienced someone I knew, at least a little, passing away. But I didn't like seeing her body in a casket then, and I didn't like the idea of Archer's body lying cold somewhere now.

Burrowing underneath the covers, I shoved my face into a pillow and I finally started to cry.

BLINK

BLINK®